£3

Sitting

Pretty

APRIL HARDY

ACKNOWLEDGEMENTS

My first thanks go to Barbara Large for her wonderful Winchester Writers' Conferences, and Allie Spencer, whom I met at my first one, for recommending I join the Romantic Novelists' Association's New Writers' Scheme, who also deserve a heartfelt thank you.

Anne Bennett, Trisha Ashley and the late Catherine King took me under their wing at my very first RNA event. I have fond memories of our stays at the New Cavendish and want to thank them for the writerly wisdom they imparted in the bar and across the breakfast table. They treated me as if I were already one of the gang!

Amanda Jennings and Lucy Diamond gave me generous critical help (literally), thanks to the charity auction, Authors for the Philippines. Ditto Joanne Grant thanks to Authors for Nepal. Very much appreciated!

Special thanks to Emirates Airline Festival of Literature, for introducing me to my agent, Alison Bonomi of LBA Books. And to Judy Finnegan and Francesca Main, for choosing one of my stories as the winner of its first Literary Idol Competition in 2014.

Also Yvette Judge and all at Dubai International Writers' Centre, where talented tutors Sherry Ashworth and Jo Wroe provided plenty of inspiration.

Cathie Hartigan, Margaret James and Sophie Duffy – thank you for organising the annual Exeter Novel Prize, and Broo Doherty, for judging the finalists. It was a great experience!

Much gratitude to my long-suffering editor, Alexandra Davies who, if there was a Nobel prize for patience, would deserve to win it. Thanks too, Hazel Cushion, Bethan James, Rebecca Lloyd and everyone behind the scenes at Accent. Also Cat Camacho, who was my first editor there.

Much appreciation to Daunt Books Chelsea, for hosting my London launch, and Jane Northcote at Dubai World Trade Centre Club, for hosting my Dubai one.

Enormous hugs for my ever so supportive writing pals, both in UK and Dubai, Sue Mackender, the Tonbridge Diamonds, Sharmila Mohan and Linda MacConnell. You've all helped me more than you know.

Thanks and love to my family, who've been there at every turn and done everything they could to help me on my way.

And last but not least, my husband, Andrew, for making it all possible – and for his new-found interest in cooking which couldn't have come at a better time!

CHAPTER ONE

'I don't understand.' My voice echoed loudly in the empty flat. 'What do you mean, I'm not coming with you? Alex?'

The voice on the other end of my mobile was quiet now he'd delivered his bombshell. Now he'd told me that our marriage was a mistake and we'd be better off apart. But I knew he was still there. 'You can't just bugger off to Dubai without me. I'm your wife. We got married so I could come with you!' The hammer of my heartbeat rang in my head, drowning out any sound he might have made.

'We've given up the lease on this place.' I looked around in panic. 'The shipping company have just gone with all our stuff. What am I supposed to …' *All our stuff.* The penny finally dropped, ice-cold and slow, all the way down my back. The movers had boxed up all the furniture and household goods, all the things Alex, with his much bigger salary, had paid for.

When he left for work this morning, he took his clothes and personal things with him. 'So they wouldn't be in the way', he'd said. I'd carefully packed his shirts in tissue paper - in the fancy Kipling travel bags I'd given him as a wedding present. In my Sitting Pretty car downstairs, my clothes, toiletries, and accessories were crammed into an elderly case on dodgy wheels and a couple of big, nylon zip-up sports bags. I was supposed to be driving my work vehicle back to the office for the last time, then Alex was going to pick me up and drive us to the airport.

The muffled sound of an announcement telling passengers to switch off their mobiles for take-off sent my stomach into freefall.

'You're on the plane!' I panted down the phone. 'You changed the flight! You bastard! How long have you been planning this?'

'*Einai kallitera etsi*, it's better this way … Goodbye, Beth.' And he hung up. Nothing else. No apology, no explanation. What the hell was I supposed to do now?

I stared blindly through the curtain-less window at the half fresh-green, half reddish-brown, not ready to admit it's autumn, view of the park. Wintertown Park, with the lake in the distance, had enticed us into paying a small fortune in rent. Today it mocked me. *You don't belong here. You never did.* Then it blurred as tears filled my eyes. I'd loved living here. It had been our first marital home.

We'd sort of lived together in London, where we met, courtesy of one of the dogs I was walking for a living escaping my grip and hurtling into Alex on his way to work one morning. The dopey Labrador had been eager for a quick hook-up with a pretty poodle being walked on the other side of the road. In one clumsy collision, Alex had managed to capture both the Labrador and my heart, and we'd been more or less inseparable ever since.

We were lucky that his parents lived far enough away to remain in blissful ignorance. They would've had a fit at the thought of their precious son living in sin with a non-Greek; especially when Tula, his Athenian ex-girlfriend – the future daughter-in-law of their dreams – was apparently still single. And following his every move via Facebook. He'd had to be very careful what he put on his page and, until we were actually engaged, I was only allowed to be on there as a friend.

When Alex was asked to head up his company's new office in Wintertown, we headed there together and they were none the wiser. When he was offered a transfer to Dubai, however, we'd had to make a choice. I couldn't go with him as his girlfriend; living in sin there really meant *in sin* and you could go to prison for it. Looking back, it was way too soon to make a commitment like that. His parents and my mum had tried to convince us of it at the time, but we'd ignored them and made it anyway. And now Alex had unmade it. By *phone*. Furious tears spilled over and I wiped them away with my hands. I didn't even have a tissue to use. I stood up to get some toilet roll from the bathroom, then sat back down, remembering the packers had used the last of it. Typical.

Slumped on the edge of the window ledge, I sat with my forehead pressed against the cool glass. What did he expect me to do? Go back to London, to my mum's place and tell her she was right? Move into her spare bedroom and have to watch her not say 'I told you so' while I looked for another job and somewhere to live that I could even pretend to be able to afford? If I had any money in my bank account, or a credit card rather than a debit one with nothing behind it, I'd buy my own ticket, get myself over to Dubai and … and what? I wiped my runny nose on my arm. As I got up to see if there was a stray coffee shop napkin scrunched up in my bag, my phone rang again.

'Alex!' I yelped, snatching it to my ear. It had been a joke … He was on his way to meet me …

'Beth, darling?' My heart sank. It wasn't him. 'Beth? Are you there, sweetie?' It was Davina, my ex-boss. 'Don't suppose you're still in the area, hun?'

What did she want? I couldn't handle a faux luvvy conversation with her right now.

'Major *cats-trophy* here, darling,' she carried on, oblivious to my silence, as she was to most things. 'That silly girl who's supposed to take over your clients has only gone and lost the Parkers' poodle. You couldn't pop round and feed Henry Halliday's cat, could you, sweetie? You're an angel. Give my love to that handsome husband of yours.' And she hung up, without even waiting for a reply.

So, my husband had just left me, I was about to be officially homeless, and now I had to go and feed someone's pampered pet. Maybe I'd wake up soon. Maybe this was a nightmare brought on by the strange concoction I'd put together for last night's dinner to use up the last bits and pieces in the fridge.

I pinched my arm. It hurt. This was real.

Grabbing my shoulder bag from the window ledge, I marched out the front door. I didn't even check the rooms to see that nothing had been forgotten. What was the point?

Henry Halliday's chocolate box cottage overlooked the end of Netley Parva village green and backed on to a thicket of trees and Netley Common. During my time at Sitting Pretty I'd fed and walked quite a few pets from the picturesque Netley villages: Netley Magna, Netley Parva, and Netley Mallow, but Henry and his smoky grey cat were long-term regulars. I knew that Eleanor at the tiny post office and general store would have no problem handing me the key she kept for him in case of emergency. I parked the little car and scuttled inside for it, thankful she was busy and didn't have time to comment on why I was there instead of my replacement. As soon as the key went into the lock, Talisker began meowing on the other side.

'Sorry to keep you waiting, your lordship.' I pulled the door behind me, made for the utility room, and opened a tin of salmon flavoured Sheba. He followed me, tail in the air, purring like a steam engine, but instead of tucking into his meal, he wound himself like a feline Slinky round my ankles, then rubbed the sides of his face against my knees, almost pushing me over. I stroked his silky head and back, his warm, furry body vibrating in pleasure. At least someone was pleased to see me.

'Oh, Tal,' I sighed as fresh tears blurred his image. Brushing my free arm across my eyes, my vision cleared enough momentarily to see the smudged mascara on it. I briefly wondered if it had been there when I'd gone to pick up the key, but I couldn't bring myself to care.

'Eat up, Tal.' Slowly I stood up, disengaging myself from his comforting presence. I groped my way to the little cloakroom and turned on the tap, splashing cool water over my face and arms until my eyes were red, but clean looking. Then I buried my face in the spotlessly white, fabric-softener-scented hand towel.

Talisker meowed from the doorway then re-launched his friendly assault on my legs. I took my face out of the towel. It looked like somebody had cleaned their shoes with it.

'Your dad's going to love me,' I said to him, wondering if the black marks would rinse out.

'Come on, fella,' I stepped carefully round him. 'I'm sure he won't mind me making myself a cup of tea.' The kitchen, like everything in this cottage, was sparklingly clean and fresh smelling. It's the only home with a pet I've ever been in where you can't immediately smell the presence of a furry animal.

Half-filling the kettle from the tap, I looked for the tea bags. There were tins of Lapsang Souchong, Earl Grey, Orange Pekoe, and Darjeeling. I opened the Darjeeling, but it was loose leaves, not bags. The others turned out to be just the same. Trust Henry Halliday to only have the sort of tea you needed a teapot for. The kettle boiled and switched itself off and I poured a little into the pot to warm it, then made myself half a pot. There was no milk in the fridge. I didn't have the energy to go back to Eleanor's to get some – I'd just have to have it black.

I carefully carried the Royal Worcester mug – no chunky Keep Calm and Carry On china for Henry Halliday – into the front room and sat on the sofa. Talisker jumped onto my lap, kneading my thighs like a master bread maker. Leaning my chin on the top of his head, thinking I should be halfway to Heathrow with my husband by now, looking forward to getting rid of our luggage and having a wander round Duty Free, it occurred to me to wonder how Alex was already on a flight just hours before we were supposed to check in for the one we were booked on? They don't fly that frequently, do they? Had he changed airlines as well as times? I suddenly realised I'd never actually seen the tickets – they were at Alex's office. I'd just taken everything he said as gospel. When had he decided he wasn't taking me with him? It couldn't have been that long ago, or why bother going ahead with the wedding?

The tears threatened to start up again but Talisker sat there patiently, rubbing the top of his head against my lower jaw. It was almost as if he were saying 'There, there, it'll be all right'. I could have sat there all night. I wished I could, but I had to return the car. Davina was expecting me to drop it off at the Sitting Pretty office, ready for her to pass on to my replacement. I sighed heavily; this wasn't how today was supposed to end up at all. The tears welled up and I blinked them back furiously. Damn Alex!

I left good friends and a job I loved in London to move to Hampshire with him, but that was all right because I'd loved it once we got here. And now I'd left another job and another set of friends, and even married him, to follow him further afield. Only this time he'd decided he didn't want me tagging along. Had being married suddenly felt a bit too real for him? A bit too much like a noose tightening? Was that why he'd done the cowardly thing?

My watch said it was gone six, and I was already exhausted. I didn't think I could face seeing Davina and pretending everything was all right. And I certainly couldn't face the journey to London and the painful conversation that would be at the end of it. Wasn't it a shame this couldn't have been one of those nights when a client needed a sitter to stay over. The last one had been when old Mrs Williams had to go and take care of an even older relative who'd had a fall and was unable to take Lulu, her Siamese cat, with her but couldn't bear to leave her alone for a night. The fifth of November would always provide a few overnight sits, when an owner had to be away but was worried that the whizzing and banging of fireworks might upset their beloved pet. We fought over those jobs – watching TV with a little fluff-ball snuggling on your lap and trying to stick its head up your jumper – it was just like babysitting. And we got paid time and a half for it. Between us we'd fallen asleep on more than one sofa.

The sofa here was really comfortable. Would anyone know if I just stayed here tonight? Admitting my world had fallen apart could wait until tomorrow, couldn't it?

Oh God, it was so tempting to lie down and put my head on that plump, velvety cushion.

Talisker head-butted my cheek as if he knew what I was thinking and was saying 'Yeah, stay with me. Rub my head. You look after me and I'll look after you'. Did I dare? What were the chances of Eleanor coming to check I'd left? As long as I didn't make any noise or mess, no one would even know I was here. And I really ought to put that little towel in the washing machine, I reasoned, like a dieter trying to justify having a biscuit. How much noise would the washing machine make?

At that moment the doorbell rang. The mug nearly slipped out of my hand. Had I locked the door when I arrived? Oh God! Holding my breath, Talisker dug a claw in my thigh. I stifled a gasp and the bell rang again. Then, slowly at first, the handle started to rattle.

CHAPTER TWO

The most revolting smell woke me up, rotting fish with a hint of something else, wafting straight in my face. I tried to move but I was pinned down by a heavy weight on my chest. As I opened my eyes, Talisker yawned again.

'Talisker! Eugh! I managed to turn my head in time to miss most of the toxic blast: last night's Sheba and cat breath. 'Stinky cat!' I eased him, gently but firmly, off me and onto the floor. He seemed more surprised I wasn't delighted by his morning greeting than offended by my slur against his personal hygiene. I couldn't imagine Henry Halliday putting up with that. This is a man who pays a woman to come in and iron his tea towels.

I sat up, stretching my arms above my head. The sofa I'd fallen asleep on had actually been more comfortable than our bed. I gritted my teeth; *our bed*. It was Alex's bed now. As I tried to push the image out of my head, Talisker jumped back up on my lap.

'Oh no you don't, mister,' I turned him round, so his face was away from me. 'You may be gorgeous' I rubbed his ears, 'and you may be the cleanest cat in the world, but seriously, they could bottle your breath and use it for chemical warfare.' He purred, so I knew I hadn't offended him.

After Eleanor, or whoever it was, had tried the door last night, I'd been too nervous to move about too much, in case a neighbour heard me and, knowing Henry to be away, brought it to Eleanor's attention, or even called the police. I thanked my lucky stars that I must have automatically locked the door when I arrived. It's a company rule that to keep the clients' homes as secure as possible when we are looking after their pets, we lock doors on arrival. I must have been running on autopilot. And Eleanor must have assumed I'd just forgotten to drop the key back when I left. That would have to be sorted out when I went back later today in my proper role as professional cat sitter. As long as Davina gave me my job back.

That was the plan I'd come up with to stay and carry on working while I saved up some money and decided what I wanted to do about all this. Henry Halliday was my most regular client. He was away on business for one entire week, every three weeks. That meant, if I didn't manage to get myself caught, I could camp out in his cottage for the whole of every third week. I'd gotten away with it this time, hadn't I? And that was without any kind of planning or forethought. It would be much easier next time, wouldn't it? And I was sure there were plenty of other clients whose homes I could sleep in for the odd week, or weekend, or even just a night. Because one thing was certain – I was damned if I was going to leave the job I loved only to move back to London and stay with my mum just because Alex had decided marriage wasn't for him after all. I would be the one to decide what happened next, thank you very much.

My wages from Sitting Pretty, however, wouldn't cover the rent of a new flat, even a tiny bedsit. And as for the upfront deposit? Forget it! Because Alex had always been a big spender and I'd preferred to pay my way, I'd not only stopped saving any money, but the little bit I'd previously saved had all but evaporated. I had plenty of zeros in my bank balance – it's just that the decimal point was on the wrong side of them. There were always friends' spare rooms and sofas where I could crash, but that would be too awkward. I didn't want any of them knowing any more about Alex going to Dubai without me than they had to. I refused to be pitied as the girl whose husband had flown to Dubai without her and had ended their marriage with a phone call from the plane. That was not going to be me. I knew I'd have to give all of this a lot more thought later, but for now I wanted to keep what Alex had done to me to myself.

That reminded me, I really needed to call my mum and somehow tell her the change of circumstances without worrying her and without actually telling any lies. I'd have to choose my words carefully. At least I knew Alex wouldn't be calling her. They'd always been polite to each other for my sake, but they never really hit it off and neither had ever gone out of their way to start a conversation with the other. That should have told me a lot.

I wondered if he'd at least call me to see that I was OK. Somehow I doubted it. If he'd been too chicken to tell me face to face, he'd be too chicken to call me again, knowing I'd had time to think up plenty to say back to him.

'So,' my fingers raked their way down Talisker's back, 'you're probably ready for some breakfast.' I got up and followed him to the utility room, where he looked up, expectantly, at the click-lock container of top quality cat biscuits. I tipped some into his bowl. He nudged my hand in thanks and dipped his head towards his breakfast, taking this extra meal as nothing more than his due for sharing the sofa with me last night.

I was starving. Yesterday's events had obliterated my appetite and food hadn't even crossed my mind as I spent the evening being as quiet as possible.

Once it had started to get dark, I'd moved myself into the cosy back room and pulled the curtains together, thankful for their thickness, the dense greenery at the bottom of the garden and the many trees on the common beyond that, which meant it would be safe to put a lamp on. I'd also pushed Henry's carrier-bag holder, one of those sausage-shaped, cloth things you see at craft fairs, against the bottom of the front door just in case any light showed on the other side. Then I'd pretty much spent the evening huddled on the sofa in there with Talisker, my mind whirring, trying to make sense of what Alex had done to me.

It was surreal. If you watched a trailer for a film where a husband dumped his wife the way Alex had dumped me, you'd think it was a bit silly and probably not worth watching.

It was cruel. How could he let me give up a job he knew I loved, in the expectation of a move to another country, when he knew all along, he wasn't taking me with him?

It was bloody cowardly. Telling me over the phone. What did he think I'd do if he'd told me face to face? Hit him? He's a foot taller and stronger than me. Scream and shout? He's known me long enough to know I'm not the hysterical type. Or maybe he hasn't. Was he afraid I'd try and talk him round? Make him change his mind and take me with him after all?

My stomach grumbled. I had to have something to eat, then go straight to the Sitting Pretty office and get my job back. A quick look in the kitchen cupboards revealed nothing that didn't require cooking, nothing I could eat and replace. Henry Halliday, it turned out, wasn't a buyer of biscuits and snacks. The only breakfast cereal in the place was porridge – organic, of course. And there was no milk in the fridge anyway. Or yoghurt, or fruit or anything remotely edible. Not even a piece of obsessive-compulsively over-cling-filmed cheese. Just vacuum packed containers of fancy coffees and a row of expensive-looking jars, all their labels facing exactly the same way, containing black and green olives, and various pickled things – onions, beetroot, walnuts, and piccalilli – yuck!

So breakfast would be another half pot of black tea. At least it would stop me being dehydrated from all the bouts of crying. Taking it with me, I tip-toed up the stairs and stopped, wondering which bathroom would be best for me to use for a quick shower. The washing machine would have to go on anyway for the towel I'd covered in mascara yesterday. I'd worked out that this could be done later when I, fingers crossed, came back to feed Talisker. If any nosy neighbour could hear the washing machine and cared enough to come and investigate, I could always say Talisker had knocked something over and I didn't want to leave a mess for Mr Halliday to come back to.

Because Sitting Pretty always had a lot of clients around these villages, I knew the layouts of probably most of the cottages. The en-suite bathroom for the guest bedroom at the back didn't share an adjoining wall with the cottage next door, so it should be all right to use the shower in there. It was, of course, spotlessly clean but there were no toiletries in there, and all mine were in the car. So I took a deep breath and ventured through Mr Halliday's bedroom, hoping to borrow a few essentials from his bathroom.

The photographs, on his bedside table and chest of drawers, of him with the cutest little curly-haired girl, holding ice creams outside a monkey enclosure at a zoo, took me by surprise. There weren't any photographs downstairs, and the couple of times I'd met Henry Halliday he hadn't given the impression of being a monkeying around, ice cream-buying, favourite uncle kind of man. He looked younger and surprisingly dishy in casual clothes – they suited him far better than the stuffy suits I'd only ever seen him in.

I carried on to the en-suite bathroom. Catching sight of myself in the mirror as I squeezed a small blob of toothpaste onto my finger, my puffy eyes gleamed back at me. The red rims made their usual blue-green even greener. My dark chestnut hair, that slinky, sleek bob I'd had done for the wedding and had kept because Alex liked it, looked like a birds' nest. No wonder Talisker had slept on my chest. He'd probably been waiting for a bird to pop out of there.

It was highly unlikely Henry Halliday would possess any hair smoothing products. He wouldn't need anything like that, with his hair almost militarily short. He was clearly a fan of L'Occitane toiletries, though. Very nice. But he didn't seem to have any conditioner, so hair-washing would have to wait until tomorrow. A comb-through with wet fingers would have to do for today. I left the shampoo alone and just took his citrus verbena shower gel with me, feeling like a thief. This was expensive stuff. I really would only use a tiny bit and tomorrow I'd make sure to have my usual Frizz Ease and Body Shop bits and pieces with me.

After looking as far up and down the little street as I could, from the front door's spy-hole, to make sure there was nobody about, I took the back door key from its hook and nipped outside, locking the door and tiptoeing down the side of the cottage, all as silently as possible, feeling like a criminal about to get caught. It was a relief to get into the car uncontested and drive away.

Davina's vermilion red BMW was already parked in the space nearest the office. I don't know how she always managed to get that space, whatever time of day she came and went.

I eased Harriet, my little Honda, into a spot further away, between an Oops-a-Daisy delivery van and three pizza delivery motorbikes. Time to go and dazzle Davina into rehiring me.

CHAPTER THREE

'So, you're not jetting off to Dubai after all?' Davina cooed, clapping her slender hands together as if I'd just told her we'd communally won the lottery. Anyone else might have questioned my story about us deciding at the last minute that it would be better if I stayed put in good ol' Blighty for now and carried on working while my husband went to Dubai alone and sorted out somewhere for us to live. It suited her that I was staying and that was all that mattered. Davina was all about the business.

'Yes,' I breathed, thanking God for Davina being so, well ... Davina. 'That's right, so if it's all right ...'

'Katya can reschedule your regular clients as soon as she gets in. And we can lose that silly girl, whatever her name is.' She tapped her hot pink nails on her desk. 'Honestly, if she can't keep hold of a tiny little poodle, I can't imagine what use she thought she'd be to me.' Davina rolled her perfectly made-up eyes. 'You'd better call Mrs. Parker and tell her you'll be back walking Bubbles from today.'

'I'll call her now ...'

'What a good thing I didn't let Henry Halliday know you were thinking of leaving us. You know what a stick-in-the-mud he is about having people he doesn't know in his home.' Davina treated me to one of her dazzlingly white-toothed smiles, her glossy lipstick, as always, matching her nail polish. 'It's almost as if I knew you wouldn't really toddle off and leave me in the lurch.'

A grin spread across my face as I made myself a large mug of tea and took an even larger handful of biscuits from the tin. My job back with no questions and biscuits for breakfast. This day was already about a million percent better than yesterday. Yesterday – that wiped the stupid grin straight back off again. All I'd done was get my job back. The time for grinning would be when Alex stopped arsing about and called me with the mother of all grovelling apologies and I'd told him to get stuffed. Either that or when I'd saved up enough for the air fare and gone out to Dubai and found a high enough balcony to push him off – I gathered they had quite a lot of those over there.

Katya wasn't in yet, so I sat at her desk to phone Mrs. Parker. But while nobody else was in the outer office to see me, I logged into my email account, wishing I'd let Alex have his own way and buy me the latest smart phone for my birthday so I could do this in private. I must be the last person under the age of a hundred and five in the whole phone-owning world with such an old mobile, but it worked perfectly and I liked it. Being low maintenance hadn't done me any favours. That bottle of perfume I'd asked for instead seemed like a huge mistake now. It certainly hadn't made me smell so nice my husband wanted to be on the same continent as me.

There was nothing from him and I didn't dare write anything to him just yet, as I was pretty sure anything I composed right now would get me arrested. While I still had the computer to myself I logged into my Facebook account too. No personal message. Just the usual crap. Half of me wanted to see Alex's page. Would it still say *Relationship Status – Married to Beth Dixon* with the photo of us, all tanned and happy, petting Santorini donkeys on our honeymoon at the top of the page? I was half convinced that he'd arrive there and realise he'd just had a wobble. Well he could wobble right off for all I cared. Angry? Moi? My finger was still hovering over the mouse when I heard Davina coming towards her office door. I logged off and picked up the phone to call the owner of the disappearing dog.

Far from a tiny little poodle, Bubbles was a large standard size, wilful as a stroppy teenager and surprisingly strong. The first time I took him out, he nearly yanked my arm out of its socket when he caught sight of an unfortunate cat in the distance. If that poor girl yesterday hadn't been warned, then it really wasn't her fault she'd briefly lost him. I'd try and talk Davina into giving her another chance.

My first call of the day took me back to the Netley Villages. They were like the three bears of villages – Netley Magna being the big daddy bear, Netley Mallow, the medium sized mummy bear, and Netley Parva, where Talisker lived, the baby bear. Right now I was off to one of a pair of 1930s bungalows overlooking the duck pond in Netley Mallow, to visit Anthony and Cleopatra. Yes, seriously.

Tony and Cleo, the names they actually answer to, are brother and sister, two beautiful ginger cats. I reckon I'd have called them Hudson and Mrs Bridges if they were mine – I bought Mum the fortieth anniversary DVD box set of the original *Upstairs Downstairs* after the new version came out. He has a white smudge on the front of his neck, like a little bow tie, and white back paws as if he's wearing spats. She has a white belly and white smudges on her cheeks like she's wearing an apron and has flour on her face. And if Cleopatra/Mrs Bridges had ever had kittens, I'd have kept a female one and called her Ruby – yes, fanciful I know. But, like Talisker, they're regular customers and I've had time to get rather fond of them.

I let myself into their bungalow. Anthony was stretched out on the arm of the sofa. He opened a lazy eye as I walked over to him, closed it again, and stretched himself even longer.

'Hello, handsome,' I dropped my bag on the ottoman and stood over him. 'Where's your sister?'

Behind me, Cleopatra meowed as she pitter-pattered out of the bedroom, where I knew she liked the king size bed to herself.

'I trust madam had a comfortable night?' Kneeling down, I stroked her. She paused to lean her head into my hand for a moment before meowing at her brother, telling him, I imagine, to get up, which he did, stretching and yawning as he went. Both of them escorted me into the kitchen and watched to make sure they were getting the right flavour Fancy Feast, the right amount of biscuits, and that their water was changed properly. As they tucked into their breakfast, I ran myself a glass of water from the tap and went to sit on the ottoman.

This could really work, I thought as I sat there, sipping my water. OK, the Steadmans, Tony and Cleo's owners, had an erratic schedule, filming documentaries. They could go weeks without needing us and then call us at the last minute to feed their pets for two days. There were also times they needed us a couple of days a week for a month or so. But for the weeks when I couldn't camp out at Henry Halliday's cottage, this could definitely be somewhere I could spend the odd night.

I entertained the cats, playing with a couple of their toy mice. Anthony joined in, dashing back and forth trying to catch them, while Cleopatra washed her face and watched us. Then I picked each of them up for a cuddle, tidied up their His and Hers litter trays, and headed off to my next call.

Yes, I could definitely do this.

CHAPTER FOUR

I can't do this. It's breaking the law. It's like squatting. Maybe it even is squatting. Whatever it is, I just know I'm going to get caught and go to jail. I'm not clever enough to get away with it. Oh my God! What was I thinking!

It was all right during the working day. It was so easy to bravely plan my victimless crime that it didn't even feel like a crime. And it would be victimless. I wouldn't be eating any of their food or running up their utility bills. I would literally be having the odd cup of tea, sleeping, and showering. All right, the showers would use some water and electricity, but I'd keep them as short as possible. And I could do something nice for each of the clients whose homes I borrowed, something they wouldn't notice, like top up their pet food supplies or clean the kitchens of those who didn't have cleaners or something.

There was a key cutting place at one of the entrances to Wintertown shopping centre. During my lunch break, when I would normally be popping home for a couple of slices of cheese on toast or eating a sandwich in the nearest coffee shop to wherever my last client had been, I drove there. The closer I got to getting a copy of Henry Halliday's key cut, the more I felt how I imagined shoplifters or fraudsters might feel. At any moment, I was expecting the long arm of the law to tap me on my shoulder and to be asked to prove my legal and rightful ownership of this key; then be carted off to prison because I couldn't. My mouth was getting drier and I could feel my heart racing as I dithered about. The young man behind the counter had to have realised I was acting suspiciously – I could all but see my face on *Crimewatch*. It was just as he opened his mouth to speak to me that my nerve left me completely and I turned and fled. My feet took me to Dominic's Café where the prices are reasonable and they do a great all day breakfast, not that I could have faced one right then. I had a large decaf latte to calm my nerves and ordered a bowl of fusilli with pesto sauce, their pasta dish of the day, to settle my churning stomach. I'd have to have my main meal at lunchtimes for now. If I was still going to do this.

As I sat there, moving my food around its bowl and forcing down a few mouthfuls, I gave the key situation a rethink. Getting one cut was definitely illegal. And premeditated. If I could just keep Henry Halliday's with me at the end of the day, it felt a bit less like something that would see me spending Christmas in HMP Parkhurst. But how would I manage it?

The afternoon flew by. Firstly just feeding and playing with the cats. Then, later on when it was getting towards tea time, the return visits to the dogs for their dinners and second walks of the day. I'd given Bubbles a stern talking to, when I went for his morning visit, but by the evening he'd completely forgotten our agreement that he was going to behave himself. The neighbourhood cats were all thoroughly terrorised by the time we got back to the Parkers' house.

After going back to Sitting Pretty to give back the keys, with my key for my mum's place swapped for Henry Halliday's, I was at a bit of a loose end. I didn't want to go straight to the cottage for a long, silent evening of reading or playing on my laptop. I'd recharged the laptop in the office so it wouldn't need plugging in. There had been too many people about, otherwise I might have taken a deep breath and forced myself to have a look at Alex's Facebook page. So the supermarket seemed the sensible place to go, to pick up a few bits and pieces, maybe a salad and some fruit for my dinner. I could torture myself later.

It wasn't until I was walking out of Asda with my half price chicken Caesar salad, a Greek yoghurt, a couple of bananas, some instant hot chocolate sachets, and a bag of crisps, that the nerves kicked in again. Yesterday I'd gone to feed Talisker legitimately. It was only after I'd got there that the decision to stay had come about. This afternoon I'd been to feed him just like yesterday, only making sure to take the key back to Eleanor, apologising for forgetting to return it the day before. But today I would be going there out of my usual work time. And with the express intention of spending the night there, uninvited.

Wandering round the shops had killed a bit of time, but it felt a bit pointless, not wanting to buy anything because firstly, I couldn't afford it, and secondly, there was currently nowhere to put it. I went back to Dominic's for another latte, wondering how long I could make it last. There was a man at another table who looked, from sideways on, a lot like Alex. He had the same, brown-so-dark-it-was-almost-black, thick, wavy hair resting on his collar, and the same aquiline nose. He was even wearing a cornflower blue shirt – Alex's preferred colour of work shirt, although to him it was just a light blue chambray. I nearly choked on my coffee. I had to stop myself marching over and asking him what the hell he thought he was playing at, while tipping whatever was in his mug over his head. Thoughts of my husband, which I'd managed to keep out of my head all day – well, since this morning anyway – came crashing in. What was he doing right now? Not that I cared. Of course he hadn't phoned me – but had he even thought about what he'd done to me? Was he alone? Had he left me behind because there was someone else and she was going to be there in my place? Had Tula, that Greek goddess his parents adored, somehow finally got her claws into him? Well she was welcome to him.

There was no one about on Netley Parva's perfectly manicured village green when I got there, even though it was quite a fine evening. It looked like a film set of a village ready for the extras in a *Miss Marple* mystery to come walking along and as I parked further down the street, I wondered if anyone had noticed that my car had been parked not far from Henry Halliday's cottage for the whole of the previous night. Could there be a sweet, little, old lady or two knitting away behind any of those lace curtains with one eye on what was going on outside? Taking a deep breath, I grabbed my bag and walked as nonchalantly and as quietly as I could, slipping up the side of the cottage and letting myself in through the back door, locking it behind me again. Yes, I thought. I've done it!

I hadn't realised how much my heart was racing until I got through that door. I was gripping my bag so tightly my nails were digging in to my palm. My mouth was dry again too. With a flashback to the key cutting place, I put my bag down and went to the kitchen sink to run a glass of water. I was drinking it down gratefully when the near silence was snatched away by the shrill ring of the telephone in the hallway. And the sound of my choking as the water went down the wrong way. Who on earth could that be? Had my imagination conjured up a real little old lady who'd seen me coming in and had put down her knitting to phone and check up on me? Would it look suspicious if I didn't answer it? But it would give the whole game away if I did.

Great! Day one of my plan and I was already falling at the first hurdle.

CHAPTER FIVE

I didn't breathe again until I'd checked the lock on Henry Halliday's door for what felt like the twentieth time, and was leaning against it, eyes closed, heart going nineteen to the dozen. The window cleaner who'd just left a message on the answer phone would never know what a fright he'd given me. I'd been so sure he was someone from the local Neighbourhood Watch, suspecting someone was in here and waiting to see if they'd answer the phone. First night in and I'd already been caught red handed. Except, thank God, I hadn't.

Talisker trotted down the stairs and meowed in greeting, completely unaware of my state of near panic. He head-butted my shin and I slid down the door, nudging my Asda carrier bag across the floor so I could stroke his head. He then decided to take an interest in my shopping and I had to stop him staking a claim on my chicken salad.

'I don't think so, mister,' I whispered to him, getting up and taking my dinner and tomorrow's breakfast through to the kitchen. I put the salad and Greek yoghurt straight in the fridge. 'You've got your own food. This is mine.' I took the carrier bag holder and laid it against the bottom of the door again like last night and went into the utility room to give him a snack. It had been my intention to get him something as a treat while I was in Asda but, in deference to my new budget restrictions, I'd been seduced by the lure of following a member of staff with a reduced-price sticker gun while of course, pretending to be doing no such thing, and I'd forgotten. I'd have to get him something from Lidl, or Aldi, or The 99p Shop. There'd be no more food shopping in Waitrose for now.

I tipped some fresh biscuits into his bowl and left him crunching away while I took my shoulder bag upstairs. Not wanting to look like I was taking a lot of stuff in with me, I'd managed to cram a clean T-shirt and undies for tomorrow, a pair of pyjama bottoms, basic toiletries, and a book into the thankfully roomy bag. I'd padded the clothes around my little laptop. It's a good thing that in my job, neatly ironed clothes aren't a necessity.

The sofa had been great for one night, but I'd decided if I was going to be using the spare room's bathroom, I might as well sleep in the spare bed. The thought of using Henry Halliday's bedding made me feel a little uncomfortable, but it was warm for October and if I took the fancy bedspread and extra pillows and cushions off, I'd be more than comfortable with just a sheet over me. I could wash it with the bottom sheet, pillowcase, and towel the day before he was due back.

I drew the heavy curtains across the window and turned on the bedside lamp. The little travel alarm clock on the bedside table read half past seven. It couldn't still be that early. I'd really taken my time at the shopping centre and sat for ages over my coffee. But one glance at my watch confirmed it. I wondered what I was missing on *EastEnders*. And wasn't *Waking the Dead* on tonight? All the times I'd cursed the programme schedulers for showing repeats all the time and right now I'd happily give my past-its-freshest chicken salad for a couple of hours as a couch potato in front of the telly. Not that I'd take any of it in, but there was something comforting about the familiar, wasn't there?

Emptying the contents of my bag onto the chair by the dressing table, I picked up the book I was halfway through. Talisker wandered in through the door and rubbed his head against my ankle. He looked very pleased with himself, as he prepared to jump onto the bed. Of course, the door to this room was usually kept shut, I remembered. This was usually forbidden territory.

'Come on, Tal.' I picked him up and carried him out of the room with me and down the stairs. 'Don't you think cat hairs are going to be a bit of a giveaway?' His purring indicated his complete lack of concern in the matter.

Downstairs, I took my salad out of the fridge. It looked a lot less appetising than it had in the shop.

Half past seven. Much as I loved reading and playing computer Solitaire and Minesweeper, I was going to have to find a better way than this to spend the evenings. If I didn't, the alternating cine-film flickering through my head – one reel flashing up memories of Alex and I together, the other making up trailers of him in Dubai having a fantastic time without me – possibly with someone else – would drive me insane.

CHAPTER SIX

In my dreams that night, I was chasing a beautiful, faceless Greek woman carrying a huge watermelon. Don't ask me how I knew she was beautiful if she didn't have a face, or why she was running away from me with a large piece of fruit – you just know things in dreams, the ridiculous makes perfect sense – a bit like my life right now.

We were in a market – it must have been in Greece as there were lots of little, wrinkled old ladies dressed in black, bashing people in the shins with those shopping bag things on wheels and shrieking that all-encompassing phrase, *Ella paithi mou!* to anyone who got in their way. It was a bit like stumbling across the village ladies in *Mamma Mia!* while they were in a collective bad mood.

The beautiful but faceless woman kept darting ahead of me through the crowds. I'd nearly catch her and then she'd be gone and my eyes would have to start scanning the crowds for her again.

There were stalls and stalls around me of shiny, ripe watermelons but, for some reason, I knew that the one she had was mine and I had to have it back. Market traders kept thrusting olives, trays of baklava, and bunches of dried herbs at me but all I wanted was that damned watermelon. My damned watermelon.

Up and down, round and round those stalls I ran, until I saw her slide through a slender gap between two of them. Following her through, I saw her enter a little white church in the distance and ran faster to try and catch her. That was when I noticed her dress. It was a wedding dress. And the watermelon was a bouquet of flowers.

Still I didn't stop running – all the way to the church door. And then I saw him. It was only the back of his head, his dark, wavy hair just resting on his collar, but I knew it was him.

'Alex!' I cried. But he carried on, walking down the aisle with her. 'Alex!' I cried again, and that was what woke me up.

CHAPTER SEVEN

I propped the last cushion on its corner so it matched the one next to it and stood back. The bed looked pretty perfect to me, but what if I hadn't remembered how it looked exactly and Henry Halliday noticed something was different? Why hadn't I thought of taking a photo on my phone? Oh well, too late now. Taking one last look around the room to make sure I hadn't left anything of mine there, I closed the door and went downstairs.

Last night had been my final night here until Talisker's owner went away again after a few more weeks. I'd rearranged my appointments and come back to feed the cat earlier than usual this morning. Staying longer than normal while the bedding went through the quickest wash, spin, and tumble dry cycles I could work on Henry Halliday's washer/dryer, I'd cleaned up and made sure no trace remained of my overnight stays. I'd also checked my emails – nothing from Alex of course. I'd then checked Alex's Facebook page – *Relationship Status – Married to Beth Dixon* was still there. In fact, he hadn't added, shared, or changed anything on it since he left. Was that because he was so busy settling into his new job that there wasn't time for social media? Or was it because he was even busier having a good time and living his life rather than writing it up on his laptop? He'd always scoffed at people on Twitter, saying they were so sad that they thought the rest of the world would be interested in what they had for breakfast, but he had always logged into his

Facebook page every now and then.

I'd ironed both sheets and the one pillow case I'd used far more carefully than I'd ever ironed anything in my life, and made up the bed again. I had my story ready just in case any nosy neighbours came by wanting to know why I was doing laundry. I would say that Talisker had been sick on Mr Halliday's bed and I hadn't wanted him to come home to a mess. But it wasn't likely that anybody would ask. Not here. Netley Parva was one of the quietest villages I'd ever been to. It was more of a street with a little village green in front of it. There was the post office and general store on one corner of the green and the little Norman church on the other, and that was about it. Not even a pub or a phone box. Of course, a stranger would stand out at once, but my face was known round here. It was a peaceful community, where people in the surrounding lanes could put six boxes of their hens' freshly laid eggs outside their gates in the morning and later, collect six unmolested pound coins left in their place. I would be recognised as Henry Halliday's cat sitter, and very likely waved at, but beyond that nobody would pay much attention to my comings and goings. Even though it looked as if there should be, I was pretty sure there were no Miss Marple characters here, and at the moment I was very glad of it.

Talisker lifted his paw and padded at my ankle, so I picked him up for a cuddle while having a last look around downstairs. The place was as clean as possible – to my eyes at least – and nothing looked out of the ordinary that I could see.

I'd been and bought a bag of cat litter and small refill versions of the hypo-allergenic, ecologically-sound, wouldn't-hurt-an-ant laundry liquid and fabric softener that Henry Halliday always used and tipped them into the existing bottles. I was hoping he wouldn't notice that Talisker's newly topped up biscuit container didn't look any emptier than when he left, or that the number of tins and sachets of cat food on the tray in the utility room hadn't gone down much either. Surely nobody counts tins of cat food.

Planting a couple of kisses on top of Talisker's velvety head, I put him down on the sofa and rubbed his ear.

'OK, Tal. I'll see you in a few weeks, fella.' He winked at me as if to say 'Don't worry, I'll keep your secret,' then leaned on his side, stuck his back foot in his ear, and started to have a good scratch.

The rest of the day went by quickly, catching up with my other clients, and I was quite breathless as I dashed into the office at half past six. It was Katya's birthday and we were all meeting up for cake and a glass of fizz as Davina had another engagement and couldn't join us for the evening. Katya was flushed already and I guessed there'd been some fizz at lunchtime too. Davina, in coral pink today, was elegant as ever.

'There you are, Beth darling!' She thrust the last champagne flute in my hand. 'Thank God! We're all absolutely gasping with thirst!'

I smiled self-consciously. It seemed to me I was always the one rushing in late and looking like I'd just been dragged through a hedge backwards.

We sang *Happy Birthday To You* as Natalia, the longest standing member of the team, carried a Croquembouche out from the kitchen, a tall sparkler doing its thing in the top. Trust Davina – no ordinary birthday cake if she was in charge.

Once the sparkler went out, Natalia dismantled the glistening profiteroles and dished them up. They were so good I could have eaten the whole thing. This was the second weekday birthday in the office since I'd joined Sitting Pretty. The first had been Natalia's, and Davina had arranged for a chocolate fountain to be brought in, complete with marshmallows, strawberries, chunks of banana, and little cubes of cake on sticks. She hadn't been able to come out with us in the evening for that one either.

We were going to some fancy cocktail bar in Southampton. It was Katya's favourite place to party at the moment, probably because Katya's current favourite barman worked there. I'd only ever been once, as Alex – who probably spent more on hair products in a month than I did in a year – had decided it was full of posers. I remembered heartily but silently agreeing with him at the time, a bit miffed though, that it sounded like he was including my friends in that judgement.

Katya had reserved a seating area for us last time she was there so we didn't have to worry about not being able to get in. The arrangement was for us all to meet there. I was going back to Katya's place with her to get ready and then I was going to stay the night. It was pretty certain the birthday girl wouldn't be in any fit state to find her own way home at the end of the night, so I'd offered to be the one to make sure she got home all right. It was the sort of thing I'd do anyway. I'd got her a nice bag, in the sale in Debenhams that I knew she'd love, to stop myself feeling guilty about inviting myself for a sleepover. I was so looking forward to spending a night in a bed without worrying that I wasn't supposed to be there. And having a proper shower, rather than the quickest I could manage. Or even a bath. I never thought I'd find myself getting so excited at the thought of having a bath. Well, not one on my own, anyway.

CHAPTER EIGHT

The music was thumping. From the moment we stepped out of the taxi, I could feel it vibrating up from my feet, through my entire body. At least it was music I recognised. I'd half expected an eclectic mix of techno, rap, garage, funk, and house, none of which I was into, and quite possibly none of which was even played any more. Looking at all the notice boards adorning the entrance, however, I realised that Wednesdays were 80s nights. I was so glad Katya had insisted on going out on the night of her actual birthday and not waiting a couple of days until the weekend. Although, if I knew Katya, there'd probably be some hard partying going on from Friday night through to Monday morning.

'Woo-hoo!' Katya and Natalia chorused. 'Time to *party*!' They tottered towards the entrance in their six inch heels while I struggled to keep up in my three-inchers, my one pair of shoes that weren't flat and dog walk friendly.

'Good evening, ladies,' the doorman cast the two Eastern European beauties an approving once-over. He ignored me – less tall, less leggy with a lot less flesh on show – completely.

'Katya Radanovich,' Katya shrieked over the music. 'Party of twenty-two … '

'Birthday party,' added Natalia, pouting for good measure. I could see I was in for a night of watching the handbags if these two and their friends were going to spend the whole evening on the pull.

A smiling waiter came over and we were shown to a corner of the outside seating area overlooking the Port of Southampton. There were Reserved signs on the low tables, balloons with Happy Birthday on them tied to the cushions of the curved divans and a few strategically placed outdoor heaters. Some of Katya's friends from outside work were already there, a three quarters empty Russian Standard vodka bottle and some half-eaten dishes of nuts and olives on the table in front of them.

'Katya! *Preevyet*!' one of them cried out and they all stood up to greet the birthday girl, all long legs, short skirts, teeny tiny waists, and huge hair. '*Dobriy vyecher*!' was the only greeting I recognised – good evening.

A second bottle of Russian Standard appeared on the table with a couple of ice buckets and a few mixers. I could have murdered a glass of wine, but it seemed everyone was drinking vodka and I didn't want to be the odd one out. As it was, I was the only Brit in our party so far. I hoped the girls from work weren't going to be much longer. No one was speaking a word of English now.

A bag of presents appeared from the side of the divan and Katya fell on them excitedly. A pair of huge, gaudy earrings were the first gift she opened. I thought they looked like something Pat Butcher would have worn on EastEnders, but Katya seemed to like them.

'*Spaseeba*! *Bal'shoye spaseeba*!' she yelled over the music. I knew *spaseeba* meant thank you. I guessed *bal'shoye* didn't mean they're horrible and you obviously hate me to have given me these but …

'Hey!' A voice I recognised shouted over my shoulder. 'How did I know this would be the most glam table in the whole place?' Daisy, the new girl who'd almost lost Bubbles the poodle, appeared with a man I didn't know. 'Happy Birthday, Katya!' She kissed Katya on both cheeks. She'd given Katya a pretty pashmina before we left the office, in the same colour as the bag I'd given her.

'Hi, Daisy,' I hoped I didn't sound too relieved at finally having someone else to talk to. It wasn't that the Russian girls were unfriendly, they were just excited to celebrate their friend's birthday and to them, I was the foreigner who didn't speak their language.

'Hey, Beth! How's it going?' she gushed. 'This is Nick. Nick, this is Beth from work. She's the one who stopped me getting the sack when that poodle ran off on my first day.'

'Nice to meet you, Beth,' Nick smiled. 'Is it just vodka, or is there any beer?'

'I don't know,' I looked around our party. 'I'd prefer a glass of wine myself. I'm not really a spirit drinker.'

'I'll go to the bar and get us some drinks,' Nick offered. 'Daisy?'

'I fancy a cold glass of white,' Daisy looked at me. 'Beth?'

'Sounds good to me. Sauvignon Blanc if they have it. Thanks.' Nick made his way towards the bar. 'You've got him well trained,' I told Daisy, thinking Alex would have clicked his fingers and expected to be waited on. I shook the thought out of my head. This was Katya's birthday and the first time I'd been on a proper night out without Alex, probably since I'd started going out with him. He wasn't a fan of girls' nights out. In fact, back in London, whenever we'd gone somewhere and there'd been a hen party present, we'd turn round and leave. If he'd been here rather than in Dubai now, I probably wouldn't have come here tonight – he wouldn't have stopped me, but it would have been easier not to.

'Are you OK?' Daisy asked me, touching my arm.

'I'm fine,' I smiled back at her.

'Missing Alex?'

'Oh … you know …' I mumbled. I'd have to come up with something better than that to say whenever anyone asked me about my errant husband.

Daisy was looking very 80s Madonna tonight. Or was it Cyndi Lauper? Her normally swingy ponytail was fluffed to within an inch of its life and had lots of little plaited bits and ribbons in it. Her makeup was much bolder than usual and she was wearing a cute pair of lace gloves. I wished I'd known about the 80s thing, not that I really had anything suitable for it.

The rest of the girls from work arrived along with more of Katya's friends and our corner suddenly felt very crowded.

'I got you a bottle,' Nick yelled over the music, clutching a tray and edging his way out of the heaving crowd. 'Made more sense than going back and forth with glasses.' He put the tray on the table. 'It's Chilean, hope it's all right.'

'Mmm, lovely,' Daisy picked up the bottle and looked at the back label. 'Attractive, fragrant nose,' she read. 'A tropical fruit salad, with underlying typical Sauvignon Blanc aromas of fresh cut grass.' She grinned at me. 'I think they should have stopped while they were ahead, after tropical fruit salad.' She poured the wine. 'Cheers!'

Nick clinked his Stella bottle with our glasses.

'It's starting to get lively,' I commented.

Katya's friends were all gyrating to David Bowie's *Let's Dance*. Their arms all seemed as long as their legs.

'I wonder if they do requests?' Daisy looked at Nick, who winked back at her.

'The first time I saw Daisy,' he explained to me, 'was at an 80s night. She and her mates were dancing to *Girls*

Just Wanna Have Fun and I couldn't take my eyes off her.'

'Ah,' Daisy ruffled his hair. 'It was love at first sight, wasn't it?'

'Yeah. That and the back of your ra-ra skirt being tucked in your knickers!'

'No!' I chuckled as Daisy blushed.

'But they were very nice knickers.'

'Stop it, Nick!' Daisy cuffed him, playfully, round the head. 'Or I'll ask for *Prince Charming* and make you do your Adam Ant impression.'

At that moment Kool and the Gang's *Celebrate* came on and the three of us were swept up in the dancing.

CHAPTER NINE

Katya, Natalia, and the other girls were shrieking with laughter as I pushed, pulled, and persuaded them into the back of our taxi, thankful there'd been a people carrier available. Come to think of it, though, the birthday girl and her compatriots never seemed to have any trouble finding taxis. Climbing into the front and apologising in advance to the driver, I gave him Katya's address. I didn't blame Daisy and Nick for not coming back with us. I wouldn't have been coming back with us if there had anywhere else for me to come back to.

Behind me, the girls were laughing their heads off and singing something that was probably the Russian equivalent of *Four and Twenty Virgins went down to Inverness*. I just concentrated on looking out of the window and pretending I didn't know them.

When we reached Katya's address, getting them out of the taxi with what was left of their dignity intact was nigh on impossible. Both the taxi driver and a loved-up couple walking along feeding steaming hot chips to each other out of a paper cone were treated to the sight of highly toned upper inner thigh. And there were enough flashes of Natalia's red lacy knickers to get us all arrested. Though I suppose I should be thankful that she was wearing any at all.

'*Nazdorovie!*' Katya waved an imaginary glass at the driver. As if he and the whole street didn't already know she was drunk.

'*Nazdorovie!*' joined in the other two, clearly not wanting to be left out.

The driver sped off and I started herding them into the front door of her building. It was like herding cats and I couldn't wait to get inside and get my shoes off.

'*Nazdorovie!*' Katya grinned and gave me a mock salute.

'Yep, *Nazdorovie* to you too. Come on,' I cajoled, steering them towards the lift. 'There's nothing to drink down here.'

That worked. They staggered into the lift and I pressed the button for Katya's floor before anything else could stop us. I was shattered. It was gone half past three and my first appointment tomorrow, on Natalia's behalf, was supposed to be at eight o'clock. All I wanted to do was get them behind Katya's front door before they upset any of her neighbours, though if they were male they'd probably be more than forgiving.

Katya dropped her key as she tried to get it in the lock. I picked it up, let us all in, and locked the door. While Katya made straight for the kitchen, no doubt to get vodka and glasses, I headed down the hallway to the spare room. The bed was such a welcome sight, I could have just pulled the cover over me and fallen asleep, but I knew how rough I'd feel in the morning if I didn't take my makeup off and have a large glass of water before going to bed. I grabbed my sponge bag and went to the bathroom.

When I came out, the one girl who's name I didn't know was weaving her way towards Katya's bedroom. I went and got a glass of water from the kitchen and found Katya spark out on the sofa, mouth open, half full tumbler in her hand. I peeled her fingers from around it and put it on the coffee table. Natalia was nowhere to be seen.

I drank my water, filled the glass again, and took it back to the spare room. The light was off. Did I do that? I turned it back on and was greeted with the sight of Natalia, shoes still on, sprawled face-down, diagonally across the bed.

'Natalia,' I tapped her shoulder. Nothing. 'Natalia!' I wasn't as gentle the second time. It didn't make any difference. She was out cold. I couldn't believe it – both of them, loud as you like one minute and comatose the next.

Then I remembered the other girl. I went to Katya's room and there she was, spread-eagled across Katya's bed. I tried to wake her. She might as well have been dead. And the way she was lying, there wasn't even a corner for me to curl up in.

I went back to the room I was supposed to be sleeping in. The lovely bed looked so comfortable, but it was only a single. There was no way I could squeeze onto it with Natalia there. Cursing my goody-two-shoes need to take my makeup off, I switched off the light and left her to it. Those precious seconds in the bathroom and kitchen had cost me a place to sleep.

All I'd wanted for the last few hours was to come back and get into that lovely bed. Now I just wanted to cry.

CHAPTER TEN

Twenty-five past seven found me folded like a badly arranged concertina on an armchair that had clearly been designed with style in mind rather than comfort. In fact, going by the rest of the furnishings in the room, it might actually have been made for looking at rather than sitting on – Katya's parents had certainly thrown plenty of money at their daughter's home, but I doubted they'd spent any time in it.

Tired as I'd been, it had taken me ages to grab any kind of sleep. I'd spent what felt like hours doing that bum shuffle you do on a budget flight, when your seat back won't recline and you just can't get comfortable. I had briefly considered lining the bath tub with Katya's fluffy cranberry-coloured towels and sleeping in there, but the thought of any of the girls coming in to use the loo during what was left of the night had put me off. And now my phone was bleeping at me to wake up and make me go and walk dogs who'd spent the night in fleece-lined dog beds. I wondered if any of them would mind if I nudged them over and got in with them. That had to be a new low, when a hairy dog bed started to look attractive.

I tiptoed as quietly as I could into the spare room to retrieve my sponge bag and clean clothes without waking Natalia. Why I was bothering I don't know, as she was snoring like a fog horn in the very bed she'd pinched from me. Half of me wanted to get a couple of saucepans from the kitchen and bash them together next to her head – the nicer half made me pick up my things and tiptoe back out. Then I cannoned into the locked bathroom door. The low groaning noise coming from inside told me that a shower wasn't going to be possible. This staying over at Katya's really hadn't gone to plan. A comfy, and more importantly, legitimate bed for the night followed by a decent hot shower had turned into a cricked neck and back, which was now going to be followed by a quick brush of the teeth at the kitchen sink. I supposed this was karma for my misdeeds.

My eight o' clock appointment was with the Doberman pinscher Natalia was currently walking five mornings and five afternoons a week. Apparently Mr DP worked away during the week and Mrs DP had broken both her wrist and her ankle and so couldn't walk him herself. I'd offered to see to him this morning as I'd known Nat would be in no fit state to control a large animal. I instantly regretted my kindness as it leapt up at me, paws on shoulders – mine, not his – and started barking in my face while pushing me backwards in an awkward kind of tango. I felt like a contestant on *Strictly Come Dancing* who'd forgotten the routine and had ended up with a very bad-tempered partner with halitosis, shouting the steps out loud as the dance stumbled across the floor.

'Oh, do get down, Wendell,' a harassed-looking middle-aged woman, hanging on to the door handle with the arm which didn't have a plaster cast on it, admonished him. Fair enough, he did actually get down, although not until I'd inhaled enough of his breath to decide that Natalia owed me almost as much for this as she did for nicking my bed last night.

'Hello,' I breathed out. 'I'm Beth …'

'Sorry about Wendell.' She opened the door wide

enough for me to get in. 'He gets very excited at meeting new people. He jumped up at Natalia to begin with but he's good as gold with her now.' She handed me Wendell's lead, turned her head to him, and told him to be a good boy for me. He gave her a look that said 'Yes, of course I will. I'm lovely. I'm the most obedient dog in the whole wide world', and me one that said 'Don't you believe it, sweet cheeks – that tango was just me warming up. You wait 'til we're round the corner – you ain't seen nothin' yet, lady.'

I'd thought Bubbles was a wilful so and so, but at least he only weighed about half to a third of what this beast must weigh. He nearly wrenched both my arms out of their sockets as we got to the entrance to Wintertown Park and near to what turned out to be his favourite tree. It seemed the next port of call on his agenda was the lake.

'Stop, Wendell!' I yelled as he careered towards it. I could see us both ending up doggy paddling among the ducks but he stopped just short of it, at a litter bin by one of the dozen or so benches dotted around it. The tops of my thighs slammed into the bench and I nearly went flying over the top like a cyclist who'd braked too hard on the front wheel. Natalia was going to be in for some good old-fashioned Anglo Saxon English when I caught up with her. I bet I could teach her a few words she hadn't come across before.

'You all right there?' A ruddy-faced man on the next bench along, smoking a pungent brown cigarette, was watching me over the top of his *Lymington Times*. He looked like he was trying very hard not to laugh.

'Fine thanks,' I gasped, unwinding myself from my own bench while Wendell, tail beating from side to side like a short, sturdy whip, buried his face in the treasure trove of the bin. 'Come out of there, Wendell,' I commanded. The only reply I got was the tail whipping even harder.

'Bet he's found the remains of someone's burger,' the ruddy-faced man nodded at the bin. That was all I needed, for this damn dog to eat something that would make him throw up while I was in charge of him.

'Wendell!' I did my best Barbara Woodhouse impression. The tail just went into an even bigger frenzy.

'You want to watch he doesn't eat something that disagrees with him,' Mr Ruddy Face continued his running commentary. I must have looked like I didn't have a clue what I was doing. Especially as that was the moment Wendell chose to drag his haul out of the bin. Out he came, with a mangled, yellow polystyrene takeaway fish and chip carton attached to his face. As he dropped it on the ground I could see the end of a congealed saveloy and a handful of hard chips. He grinned at me with his eyes over the top of the carton, as if daring me to even try taking his prize away from him and promising me the paso doble to end all paso dobles if I was daft enough to try.

After being dragged around most of the lake, I was dusty, sweaty, and five minutes late, by the time I got Wendell back to his owner. An extra minute to apologise for being late made me six minutes late getting to the Parkers to walk Bubbles. And that was pretty much how the rest of the morning went along. When it was time to break for lunch I felt too dirty, even by my usual dog walking, cat cuddling, and poo scooping standards, to risk offending Dominic's customers by going there for something to eat, so I drove back to the Sitting Pretty office and ordered a pizza.

It's funny how the smell of freshly delivered food brings everybody out of their hiding places. The office had been empty apart from Davina, who was allergic to carbs unless it was a special occasion, so I'd just ordered an individual ham and bacon with a side salad and a diet Pepsi. As soon as it arrived, however, Katya and Natalia appeared, both hung-over and hungry. Natalia, the bed thief, was first to reach out her hand towards my little box.

'I don't bloody think so! You … you …' I squeaked, pulling the box out of her reach, realising full well that she wouldn't have any idea she'd done anything wrong.

'What is matter?' She did indeed look completely baffled.

'You took my bed last night!' I tried for a slightly lower register but it still came out as a squeak. 'I had to sleep folded up on that hard arm chair, like …'

'Why you don't sleep on sofa?'

'Katya was passed out on the sofa and …'

'Why you don't sleep in Katya's bed?' They looked at each other as if they couldn't believe I hadn't thought of that for myself.

'Because that other girl took it and …'

'Irina? Why you don't share with her? She won't mind.'

'She was spread out over the whole bloomin' bed like a starfish. There wasn't room for me.'

'Ah. Yes. Irina is quite tall. Never mind.' She reached out and hooked herself a slice of pizza and lifted it to her lips. 'I make it up to you. You come dancing with us tonight, drink vodka, have good time! We help you forget you miss Alex.'

I plastered on a smile as I sighed and shook my head, ignoring the wave of anger brought on by the mention of Alex's name. He was the one to blame for my discomfort. Natalia meant well, and of course she couldn't have known how important that bed for the night had been to me. But there was no way I was up for a second night of that. No way at all.

CHAPTER ELEVEN

Bedding down on the Garrison's sofa later that night, I wished I'd gone out with the girls after all. Bart, their elderly Irish Wolfhound, had an aversion to clean water, an even bigger one to dog shampoo, and a bottom that could understudy for the wind section of any amateur orchestra, just so long as all the other musicians had no sense of smell. But this was all that had been available to me for tonight and, if Mrs Garrison's sister and brother-in-law hadn't been celebrating their ruby wedding anniversary with a big family party at a hotel in the Cotswolds, I wouldn't even have had this option.

I was beginning to wonder how long I could keep this up. I didn't know much about the stages of grief, or whatever it was you were supposed to go through after a break-up. There had been tears, there had been disbelief and then I seemed to have reached the angry stage and stayed there. The adrenalin of anger had got me this far, but how long could I really keep doing this?

Tomorrow I had to get off this sofa and do today all over again, only minus Wendell, thank goodness, but then what? Invite myself for another night out with the girls where I might or might not end up perched on a hard armchair again?

This had been a stupid plan. I should have gone straight to London and told Mum what had happened. Why hadn't I done that? Because I'd have had to see that 'I'm not going to say it but I did tell you so' look flash across her eyes before she could stop it? She'd bite her tongue, of course, and not actually say it to me. Mum wasn't like that – she would always try and talk me out of making a mistake, but once I'd made it, she wasn't one to sit about rehashing things. But I'd know it was at the back of her mind and that she'd be worried about me. I didn't want that. So I'd kept her in the dark.

But there are times when a girl could really do with her mum. I wondered what she was doing this weekend.

CHAPTER TWELVE

My decision to spend the weekend at my mum's had taken me by surprise. But the more I thought about it, the more sense it made to head up to London after my last client on Friday night and come back early Monday morning in time, hopefully, for the first one. Three nights of comfortable bed, cooked breakfast, as much loud TV and all the hot water I could wish for. All I had to do was not let Mum realise the real reason I had stayed behind when Alex left for Dubai.

Of course he still hadn't called and, of course, when I had given into temptation and tried his old number, I'd had to listen to that *The number you have dialled is not in service* message. How did that message always manage to sound like it was saying 'The person you have dialled does not want to speak to you'? I'd written and deleted a hundred and one emails to him, not being able to bring myself to press Send. His Facebook page still said *Relationship Status – Married to Beth Dixon.* And our honeymoon photo was still there. Nothing added, nothing changed, nothing taken away. I wondered again if he just couldn't be bothered with it, or if he was so busy enjoying his new life that he didn't have time for bothering with social media. Or was the coward in him worried what Mama Petropoulos would say when she found out?

Anyway, I had to forget about that while I was at Mum's or she'd know something was up. I hated lying to her as it was, but at least the little white lies I'd be telling her would be told with the intention of not worrying her.

I'd left it too late to book a cheap advance train fare, and there was nowhere to park outside Mum's, even if Davina let me borrow the car for the weekend and I could afford the petrol. So I booked a return ticket to Victoria on the coach from Southampton, as that was the only one that would get me back anywhere near in time on Monday morning, but I would be getting on at Winchester. Natalia did my last client of the day in return for my walking Wendell so Davina could drop me off by Kind Alfred's statue in time to catch the ten to six.

It was a long time since I'd travelled by coach, probably not since I was a student with a travel card. My chief memories were of grumpy drivers, cramped seats, and no heating or air conditioning. But a cheery driver got off this one, checked my ticket, and hoisted my bag of dirty laundry – sorry, Mum – into the luggage hold, and off we went. The coach was about a quarter full, and I got a double seat to myself. It was more comfortable than some of the places I'd been sleeping recently.

The traffic when we got into London was Friday evening bad, and we arrived at Victoria at about twenty past eight instead of ten to. Glad I didn't have to drive to North West London, I hauled my bag along to the tube station and joined the thankfully short queue to top up my old Oyster card. I was pretty sure there was no money left on it, but I was so glad I hadn't thrown it out in the big clear-out while we were packing up for Dubai. If I was going to make a habit of coming here at the weekends it would save me a lot of money.

This part of the journey didn't take long at all, especially as the Londoner that still lurked somewhere deep inside me ran, at Euston, to squeeze through the closing doors of the Edgware train that was just about to leave instead of waiting three whole minutes for the next one.

Coming out of Chalk Farm station still felt like coming home, except that home had moved itself about half a dozen buildings down the road from the house where it used to be and was now only part of a house, but still with the same postcode. Mum still lived just over the bridge from the station and, until I got to the house itself, I could pretend I was still going to my childhood home. But since Dad died, Mum had found it too big and had downsized to a two-bed, lower ground floor garden flat.

I opened the black wrought iron gate that wouldn't keep out an arthritic cat and trotted down the steps – I could almost hear Mum's bathtub calling me. She had warned me she'd be out, watching a play at the Kilburn Tricycle, so I let myself in, determined to have a cup of milky coffee and some cheese on toast, and watch something noisy on TV while the water ran for my bath. I was almost drooling, but whether for the cheese on toast or the bath, I couldn't be sure.

There was a note in Mum's spidery handwriting propped against the microwave door. *Might be late so don't wait up, love Mum xx PS We have a visitor but don't worry, I'm sure you'll get on famously!*

A visitor, eh? So after all this time, Mum had finally gone and got herself a boyfriend? Unless he'd been around a while and she was only introducing him to me because I'd decided to visit and that had forced her hand? Hmm. I wasn't sure how I felt about that. I mean, it was good that Mum wasn't lonely and had some male company, but how weird was it going to feel if he stayed over and slept with my mother while I was here? Eugh! Well, there was no point worrying now about watching my mother play footsie under the breakfast table with a man who wasn't my dad.

I shoved that image out of my head while I put a mug of milk in the microwave, and while that heated, sliced cheese, put the grill on, grabbed the TV remote and switched it on, before heading for the bathroom and getting that bath running.

There was an episode of *Only Fools and Horses* on Gold or Dave or whatever it was, so I watched the rest of that while shovelling hot cheesy toast into my mouth in a way I probably wouldn't be doing if Mum were home. I was probably going to give myself indigestion, lying down in the bath after eating that but at the moment, I didn't care.

A huge sigh escaped my lips as I sank down into the scented water. Mum had always been one for fancy bath products – stocked up on them whenever they were on three for two at Boots – there was never any Radox in our house. Mmm, Champneys' Wild Rose – I didn't think they even made that any more. It smelt like home. And the warmth of the water was so comforting. I hadn't had a bath since the night before the movers took everything away and that had only been a quick dip – I'd have made the most of it if I'd known what was about to happen – only, of course, enjoying a bath would have been the last thing on my mind. This was bliss though. I could stay submerged for hours, until my skin went all wrinkly like a pink prune, or at least until the water started to get cold.

I let my mind empty itself of my day and float, as I marinated my body in the old-fashioned fragrance and there I was, wafting through an English rose garden in a white dress and sunhat. There was a picnic laid out on a blanket next to an open wicker basket, a huge pork pie, finger sandwiches, Battenberg cake, scones and strawberry jam. A game of cricket was being played on the green on the other side of the hedge. Alex was lying in the grass, reading – no, not Alex, don't spoil it. Who was my favourite actor at the moment? That cute guy who used to be in *Spooks*, only minus the tattoos – yes, he looked like he'd be at home with a poetry book, reading out loud to me while I settled myself down in a cosy sun chair and let my eyes close ... and drift ... and ... What was that noise? Was someone trying to break in to the cricket pavilion?

I shot upright, eyes open and trying to refocus in the steamy bathroom. Then I froze. Someone was trying to break into Mum's flat.

Something smashed. It sounded like it came from the kitchen. They were breaking in through the window. Or they were already in and they'd knocked something over. Why hadn't I brought my phone in with me?

My heartbeat hammered in my ears as I heaved myself out of the water as quietly as possible and stepped out of the tub, hardly breathing as I grabbed the nearest big towel and wrapped it around myself. What was in here that I could use as a weapon? Mum's industrial size can of hairspray caught my eye. It was almost empty but the new one behind it was full. A burst of that in the face could incapacitate someone long enough for me to hit them with something, couldn't it? But what? The can was probably the heaviest thing in here. And what if there was a whole gang of them? Maybe I should just lock the door and climb out of the window and get help.

A small scuffling noise came from the hallway. In desperation, my shaking hand grabbed the tall, cream jug from the window ledge, yanked out the loofah and the couple of long-handled back scrubbing brush things Mum kept in it, and got ready to bash whoever was out there over the head with it.

I tiptoed to the door, held my breath, and listened. Somebody moved quickly and quietly outside the door. Then the noise stopped and there was a scrabbling sound. Oh God! This was it. I had to take whoever it was by surprise.

Putting the jug down where I hoped I could grab it quickly, hairspray open and at the ready in my right hand, I offered up a silent prayer.

Then, on the count of three, finger firmly on the nozzle, I yanked open the door and sprayed.

CHAPTER THIRTEEN

Adrenaline surging, I grabbed up the jug, ready to protect myself from thrashing arms. There were none. The swearing and yelling I'd expected turned into a little yelp and a snuffly sneeze at my feet, before something small and sand-coloured scampered back towards the kitchen, emitting a volley of little sneezes.

Coughing and sneezing myself, I put my weapons down. I might be having an over-inhaling of hairspray based hallucination, but I was pretty sure the little sandy scampery thing I'd just seen was the Andrex puppy. What on earth …?

I waved the bathroom door back and forth to try and disperse some of the chemicals, before tightening the towel around me and stepping into the hallway. Everything looked the same as I thought it did before. The snuffles and sneezes were getting fewer and further in between now, and I followed the sounds towards the utility room at the end of the kitchen.

From behind a little mound of broken ceramic pot, earth and basil leaves, the spitting image of the cheeky, loo paper-pulling pup looked up at me. It gave another little sneeze, and tottered towards me as if I were its long lost best friend.

'Hello there.' I quickly picked him up – yes it was definitely a boy – before he hurt himself. He started to lick my chin. 'Well, that's a lovely greeting,' I told him, snuggling him against my neck. 'And how long have you been here, eh?' I stepped over the distressed plant and looked around at the dog bed, the food and water bowls, the twelve kilo bag of Royal Canine Labrador Retriever Junior Kibble, the toys – my goodness, all those toys for one animal! This was one well shopped-for pup. 'Long enough to have made yourself at home and started wrecking the place, I see.' I tickled his ear. 'I wonder why Mum didn't tell me about you?'

The little fella wagged his tail as if he was in on whatever my mother's plan was, then started trying to nip the label sticking out from where I'd tucked my towel into itself.

'Oh no, you don't, mister. You've disrupted my bath time enough for one night.' I rewrapped myself tighter. 'You stay in here and play with your toys. I'm going to go and get dressed and then try to rescue what's left of that basil.'

He seemed to see that as an invitation to follow me, and gave out a disgruntled squeak when I gently nudged him back into the utility room with my foot before closing the door. Then he kept up a gentle whine while I pulled the bath plug out and my pyjamas on. I quickly rubbed some of Mum's Wild Rose body lotion on my arms and lower legs – which I suddenly realised, were the hairiest they'd been since before I met Alex – and some of her Estee Lauder cream on my neglected face. It was probably the wrong cream for the wrong time of day – there were half a dozen different ones – I just used the most basic looking one. She could tell me off later, although she wouldn't. Mum liked nice things but she wasn't precious about them. I think since Dad's death, she'd decided that possessions weren't important, that they were there to be enjoyed and not worried about. She was always buying nice things and then giving them away to anyone who admired them.

Once I'd swept up the mess in the kitchen I opened the door and in he tumbled, as if he'd been leant up against it, eavesdropping. He did a little half roll, tottered into the hallway and made a beeline for my pile of dirty clothes on the bathroom floor. Still, I supposed they would have a hint of dog about them so I could see the attraction. I wondered if I was going to have to spend the whole weekend with this cute little bundle of fur following me around.

He was curled up asleep on my lap when Mum got home from the theatre. The sound of her key in the lock lifted first his ear, then his head for a second or two, before looking sleepily at me and snuggling back down.

'You're still up! Hello, darling, how are you?' Mum must have had her highlights done again recently, because her blonde and honey bob – cut that way after she'd decided she liked mine so much – looked sleek and well cared for. Just like the rest of her – I hoped I still had my figure when I got to her age. She unhooked one uncomfortable-looking shoe and hobbled over to the couch to give me a hug before taking off the other. 'I see you've met our little guest.'

'Yes, but not 'til I was in the bath …'

'Oh my goodness!' Mum exclaimed. 'He didn't manage to get in the bathroom and jump into the tub with you, did he?'

'No,' I laughed, 'but you'd probably be half a can of hairspray better off if he had.' I explained what had happened, while the subject of our conversation lay in my lap, pretending to be fast asleep until my mother laughed so loud he put his right paw over his face.

Mum made us both hot chocolate and told me about the play she'd been to. It had been a comedy, but she said she'd been more entertained by the couple having an argument in the next row during the first act. They hadn't come back after the interval and she was itching to know if they'd kissed and made up or if one of them was now floating face down in the Thames.

I called her a drama queen and we were both still chuckling when we said goodnight.

CHAPTER FOURTEEN

I dreamt I was sitting in a theatre waiting for Alex, his seat empty beside me. There was a couple, in seats much closer to the stage, having an argument. I couldn't hear what they were saying and I could only see them from behind, but that was enough. He was wearing a cornflower blue shirt, his dark hair just resting on the collar, and his movements and gestures were Mediterranean. Why was he sitting with her? What were they arguing about?

I called to him but, while other people around me turned to me with disapproving shushes even though the show hadn't yet started, he didn't hear me. So I got out of my seat, edged my way past the people seated in our row, and made my way down to theirs. Except when I got to where I thought they were, I couldn't find them.

'Alex!' I started calling in one of those not quite shouts we use when we only want to attract the attention of one person and not that of everyone else around them. As if it's the human alternative to the kind of whistle that can only be heard by dogs. 'Alex!'

There was no sign of him or his companion – who I wouldn't have recognised anyway – but I kept on calling. More people were looking at me, tutting and muttering amongst themselves, but I didn't care. I ran further down and scanned the faces, all the way to the front, even though I knew they hadn't been that far down when I saw them. Not a sign of them.

I ran back up towards where my seat had been so I could look towards them and get my bearings again, but now I couldn't find my seat either. The lights were starting to dim but I couldn't stop running up that never ending aisle.

CHAPTER FIFTEEN

'Wakey wakey, rise and shine,' Mum cooed, as she brought me a cup of tea in bed the next morning. 'We've just had a little walk to the paper shop. Oh, and I've put the washing machine on, seeing as the pixies seem to have left a load of T-shirts and things in it last night.' She raised an eyebrow at me.

'Aw thanks, Mum. I was going to do it as soon as I got up,' I said, guiltily. I'd forgotten to say anything about it last night.

'Don't worry,' she waved it away with her free hand. 'It's a lovely day, so it'll dry quickly on the line. Full English in half an hour? I expect my new boyfriend will join us, but he'll only want a sausage!'

'Very funny, Mum,' I groaned, wishing I hadn't told her about my misinterpretation of her note.

'Fried eggs or scrambled?' She put my cup and saucer down on the bedside table.

'Scrambled, please,' I yawned. Nobody made scrambled eggs like my mum, all creamy and peppery and ... I snuggled back under the floral duvet and then realised what she'd just said about the dog. 'Don't give Rex any sausage,' I shouted, as she was closing the bedroom door behind her – I'd thought she was joking last night, when she told me that was what she'd called him. I wondered how many Andrex puppies there were out there called Rex.

'All right. I'll just give him some bacon,' I heard her

chuckle. She knew how to wind me up.

Damn! I was wide awake now. I'd have to have a lie in tomorrow – I certainly wouldn't be getting one on Monday. This weekend was going to turn into a busman's holiday if I wasn't careful.

Sitting up and reaching for my tea, the full daylight horror of the newly decorated guest room battered my senses. It felt as if I'd been hit around the head with the entire Diary of an Edwardian Lady catalogue from my childhood, while being kidnapped and held hostage in the floral fabrics department of Liberty's. There were enough cabbage roses, sprigs of honeysuckle, and big green leaves to give an agoraphobic nightmares. It was a bedroom that Hyacinth Bucket woman would have been proud of – and what a sad indictment of my television viewing over the years, that I knew that. It had been bad enough last night, by bedside lamplight, but in the harsh light of day it was extraordinarily claustrophobic.

I gave an involuntary shudder, took a sip of my hot tea and nipped along to the bathroom, nearly tripping over he who was not to be given bacon or sausages.

'How do you fancy a little trip along Oxford Street today?' Mum asked as she put my overloaded plate down in front of me. Two rashers of bacon – rind on. She's the only person I know who can still find that in the shops. Two sausages, a creamy cloud of scrambled eggs, grilled tomatoes and mushrooms to complete the meal and, just in case a square inch of plate should still be visible, a Daddy Bear-sized spoon of baked beans. This was a breakfast fit for a well-built workman who'd been doing manual labour since the crack of dawn. And it was the most beautiful thing I'd seen or smelled since … well … probably since last time I came home for a visit. My stomach rumbled in both anticipation and appreciation and I could feel myself salivating. Rex was salivating too, all over my feet, but he was wasting his time doing the puppy dog eyes thing with me. They reminded me of Alex's eyes, huge, soulful, the colour of dark chocolate.

'I don't know, Mum,' I hedged. 'I've done an awful lot of walking this week. Even more than usual.' Which was true if you added being dragged round Wintertown Park by Wendell to my usual dog walks. The last thing I wanted to do was wander round the shops. If I didn't buy anything myself then she'd buy something for me, and I was already keeping my entire wardrobe in the back of my Sitting Pretty car. It didn't need anything else adding to it or the suspension would go, and I'd have fun explaining the contents of my boot to Davina.

'They've got some lovely things in the sale in Debenhams at the moment,' Mum slotted the toast rack in front of me, between the salt and pepper and the butter, and sat down. 'And the Christmas mayhem hasn't started yet so you can still actually put one foot in front of the other without treading on somebody's toes. I thought we could pop in to the bistro and have a spot of lunch.'

'Mum, after this plateful I don't think I'll have room for any lunch.' I noticed she was only having scrambled eggs, mushrooms, and tomatoes.

'Well then, by the time we've done a bit of shopping we'll be in perfect time for afternoon tea there,' she smiled, a cajoling tone in her voice. How could I make her understand how much I didn't even want to set foot outside the front door until I had to on Monday morning without telling her why?

'We could do some baking and have our own afternoon tea,' I suggested. 'I was thinking,' I carried on, warming to my theme, 'about making you a nice lasagne or shepherds' pie for dinner tonight anyway,' I white-lied. 'We could make your gorgeous chocolate cake and some scones and little sandwiches?'

'I don't think I have all the ingredients. We'd need to pop out and buy some bits.' That thought seemed to perk her up. 'We'll make a list straight after breakfast. Now eat up!'

My idea of a quick food shop in this area involved one of us nipping along to Morrisons on Chalk Farm Road, blitzing the shopping list, and getting back in the time it took the kettle to boil. But Mum had other ideas. I wasn't in a position to argue too much as she insisted on paying, and I didn't want to spoil her fun so, eco-friendly carrier bags in hand – more than I thought we could possibly need, which worried me, knowing my mother – I followed her into Whole Foods Market on Parkway. I noticed a few bits of multi-coloured tinsel and other festive bits and pieces were already starting to appear in odd windows. We were never going to be nipping in and out quickly.

'Ooh, look at these gorgeous raspberries.' Mum sniffed the punnet she was holding up and sighed. 'They really smell like raspberries. They're cheaper if you get two. Let's make a Pavlova!' Two punnets of properly-smelling raspberries went into the trolley. They were not on the list.

'OK, Mum, we need,' I consulted the list, 'cocoa …'

'Don't those fresh corn on the cobs look delicious, too!'

'They won't go with lasagne, Mum …'

And so it went on, me following Mum round the shop like a parent chasing a toddler round a sweetshop. She really was determined to give us both a workout, lugging bulging bags of produce home. I was beginning to wonder if my mother was developing a shopping problem. Maybe I should buy her one of Sophie Kinsella's *Shopaholic* books. Or maybe not – if I was right, she'd probably end up going out and buying the whole set.

The kitchen looked like Mary Berry, Nigella, and the remaining Fat Lady had had a food fight in it by the time Mum and I had finished our Great Chalk Farm Bake Off. On the positive side, Mum had produced a stunning looking Pavlova, and fruit scones which would look at home served in the finest of cream teas. Slightly less positive were my efforts.

We'd forgotten the fresh lasagne sheets even though they were on the list, and my cottage pie had been cooked at too high a heat, so was a bit crisp round the edges. And my attempt at Mum's chocolate cake recipe felt like it could make a good door stop. I might just have got the plain and self-rising flour mixed up there. Mum insisted, however, that a good layer of butter cream slathered in the middle and on top, would solve all its problems. If only a good slathering of butter and icing sugar would sort my life out.

Out of nowhere, a wave of sadness about Alex had washed over me while I was mashing the potatoes for the pie. He'd always teased me about my lumpy mash. Mind you, his mother used to faff about, shoving hers through a sieve, so I'd always thought, like most Greek sons, he'd been a little bit spoilt. It took me by surprise to find a teeny tiny traitorous part of me couldn't help wishing he was here to tease me again.

If Mum had noticed anything she hadn't said. In fact, she'd barely mentioned him at all, much to my relief. She'd never been one of those mothers who asked a lot of questions, but had always encouraged me to come to her if there was anything I wanted to tell her. Growing up, my school friends had all been envious of her easy-going approach, but now it made me feel guilty that there were important things I should be telling her that I wasn't. She'd be horrified to know my recent sleeping arrangements, but I just couldn't bring myself to tell her. You'd think I was eight, not twenty-eight.

'What do you fancy in the sandwiches?' Mum asked over the top of the fridge door. 'We've got that lovely piece of Double Gloucestershire with the chives in it. And the breaded ham. I could boil up some eggs and do egg mayonnaise, and I've got a nice tin of sardines somewhere ...'

'Mum! There's only two of us,' I chuckled, making her smile too. 'Two types of sandwiches will be just fine. Let's have one round of cheese and one of ham.'

Instead of sitting at the dining table, we laid everything out on the coffee table and watched *Mamma Mia* on DVD, knees tucked under us on the sofa, while we scoffed our sandwiches, scones, and cake. The cake actually wasn't too bad now I'd stuck the one-inch-thick layers of dense sponge together with half an inch of filling and plastered a further half an inch over the top.

We sang along between mouthfuls of food and swigs of tea, Mum with some very interesting variations on the lyrics. Benny and Bjorn would be horrified if they could hear her version of *Does Your Mother Know?* I know I was.

CHAPTER SIXTEEN

My dreams that night took on a Greek theme again, with me trying to get to one of the islands to meet up with Alex, but not being able to remember which one. My ticket was only in Greek and I couldn't recognise a word on it.

There I was, running around the Port of Piraeus like a lunatic, asking anybody who looked even vaguely Greek and who'd stop a moment, to read my ticket and tell me where I was supposed to go. Nobody seemed to understand me.

Pou Einai ...? – Where is ...? That was about the only Greek phrase I could remember. Without the name of an island to tag on the end of it, however, there wasn't much point in me saying it to people.

I tried to see if I could match any of the writing on the boat signs with the writing on my ticket, but none of the letters matched to anything – they didn't even seem to be using the same alphabet. The Greek alphabet had quite a lot of our letters with some boxy ones and some angular ones. The more I looked at my ticket the more squiggly the letters became.

All I could think about was how I would ever see Alex again if I didn't find the right boat. I was already exhausted, but it felt like I was destined to run round and round this port for ever.

CHAPTER SEVENTEEN

Sunday morning, Mum very thoughtfully took Rex out for a walk. Then she shut him in the utility room and put the joint of beef she'd bought in the oven, and headed off to the half past nine service at St Marks, leaving me to my much dreamed of lie-in. At least that's what she told me she'd done – she could have gone on a shopping rampage for all I knew – I was still in the land of nod when she tapped on the door and brought me a cup of tea at ten to eleven.

I couldn't believe the time. But after our afternoon and evening of watching soppy films and stuffing our faces and a quick walk on Primrose Hill with Rex, an- uninterrupted, this time – soak in the bath tub had sent me straight to sleep. I woke up feeling refreshed and ready for anything. Which was just as well, as Mum had invited a couple of our old neighbours she'd bumped into at church round for lunch, proving she had indeed been there.

'Oh good, you're dressed.' Mum glanced up from the oven where she was shaking her roast potatoes. 'Can you lay the table, Beth? Best use the good china. Don't forget the sherry glasses.'

The need for sherry glasses told me exactly which old neighbours were coming to lunch. They had actually lived just round the corner from us while I was growing up – two little bird-like old ladies, sisters, I think, who probably weren't old at all back then but just seemed so to a child. One of them had crocheted me an orange and turquoise poncho, I remembered. It'd be nice to see the old dears, but there'd be a lot of talk about knitting patterns, the old days when we lived up the road, and telling me how much I'd grown.

Sure enough, at half past twelve on the dot, the doorbell rang. Mum was bent over the oven again, doing something with the Yorkshire puddings, so I answered it.

'Hello,' I beamed at them. Blimey! I didn't know which was the eldest, but they both looked about a hundred and three – they really must have been old ladies when I was at school. 'It's lovely to see you again. Come in.'

'Who are you?' The one in the cream cardigan blinked at me and stayed put on the doorstep. 'Who is she?' she nudged her sister.

'That's Beth, dear, Vivian's daughter,' the one in the in the peach cardigan enunciated loudly in her ear.

'Vivian's girl?' She peered at me, doubtfully.

'Hello, Doris, hello, Celia,' Mum called over my shoulder. 'Why are you keeping them on the doorstep, Beth?' She ushered them in while I shut the door. Neither of them wanted to be parted from their cardigans or the large, squishy handbags they each had hooked over their arms, so Mum led them along the hallway in a kind of slow motion, four-legged race towards the lounge. 'Would you both like a nice little glass of sherry before we eat?'

'What was that?' This was the lady in the cream cardigan – I was going to have to find out which was which. I'd only ever known them both as Miss Wilkinson.

'I'll go and pour them.' I edged back into the kitchen and lined up the four glasses – I'd have a tot of Mum's cooking whisky in mine – this was going to be a very long lunch.

'So the one in the cream cardigan who's hard of hearing is Doris and the one in peach is Celia,' Mum reminded me as I took their glasses in.

'Right,' I said, setting up a little mantra in my head. Doris is the deaf one, Doris is the deaf one.

'It's only us!' Mum called as she came back in through the front door, Rex lolloping ahead of her and barking his hello to me. 'Shall we have a cup of tea before starting on the washing up? Oh!' She followed him into the kitchen. 'You've already done it.'

'Well, you cooked. Sit down, Mum, I'll put the kettle on.'

Mum and Rex had walked Doris and Celia home, along with the remains of the roast beef for them and a couple of Mum's scones from yesterday. I suspect Rex had been disappointed that the beef wasn't a treat for him. Mum said she was being good with him, but I'd be very surprised if those puppy dog eyes of his hadn't been scoring him all sorts of things she shouldn't be giving him.

'They were pleased to have seen you. They often ask after you.' Mum hung up Rex's lead. 'Celia was wondering when you were going to be joining Alex in Dubai …' She let that sentence dangle and I knew that if I didn't say something about the situation she would definitely know that everything wasn't as rosy as I wanted her to think.

It wasn't like Mum to put me on the spot, and I suspected Celia's question had given her a nudge to do so. I didn't want to tell her any actual lies even though I'd been lying by omission. But I had to think of something to say, and I had to think quickly.

CHAPTER EIGHTEEN

That night, my dreams found me looking into a wall of televisions in an electrical shop window. Each one of them had me on the screen. I couldn't stop myself gazing at them in fascinated horror.

In some, I was stretched out on the sofa in Henry Halliday's back room with Talisker on my chest. In others, I was snuggled on his spare bed with Tal on the pillow next to me. In a few more, Anthony and Cleopatra were looking bemused to see me on their sofa. In another group of them, I was trying to escape the toxic rear end of Bart the stinky wolfhound.

And there were plenty more. The screens went on. And on. And there I was, in high definition for all the world to see – well everyone else who was on that street anyway, which was very busy, wherever it was.

Rushing inside, I tried to find somebody to turn them off, but although there were suddenly crowds of people milling about in the shop, nobody seemed to work there. I'd switch them off myself, I decided, and started to look for their cables to see where they were plugged in.

None of them had any kind of cable or lead attached to them – how was that possible? I'd look for their off switches – Yes! They had those! So I ran along the first row, switching them off, one by one as I went. Then the next row, then the next.

As I started each new row, however, the earlier rows started switching themselves back on. How was this happening? The faster I ran and switched them off, the faster they switched themselves on again. There was just no stopping them.

CHAPTER NINETEEN

On Monday morning, my bag of fresh-smelling, clean clothes – which I'd had to wrestle from my mother to stop her from ironing – and I had to get to Victoria in time for the seven o'clock coach to Southampton. Of course, after a weekend of lovely weather it had started to pee down sometime during the night, and by the time I left Mum's at six o'clock, the streets were awash with puddles the size of swimming pools and the pavements weren't much better.

I wasn't sure Mum was convinced that I was absolutely fine with Alex going to Dubai "ahead of me" . She asked me, when we said goodnight, if I was happy and I mentally crossed my fingers as I told her of course I was, and said how good it actually was to have a bit more time at Sitting Pretty because I didn't know what, if any, work would be available to me in Dubai. She must have wanted to ask more but thankfully she left it at that.

Daisy picked me up from Southampton Coach Station and drove me back to the office to pick up my car. She was playing Christmas music and grinned when I rolled my eyes.

'What? I like to get into the spirit nice and early. Anyway, it's cheerful on a ghastly day like this! How was London?' she asked, pulling her little Honda – she'd nicknamed it Hetty – out of the tiny station car park.

'Pretty much the same. The walk from the tube to the coach station at Victoria was the worst bit. The lights at the pedestrian crossing always seem to take for ever to change when it's raining. How were things here?'

'Well, yesterday Bubbles managed to pull me over in the park. I ended up grass surfing on my bum until he reached one of the bins by the lake and stopped running. I felt such a fool!' We both laughed.

'Did you have a big audience?'

'Luckily no – it was a grey day so not many people were about – just this creepy old guy with a craggy red face, smoking these really stinky cigarettes …'

'That sounds like the guy who was there when I took Wendell out for Nat the other morning. Did he say anything to you?'

'Yeah, he suggested I get a smaller dog or a skateboard – cheek!'

My first call of the day had been covered by Natalia, so after a quick coffee at the office, I drove out to the other side of Netley Mallow to meet a new customer, a gorgeous and extremely regal, long-haired tabby called Bella. Her owner was going to the States soon on her first business trip, following a promotion at work, and it was the first time she'd ever called in a pet sitting service. Explaining all our procedures to her, I told her how one of us, probably myself or Daisy, could come in either in the morning, the evening, or both, whichever she preferred, and took notes on her feeding preferences. I informed her that if she was worried about leaving her pet alone on Guy Fawkes' night, we could always arrange overnight pet sitting on that night, or indeed any other night. Then I told her about some of the other cats we looked after regularly. Anthony and Cleopatra's owners had always been happy to recommend us to any new customers, and they only lived down the road in the village itself, so I offered to give her their number in case she had any niggling doubts, just seconds before noticing on her information sheet that they'd actually been the people who had recommended us to her. She probably thought I was an idiot and hoped it wouldn't be me looking after her cat.

I slowed down as I noticed Hazards' Estate Agents on my way back through the village. I was pretty sure they did rentals as well as sales, but would there be anything there I could possibly afford to put a deposit on once I'd been paid? Where had that idea come from? The part of my brain which housed the little bit of common sense I had, probably. A voice in my head, probably from the same bit of brain, told me not to be ridiculous, anything they had on their books would be far too expensive, so I drove on. There were other agencies in Wintertown who would be more likely to have somewhere small and grotty enough for me to be able to afford, especially if it was damp, had resident rats, a hole in the ceiling, and no front door. Maybe I'd have to think again.

In the meantime, a dog walk and a couple of cat feeds and then it was lunch time. I headed back to the office, where Katya was already on the phone ordering pizzas. She put her hand over the receiver and said to me, 'Am ordering medium bacon and mushroom. You want I make it large?'

'Yes please,' I nodded.

'Drink?'

'No thanks, I'll make a coffee.' It was much too miserable a day for cold drinks. I went to put the kettle on while she went back to her order, nearly tripping over a box of Christmas decorations which Davina had asked Katya to start sorting through so she could put them up as soon as bonfire night was out of the way. Katya kept moving them from one place to another. Natalia, equally sanguine where little puppies and kittens wearing Santa Claus hats were concerned, was sitting in the corner, reading a magazine.

'Hey, Nat. Have you noticed a guy hanging around Wintertown Park when you take Wendell for his walks? Red faced, smokes strong cigarettes?'

'You mean Stinky Steve?' she looked up. 'He's harmless. Why?'

'He was there when I walked Wendell the other morning, and when Daisy walked Bubbles today.'

'So? England is free country.' She went back to her magazine and I went back to my coffee making. If he'd been young and attractive and not looked as if he'd dressed in a jumble sale I was sure she'd have been a lot more interested.

After lunch and a sneaky look on Facebook – still no change on Alex's page – I had a full early afternoon of cats to feed and play with, and late afternoon of dogs to walk and I was glad to get back to the office with my keys at the end of the day. The place I was staying in tonight was a very isolated cottage, about a hundred years old, on the way to Lyndhurst. I'd done a swap with Daisy, who didn't like going there because it was actually a bit creepy, set in its shadow-inducing, overgrown garden, even in the middle of the afternoon. The owners, however, were away for a whole week, visiting relatives in France, so this suited me down to the ground. And then I could pop up to Mum's next weekend, so that was me sorted for another week. And then I really would have to give some serious thought to the situation.

I pulled off the track and looked at my accommodation. Daisy was right. It looked *Hammer House of Horror* creepy. Parking Harriet behind the old air raid shelter that stood at the corner of the garden, I resisted the urge to turn around and drive straight off again. After all, apart from inviting myself round to Katya's or Daisy's, there was nowhere else for me to go.

At least there were three cats to keep me company. The imaginatively named Dusty, Sooty, and Smuts were each a different shade of dark grey just this side of black, Dusty being the lightest and Sooty the darkest. They'd been friendly when I'd come and fed them before, so hopefully at least one of them would stay close by during the night.

Somehow though, I couldn't help thinking a nice fierce Alsatian would have been much better.

CHAPTER TWENTY

The front door creaked open – it hadn't done that during the day. It was extremely dark in the hallway. Even in the afternoon it had been quite dark, thanks to those shadowy trees and shrubs, but now it was 'ghost train in a tunnel' dark and half of me was waiting for something cobwebby to brush past my face and a deep, hollow laugh to sound out from somewhere. I fumbled for the light switch – why hadn't I thought of looking to see where that was earlier?

'Dusty!' I called. 'Sooty! Smuts!' Silence greeted me.

Feeling the wall with my hands, I eventually found an old-fashioned Bakelite switch. I didn't think they existed any more, unless it was a reproduction, and somehow, I doubted it. It seemed totally in keeping with its setting.

I don't know why I flinched when flicking the switch, unless part of me expected it to electrocute me. After all, I was an intruder. Anyway, all that happened was a rather lacklustre light coming on in the middle of the hallway. I locked the door behind me and put my overnight bag and carrier bag of food down on the black and white tiled floor. 'Dusty!' I called again, practically tiptoeing along the hall to the living room. 'Here, puss! Puss puss puss!' In the silence, my voice sounded demented and I thought of that ghost train again. And what was that film where there was a house that nobody would go to because it was supposed to be haunted by a screaming woman in a black dress? *The Woman in Black*? I was starting to wish I hadn't come here, or at least that I could switch off my imagination.

The wooden furniture in the lounge hadn't looked quite so dark during the day, just old-fashioned but solid and well-polished. I switched on the reading lamp resting on what was probably an antique bureau and looked round the room. No cats asleep in here, unless they were hiding behind the stiff-backed sofa waiting to jump out, and I wasn't planning on finding out. The curtains at the front window had been left closed, although I didn't know why, as any self-respecting burglar coming to case the joint only had to walk round the garden to the back to see through the dining room window that there was nobody here. Except that now there was. Somebody who wasn't supposed to be here. Wasn't it always the people who were somewhere that they weren't supposed to be who copped it first in those films? And there could be anybody lurking upstairs.

Telling myself not to be so stupid I switched off the reading light and went back out to the hallway, shutting the door very firmly behind me. Then, picking up my carrier bag and not looking up the darkened stairway, I took it through to the kitchen at the back of the house. The light was brighter in here, but not by much. I didn't know if the dim lighting was due to low watt light bulbs or very dusty lampshades or both, but this place could definitely be used as a setting for a *Hammer House of Horror* film, or a *Jonathon Creek* episode. It was way too creepy for *Midsomer Murders*. I could feel the skin tingle on the back of my neck and gave myself a stern talking to – I banned myself from even thinking the word "creepy" again tonight, otherwise I'd be having all sorts of nightmares.

I unpacked my pint of milk, strawberry yoghurt, and

Salad Niçoise and put them in the ancient fridge alongside a couple of old mugs, one badly chipped and one with a broken handle that I knew, from visiting my grandparents when I was little, contained dripping – probably one beef and the other pork. I didn't think anybody used that any more, not now people knew about things like cholesterol.

The fridge had rounded edges on top and a handle you pulled down to open it, and it looked like it had been here almost as long as the house. It must have been so old it had probably become retro at least once, and the outside of it looked like it had been painted with emulsion. The yellowed cream enamel cooker was just like one my grandma had when I was tiny – gas, with an eye level grill and a plate rack on top. The sink was yellowy-cream enamel too with a huge draining board, and I knew the door next to it was a big larder because that was where I'd had to get the cat food out from earlier. Not many Sitting Pretty customers kept their pet food in the same cupboard as their own food. I wondered if they ever opened a wrong tin and didn't notice. It wouldn't be difficult given the lack of light in here.

A rustle behind me spun me round, my heart in my mouth. One of the cats – I could only tell which was which when I saw them together – had jumped up on the table where I'd left my carrier bag and was having a rummage.

'Oh no, you don't.' I pulled him back out, his claws stuck in the plastic, pulling the bag back with him. 'Hey, those bananas and crisps are mine.' The wriggling animal didn't seem to agree. 'If you're good there's some lovely chocolate cake in a box in my other bag. You can have some of the butter cream.' The cat seemed to know I was lying, and that there was no way I was giving it sugar. It hissed at me, just as the other two padded into the kitchen, probably wondering what the commotion was.

They both leapt up onto the table like ballet dancers and joined their brother in his battle to maintain control of the carrier bag. What was going on? They'd been so friendly during the day and now they all looked positively menacing, like a gang of little furry muggers. I wondered if a tin of cat food would separate them from my snacks before the bananas got all mushed up. I opened the larder door, grabbed a can of Tiger Meat Favourites in gravy, and got it open as quickly as I could.

'Here, Dusty, here, Sooty, here, Smuts,' I trilled as I spooned dollops of it out onto their tin dishes and bashed the spoon against the side of the nearest to grab their attention even more.

The two latecomers practically flew off the table and hurled themselves at their extra meal, leaving the original snack snatcher scrabbling to free his claws from the plastic. I pulled him away, shredding one side of the bag and, as he pelted after his brothers, snatched what was left of the bag, went to grab my overnight bag from the hallway, took both into the dining room, and shut the door on them.

It was only when I was in there that I remembered my salad and yoghurt in the fridge. And the milk for the coffee I hadn't made yet. And I was going to need the loo at some point. This was ridiculous – I worked with animals for a living. Most of them loved me. What the hell was wrong with these three?

One thing was certain: I wasn't going to be spending another night in this house.

CHAPTER TWENTY-ONE

When I couldn't cross my legs any longer I grabbed my sponge bag, in case this was the only chance I got, opened the door just enough to poke my head out to check if the coast was clear, and left the sanctuary of the dining room. I closed the door firmly and quietly behind me and tiptoed towards the kitchen. It appeared to be a cat free zone, so I carried on through to the bathroom, which was chilly to say the least. It must have been the only room in the house with no form of heating at all, not even one of those old Ascot water heaters that could give you carbon-monoxide poisoning but would have fitted in perfectly. The Bakelite toilet seat was like ice. I washed my hands and face in stingingly cold water and, cats or no cats, went straight back to the kitchen, where I put the kettle on for a hot coffee to warm up my hands. If the bathroom was that cold in the first week of November, what must it be like in January?

I snatched my salad and yoghurt and some cutlery while I was there and nipped back to put them in the dining room. When I turned back I nearly jumped out of my skin. There they were, the three of them, one on the bottom stair, one on the telephone table, and one blocking the kitchen doorway, all looking at me, looking ready to pounce.

We stayed like that for what felt like ages, a kind of tableau – *Woman Being Bullied By Cats*. We stayed like that until the kettle started to boil. I hadn't put a lot of water in it, just enough for one cup. It started to whistle and still the cats didn't move a muscle – they didn't even twitch their ears. I had to get into the kitchen before the water boiled dry and burnt the kettle. I took a step. The cat on the telephone table jumped down and joined the one in the doorway, not taking its eyes off me the whole time. Great. I'd have a new kettle to pay for at this rate. And how would I explain that to the owners?

I wondered if the carrier bag would distract them for a second time. It was worth a try, so I quickly opened the door behind me and dashed back through. I left one banana in the bag and slid back out with it to find all three cats in the kitchen doorway, lined up like furry bouncers, just daring me to try and get past them. I rustled the bag until I got their attention and then tossed it down the hallway towards the front door. They dived after it and I leapt into the kitchen, turning the kettle off and pouring what was left of the water into a mug hanging from a hook. It just about half filled it. That would have to do.

Keeping an eye on the cats, now rolling and tossing the banana and snowy shreds of white plastic about between them, I took my half mug of water back to the dining room and hoped I could stay there until morning.

This had to officially be the lowest point I'd reached. I couldn't live like this any more. I had to tell Mum about Alex leaving me, and I had to tell her tomorrow.

CHAPTER TWENTY-TWO

I barely got any sleep that night. Visions of them getting in and eating me alive kept running through my head. I put the radio on just to hear some human voices and keep myself sane. I played computer games until my eyes were blurry. I tried to work out what I was going to say to Davina. Then as soon as it was light, I got straight out of that house and drove away from those malevolent creatures. It was probably the first time I had ever broken a speed limit. Daisy had been more right about that place than I could ever tell her. Natalia could feed them from now on. They'd have their work cut out for them, scaring her.

It was still early when I got to the office and there was no one else there. I freshened up as best I could in the little cloakroom, made a hot coffee, and had a handful of biscuits with it while I waited for Davina to come in. I went on the computer – there hadn't been any internet in the house of evil felines and I wanted to check my emails. And, of course, check up on Alex's Facebook page.

Still nothing. It was time I gave up deluding myself.,. It was time to admit defeat, give up my job, and go back to London. All this sofa squatting, hoping I could save up enough for a deposit on a place for myself so I could keep on working here, it was all just pie in the sky. Mum would be great about it, of course, just like she was about everything. I should have gone straight there in the first place. Beth Dixon, you are an idiot.

I was going over in my head, again, what to say to Davina when the woman herself turned up – a vision in red today – looking surprised but happy to see me.

'Beth! Oh I'm so glad you're here early. That's absolutely perfect.' She clapped her hands together as if she'd just heard she'd been offered a knighthood or whatever the female version is. 'I was just about to call you. Henry Halliday rang me first thing, he's had to change his schedule as there's some problem at one of his hotels and only he can sort it out. So I'll need you to feed Talisker, probably for the rest of the week – he wasn't sure how long he would need to be away for – but with it being Bonfire Night tomorrow you'll need to stay there tomorrow night. That's all right, isn't it? I told him it would be.'

Yes, of course she did – that was typical of Davina – and right at that moment I couldn't have been happier about it. I could have kissed her.

CHAPTER TWENTY-THREE

It seemed that every time I was at my lowest ebb, Talisker – that beautiful, gorgeous knight in furry armour of a cat – came to my rescue. I could have kissed that beautiful creature. In fact, I did, several times on the top of his velvety, smoky-grey head. He seemed to take that as no more than his due and rubbed his forehead against my chin by way of telling me that I was more than welcome, and that any further such displays of gratitude would be accepted with equal pleasure.

I knew I'd have to come clean eventually about Alex – hadn't I just been about to do that very thing until fate intervened? But just this one final week doing the job I loved and getting to spend time with my favourite cat – I couldn't turn that down, could I? Henry Halliday had asked specifically for me to stay with Talisker, I couldn't let him down. And there I was again, doing the old dieter justifying the biscuit routine, but this really would be the last time.

It felt wonderful to be able to legitimately leave my things there in the spare room. OK, so I was a day early – it was tomorrow night I was officially staying, but a lot of people let fireworks off in the days running up to and after Guy Fawkes' Night, so it would be comforting for Talisker to have me there tonight too. And if I was supposed to be there tomorrow, I could make myself cheese on toast for dinner! Whoever would have thought that the notion of making myself cheese on toast would get me so excited! Of course I'd have to do a very thorough clean-up afterwards.

There were indeed a few odd fireworks going off that night – not here in Netley Parva, of course, where I would imagine the average resident was probably in bed with a mug of cocoa by half past nine. No, they seemed to be coming from the far end of Netley Common, the end closest to Wintertown, so their whizzes and bangs were quite muted by the time the airwaves brought them as far as us.

In any case, Talisker wasn't bothered in the slightest. He was far more interested in what I was having for my dinner and how many tasty morsels would be coming his way than anything going on outside. We snuggled up together on the sofa in the back room, watching television and sharing my cheese on toast before having an early night – also together – to make up for last night.

I told Talisker all about last night's cats and I must say, he did look indignant on my behalf. But after a while he leaned over on his side and started licking his nether regions with a great deal of concentration, before lying down and going to sleep. I got the distinct impression that he thought he'd done his duty by showing an interest, but the conversation was now over.

So he'd welcomed me, eaten my food, invited himself into my bed, and now I wanted more than a few seconds of attention he was snoring his little head off. Typical male.

CHAPTER TWENTY-FOUR

The next day was the fifth of November and we were being extra vigilant on our dog walks in case some idiot let off an early rocket or something. I was relieved to get Bubbles home as, if he'd been spooked by a big bang, I don't know how I'd have managed to keep hold of him.

Daisy and Nick were going to a fireworks party in Winchester in the evening. She had invited me before it turned out I was looking after Talisker.

'Tal! I'm back!' I called as I arrived that evening. He padded down the stairs and wound himself around my ankles, closing and opening his eyes in little cat smiles. 'Right, what shall we watch tonight? Something noisy to block out the bangs?'

There was going to be a big firework display at Hetherin Hall, the fancy country house hotel whose grounds were so big that they seemed to touch on the outskirts of each of the Netley villages. They didn't do anything there by halves and it wasn't that far away, so tonight would be a hell of a lot louder than last night. I switched Henry Halliday's television on and sat down on the sofa. Talisker immediately jumped up onto my lap, kneading my thighs until he got himself comfortable. I'd been into the village shop and seen Eleanor so she knew I was staying here tonight, which made it safe to leave the curtains open a little so I could see some of the firework display which, knowing the Hetherins, was bound to be extravagant and very, very impressive.

And it was. I could actually see most of the biggest ones, exploding in bursts of silver, red, gold, and green, up above the trees, lighting up the sky. Out of the window I watched enormous multi-coloured rockets jetting up into the air, little silvery things shooting up and then bursting into a multitude of colourful sparkles, dazzling rainbows shooting through the night sky seemingly out of nowhere, fountains of whooshing flare-type things – I didn't know what most of them were called but they looked spectacular. On the sofa, Talisker was curled up with his head on one paw. While I stood and watched the whole thing, he couldn't have been less bothered, even when the bangs were loud enough to be heard here.

I called Mum before I went to bed. She'd been out watching the fireworks on Primrose Hill with friends and had brought them home and made them all hot chocolate to warm up afterwards. They'd only just left. I told her I wouldn't come up this weekend as I'd be on duty, but that I'd be up to see her the following one and she seemed fine with that. I didn't tell her yet that I'd be coming up for more than just the weekend. There was no need to worry her any earlier than was strictly necessary.

When I rang off, Talisker had moved himself from the sofa and was stretched out, fast asleep, with his head on my pillow, snoring his little cat snores. It would take more than a few silly whizzes and whooshes to disturb his equilibrium.

I wondered if there were any fireworks in Dubai. There were a lot of British expats, or so I'd read. Would Alex have gone to some fancy, expensive display? He'd never been much for that kind of thing, but he might have gone to something with his new work colleagues. I wondered what they were like and what he told them when, or if, any of them asked why his wife hadn't come out with him.

My traitorous fingers itched to pick up the phone, but what would be the point? I had already heard that 'The number you have dialled is not in service' message more times than any one person should have to in a life time. So I picked up the cat instead. If Alex Petropoulos couldn't be bothered with his wife any more then that was his loss.

Of course my knee-jerk reaction to carry on working at Sitting Pretty was more to do with enjoying my job than sticking two fingers up at Alex. But there had been an element of that too. There was that stubborn streak in me that refused to just slink back to London with my tail between my legs. Staying here had been my typically quiet way of telling him to shove it. But the reality was that I couldn't afford to live here on what I was earning, and unless I took on an evening job, this was never going to have worked out.

'Make the most of me while you've got me, Tal,' I whispered into his furry head, 'because as soon as your dad comes back, I'm afraid you and I are going to have to part company.'

CHAPTER TWENTY-FIVE

My dreams took on a different turn that night, propelling me to a strange land full of tall, shiny buildings, fountains and fireworks, and elegant, happy, dancing people.

There was a party I was invited to and I was anxious to get there, but my taxi must have taken me to the wrong one because they didn't want to let me in. I didn't know anybody there, so I took another taxi to a different one. The same thing happened there. And the next one, and the one after that.

I was just about to give up and ask the driver of the taxi I was currently in to take me back to where I started from when we finally arrived at a party where I was allowed in. Someone showed me to a room, a huge kitchen. Someone else put a tray full of cocktails and glasses of champagne into my hands and pushed me back out to where the people were. I looked down and saw I was wearing a white shirt with a black bow tie, a black skirt, and a long black apron.

People were grabbing the glasses off the tray but it wasn't getting any emptier. Round and round I walked with it, supplying a never-ending round of drinks, until I spotted another door and went through it. There was a line of taxis waiting and my tray disappeared as I jumped into one.

The next party we arrived at was even fancier and in even fuller swing than the last. I walked in and a couple of girls appeared, one on either side of me, offering me a choice of drinks from their trays. I picked up a glass of something long and pink and carried on further into the room. Men with trays of canapés wandered around, but none of them stopped long enough near me for me to take one.

When I reached the centre of the room, a spotlight suddenly shone on me and everybody stopped and turned to look at me. People started pointing and sniggering. Some were laughing out loud. Was I still wearing that waitress outfit?

Looking down I saw I was in my pyjamas, my scruffiest, bobbliest, oldest pair. And they had childish pictures of kittens and puppies on them. With everybody's laughter ringing in my ears, I turned and ran for the door, but I couldn't find it. I couldn't see a door anywhere, so I just kept running.

CHAPTER TWENTY-SIX

In the office the next day, the girls were all swapping stories of how frightened, or not, their pets had been last night. I was very proud of Talisker, he'd certainly been the bravest and I told him so when I got back that evening. He slowly closed and opened his eyes in his perfect cat smile as if thanking me for the compliment, while also saying that he had, of course, expected nothing less.

I was quite sad that once Henry Halliday came back from his problem-solving trip, I wouldn't see this lovely creature any more. Then it would be time to hand in my notice properly at Sitting Pretty. And when Davina asked why – well, she didn't need to know the whole truth, just the edited version.

So I'd bought Talisker some cheap treats and a couple of toys to play with, and we had a lovely evening while he humoured me by pretending to love his new catnip-infused mouse on elastic, batting it about with his paws as if it was the best thing ever. Once he'd got bored with it, he snuggled up on my lap while we fell asleep watching an old black and white film. And of course, we both woke up, stretched, and yawned as soon as the film had finished, neither of us having a clue what it had been about.

'Come on, Tal,' I stroked his head, 'up the wooden hill. We won't be able to do this for much longer, will we?' I watched him trot up the stairs ahead of me with his tail in the air and a complete lack of concern in the matter. Maybe, like Davina, he didn't really believe that I would go away and leave him.

I went to brush my teeth then came back to the spare room. I'd just moved Talisker from where he'd stretched himself out along both pillows, given myself the one his bottom hadn't been on, got into bed, and was about to turn the bedside light off when I heard a noise. It sounded like the front door opening and closing.

Oh my God! I swung my legs back down and froze, my ears straining. Was Henry Halliday going to catch me here? Or was there a burglar downstairs?

CHAPTER TWENTY-SEVEN

'And who might you be?' asked the man standing in the middle of the stairs, a rucksack slung over one shoulder and a very puzzled expression on his face, after I'd opened the bedroom door to investigate.

My heart was pounding so hard I couldn't understand how it didn't burst. I didn't know whether to slam the bedroom door shut and start barricading it with furniture or scream and run at him, hoping he'd turn tail and make his escape back down the stairs and out of the front door. My feet, however, wouldn't move and no sound came out of my mouth.

He seemed very calm and sure of himself for a potential burglar. And, for some inexplicable reason, vaguely amused.

We just stood there, staring at each other for what felt like hours, until he carried on, 'You know, when I spoke to my brother about half an hour ago. He was in a hotel in Geneva, sacking Swiss chalet maids or something, and he's probably going to be there over the weekend and into next week. He didn't say anything about having a house guest. The crafty old beggar! So, how long's he been keeping you a secret?'

'Your brother?' I squeaked, finding part of my voice and wishing the rest of it would hurry back too.

'Yes, that's right. I'm Marvin.'

'Marvin?'

'Is there a high-pitched echo in here?' he grinned. 'I'm

Marvin Halliday. And you would be …'

'You're Mr Halliday's brother?'

'*Mister* Halliday? We're a bit formal,' he laughed, as something clanged in my head. I often picked up the post from the doormat when I came to feed Talisker. A postcard, picture side down, wafted into my mind –hadn't that been from a Marvin? Something along the lines of 'Don't you wish you were here?' Not that I'd read it of course, but there had only been those few words and the handwriting had been big. And now I'd had a chance to look at him, he did have a look of a younger, plumper, more tousled, less tie-wearing version of his brother. As if to rubber stamp his identity, Talisker padded past me, trotted down the top few stairs, meowed a greeting, and rubbed his head against the man's shin.

'Tally! Hello, old fella! How's my favourite furry friend?' He bent over and scratched the top of the cat's head with his knuckles, while Talisker went into a frenzy of purring. 'So.' Henry Halliday's brother looked back up at me expectantly, as well he might, given that I wasn't even supposed to be here. 'We've established who I am, now it's your turn, lady I've never met before who's wearing pyjamas in Henry's house while Henry's away.'

My mind had already started going into overdrive. This was the brother of the man who had no idea I was squatting in his house. Should I try and bluff my way out of this? Should I throw myself on his mercy? Should I …?

'Tally!' he turned back to the cat. 'Have you got this young lady's tongue? Where have you put it? 'Cos I think you should give it back to her so she can tell me what's going on, don't you?' He looked up at me again but carried on talking to the cat. 'Because if your dad had gone and found himself a new lady friend, I don't think she'd be calling him *Mister* Halliday, do you?'

'I'm the pet sitter, 'I blurted out before I'd managed to follow any chain of thought as to what I'd say next.

'The pet sitter?' He looked bemused. 'At,' he pulled back his sleeve and glanced at his watch, 'twenty-five past one in the morning? That's a bit over-conscientious, isn't it?'

'I … I thought Talisker seemed a bit … a bit …'

'What? Lonely?' He looked at me as if he thought I was mad. 'He's a cat! Have you got someone up there with you? Have you been using my brother's house while he's away to meet your boyfriend?'

'I'm a married woman!' I yelped, holding up my left hand which still bore my wedding and engagement rings.

'So that's your game? You're using your clients' houses to conduct an illicit affair! You're …'

'I am doing no such thing,' I interrupted him, but with slightly less conviction. After all, take away the 'conducting an illicit affair' bit and he'd pretty much got me banged to rights. I just prayed that my face wasn't giving me away.

'I'm afraid I don't believe you.' He took a couple of steps further up the stairs. 'Come on out of there!' Marvin commanded in the direction of the open door behind me.

'There's nobody else here!' I stood aside as he carried on up to the landing, marched into the room, and quickly looked round it. What was he going to do next, search the bathroom? Look in the wardrobe? Under the bed?

'Hiding in the bathroom, is he? Come out of there, you coward! What sort of man leaves a woman to face the music on her own? You should be ashamed of yourself!' The en-suite wasn't that big and it only took him a second to swish back the shower curtain and see that there was no cowardly lover concealed behind it. Would he lift the toilet seat or peer down the sink's plug hole, thinking my mystery man might be some kind of tiny contortionist who specialised in u-bends? No, he didn't actually do that. Instead, he marched towards the wardrobe and pulled the door open. This was turning into something out of the *Benny Hill Show*. He seemed quite disappointed to be confronted with half a dozen empty wooden hangers, equally spaced from each other – as they would be in Henry Halliday's house –hanging from the rail, along with one of those lavender scented, anti-moth pouches on a plastic hook. Underneath was an empty shoe rack and above them, on the top shelf, were a couple of spare hypoallergenic pillows in special hazmat-style laundry bags. But no hidden man. I was half expecting him to pull out the pillows, assuming it was a character from *The Hobbit* that I was conducting this affair with, when he ducked down and started peering under the bed. For heaven's sake!

'Right.' He jumped upright, pulled his phone out of his pocket, and looked at me. 'Shall I ring Henry now, or shall I start dialling 999, *or* are you going to tell me who you are and what you're doing in my brother's house in the middle of the night?'

This was insane. I had to tell this man the truth. It was no worse than anything he had already decided I was guilty of. I'd explain everything to him and just hope he took pity on me.

110

CHAPTER TWENTY-EIGHT

'What a tosser!' was Marvin's verdict when I'd finished telling him what had happened and how I'd ended up in this position. 'What an absolute tosser!'

It was one of the many descriptions for Alex which had run, like a loop, through my head since the day he left without me. After keeping what he'd done to myself for all this time, part of me revelled in hearing it out loud in somebody else's voice – a validation of my anger, not that one was needed after the way my so-called husband had treated me. A small, sad part of me had, at first hoped Alex would realise his mistake and that he loved me after all. Now a bigger, vengeful part of me hoped he would, but only so I could shove it right back in his face with several bells on it and see how he liked it.

'I'll go first thing in the morning,' I said. What I really wanted was to beg him not to tell his brother about me being here, but that would be too pathetic and I'd decided I was done with being pathetic. 'Unless you want me to go straight away.'

'Don't be silly,' he jumped in. 'Bloody hell, after the way your husband's treated you, the last thing you need is another man making you homeless. Bugger me,' he chuckled. 'I've got to hand it to you. I can't think of many women who would have the nerve to do what you've been doing. You've got some balls, Beth – although I don't know that Henry would see it quite like that. Look,' he said, possibly having registered the look of panic I could feel rolling across my face, 'you must be tired, you go on back to bed in the spare room. I'll kip in Henry's room until he comes back.'

'What are you going to tell him?' I heard my mouth ask, even though my brain had specifically instructed it not to.

'Don't you worry, Beth. We'll think of something.' He drained the cup of tea laced with whisky he'd made himself – I hadn't wanted one – looking like a man more at home with a big, chunky mug, a tankard, or maybe even a foaming flagon in his hand. 'It's all right. I'm not going to drop you in it.' He yawned and stretched. 'Time I was crashing. And you too,' he nodded at me. He stood up and started for the stairs, stopping briefly to call back, 'First one up makes the coffee, eh? Strong, black, and sweet for me.'

CHAPTER TWENTY-NINE

As tired as I was, the sky was starting to get light by the time I managed to fall into some kind of sleep. When I did, I dreamt that I was at an airport, somewhere abroad, but not one I'd ever been to before so it could have been Dubai. It was beyond huge and there were no signs anywhere in English, and nobody seemed able to understand a word I said.

I must have already checked in, because I had no luggage, just bags and bags of bulky shopping. I was rushing to get to my boarding gate. None of the gate numbers, however, were sequential – they seemed to be random, as if the numbers had been called out in a game of Bingo – and anybody I tried to ask just shrugged at me, or chattered away in a language I couldn't understand.

Things kept falling out of the many bags I was trying to carry – I must have bought half of Duty Free – and I had to keep stopping to pick them up again. Bottles rolled like skittles across the shiny floors, their criss-cross plastic covers doing nothing to slow their progress. I chased after them, wondering how they could roll so fast and in so many different directions and why none of them had smashed.

Cumbersome electrical items were bulging, like awkwardly shaped biceps, through the rips their pointy corners had managed to make in their bags. Posh boxes of chocolates and fancily wrapped cosmetic gift sets were tumbling about all over the place and people were starting to trip up on the things my bags were shedding around me.

An announcement shrilled through the speakers, calling my name, the final passenger for boarding. I had to hurry. The gate was going to close.

I had to leave everything and run. But which way?

CHAPTER THIRTY

A knock at my door woke me from my dream. My confused brain couldn't work out whether it was part of it or not. By the time it had realised it wasn't, I was absolutely exhausted.

'Well, lazy bones, I gave up waiting for you to make the coffee.' Marvin wandered in with a cup of black coffee for me in one hand and a pint of milk in the other with Henry Halliday's probably very expensive sugar bowl and its silver spoon balanced precariously on top. 'That Elaine at the shop's a funny old bird, isn't she? I haven't been there often, and when I have I think it must have been her husband serving me. I went to get this.' He jiggled the milk, nearly tipping the sugar bowl onto the floor. 'I half expected her to say "This is a local shop, for local people!" and not let me buy anything.'

'Do you mean Eleanor?' I asked, wondering if Eleanor had a sister I hadn't met.

'That's the one! I grabbed this and paid before I found myself locked in and forced to watch her feeding a piglet or something.' He shuddered dramatically. I reached out and rescued the sugar bowl and put it down on the bedside table before anything happened to it. 'I didn't know how you liked it.' He put the coffee down and the milk next to it. 'It might be a bit strong.'

'Thanks, that's very kind of you.' I was glad my T-shirt was thick. It felt a bit ... not uncomfortable exactly, but there was something rather bizarre about sitting in a bed I wasn't supposed to be in, while a man I'd only met a few hours ago brought me coffee. Alex would have had a fit. Huh! I pushed that thought aside as it was his fault I was here in the first place, and he had no business having an opinion on anything I did any more. In fact, I wished he could see me here. 'That would show him,' one half of my brain said, while the other half asked, 'Show him what, exactly?'

'Anyway, I'll leave you to it.' Marvin turned to go, got as far as the door, and said, 'I suppose you have to go to work today?'

'Yes, of course I do, and actually,' I glanced at the little clock on the bedside table, 'I'll need to get going soon.' Would he take the hint and leave me to go and have a quick shower?

'Well, do you have any plans for tomorrow, Beth? You know,' he grinned, 'other than pretending not to be here?'

'Well …' I was embarrassed to admit my not very exciting plans for a Saturday. 'It's my weekend to be on duty, although it's not busy. I have a few cats to feed at some point during the morning – their owners are all away, so there's no fixed time. And one dog to walk. Then I was thinking of going into Wintertown. I was going to call some of my friends from work and see if they wanted to meet up for lunch, then I thought I'd find out what was on at the cinema, and then pop in on the cats again in the evening and give the dog a walk on my way back here …'

'So, apart from some hungry cats and a dog wanting a walk, there's nothing that can't wait until next weekend?

'Well,' I hedged, wondering what on earth he was going to suggest. The fact that he'd thought my recent bout of borrowing other people's sofas while they were away was ballsy and worthy of some sort of admiration was a rather worrying barometer of what he might think was a fun way to spend a Saturday. He wasn't going to ask me to don a Margaret Thatcher mask and help him rob a building society, was he? Or break into a medical laboratory to rescue a load of test rats?

'How do you fancy the Isle of Wight?' His question came as something of an anti-climax. Unless he'd been in the middle of organising a jail break from Parkhurst and just waiting for the perfect accomplice to come along, which happened to be me.

'What?' He had just asked me to go to the Isle of Wight with him, hadn't he?

'I need to take Lizzy over to Yarmouth for a few hours. Got some bits and pieces to do there. I was going to do it today, but tomorrow would do just as well. We could have a nice lunch, go for a walk, take a look around …'

'Isn't it a bit cold for sightseeing?' I asked, hoping I didn't sound ungrateful for the offer. And anyway, this Lizzy might not want me tagging along.

'Cold?' he laughed good naturedly. 'Don't you walk dogs in all weathers for a living? You don't tell the poor little mutts they have to hold it in because it's snowing out and you don't want to get your little tootsies cold, do you?'

'Well, that's true,' I laughed. He had a point – when a dog had to go, it had to go, there was no waiting until the weather got a bit nicer. I'd walked my charges round parts of the New Forest through howling gales, rain, snow, and sleet. I'd slid along icy paths while they'd sniffed at frost-covered trees, waiting for them to do their business. The only type of weather that got in the way of our walks was thunder and lightning. If anybody who did my job wasn't quickly toughened up to a bit of cold then nobody was.

'So?' he chivvied me. 'We'll go tomorrow, then? We

can have a bit of toast or something for breakfast, feed your cats and give the mutt a quick walk on the way, and be there by lunchtime. Then we can do the same on the way back. What do you think?'

CHAPTER THIRTY-ONE

What did I think? As I drove out of pretty Netley Parva, its village green showing even more bright emerald against the now half-dressed November trees, and on through the autumnal New Forest lanes, I thought I must be in the middle of another weird dream. I could just imagine the bronze and copper foliage on either side of me, punctuated by little strings of temperamental ponies, going on and on for ever, the turnings and forks in the roads that I usually turned off disappearing into thin air. I could be driving along this lane for what felt like for ever, until I eventually woke up in Henry Halliday's spare bed, with Talisker purring his little furry head off on the pillow next to me and no sign of any previously unmet Halliday relations.

There was an air of surrealism to being invited out for a jolly Saturday jaunt by Marvin –as if I was somebody he'd met at a social event and found he'd got something in common with – literally hours after him finding me squatting in his brother's house. From what I knew of Henry Halliday, he must be the stiff, white stick of chalk standing to attention in its pristine box to Marvin's squidgy chunk of Camembert oozing messily all over the cheese board.

'Are you all right?' Daisy asked me as we bumped into each other outside the door to the Sitting Pretty office. 'You look a bit preoccupied.'

'No, no, I'm fine, thanks. What are you and Nick up to this weekend?' I hoped she didn't notice how eagerly I'd changed the subject. She was a kind and empathetic girl and I'd hated not to be able to tell her the truth about my situation. I would miss her most of all my work mates when I went back to London.

'There's a gig on at Southampton uni that Nick wants us to go to – some band I've never heard of, but he seems very keen. What about you?'

Damn! I should have realised she'd ask me that. Unlike Katya and Natalia, Daisy actually took an interest in other people's lives. 'Well ...' Should I tell her about the trip to Lymington or not? 'I might be going to Lymington for ... for lunch tomorrow, once I've fed the cats and walked Bubbles.' Apparently my mouth had decided for me. I wished it would stop doing that; one of these days it was going to get me into real trouble – and the rest of me was quite capable enough of doing that, all by itself.

'That's a long way to go just for lunch,' she said as she signed for her pack of keys for the day and handed me mine and the pen. Katya was missing from her desk. It didn't look like she was in yet and I was more than happy about that. 'Look,' Daisy carried on, 'I'm not doing anything much tomorrow until the evening. If you like, I could do the morning and late afternoon feeds and give Bubbles his walks, then you can set off whatever time you want and don't have to rush back.'

That's really kind of you, Daisy,' I told her,' but Bubbles? Do you really want to risk walking him again?'

'Hey! That was my first day! I'm more experienced now. And don't forget I did walk him that weekend ...'

'Didn't he end up dragging you through Wintertown Park on your bum?' I chuckled.

She joined in too, then gave a little shudder, 'Eugh, and that horrible man with those cigarettes started making comments.'

'Yes, he seems to lurk about the park like some kind of giant, smelly, garden gnome,' I felt my nose wrinkle up at the memory of those cigarettes. What were they, Gauloise or Gitanes or something? Or they could be Turkish ones? They whiff too don't they?

'Gnome Man! I like that,' Daisy chuckled again. 'Nat calls him Stinky Steve, but I think I'm going to call him Gnome Man from now on.'

We settled on Daisy giving Bubbles both his morning and afternoon walks for me on Saturday. I'd feed the cats on the way and they'd be fine, even if we got back a bit late. I didn't want the favour Daisy was doing me to get any bigger as I knew it was highly unlikely I would be here long enough to pay it back. I still had Daisy's Gnome Man chuckles in my ears as I went off to walk Bubbles. The disobedient dog was waiting for me when I got there, paws up on the little window sill next to the front door, barking for all he was worth. Mrs Parker opened the door just enough for me slide in without Bubbles making his escape.

'Good morning, Beth,' she smiled, and stood back as I clipped on the dog's lead. She was a lovely lady, Mrs Parker. I guessed she was only in her fifties, but she had been diagnosed with osteoporosis and she was afraid to walk her much loved but very wilful dog in case he pulled her too hard and she broke a bone. She could manage Bubbles in the confines of her house, but outdoors he was just too much for her to manage, so when it came to walkies, Sitting Pretty had been called in. 'I hope he won't be any trouble today.' Bless her, she always hoped that. And nine times out of ten he was – although most of those times I didn't tell her – but you had to love her optimism.

'I'm sure he'll be fine,' I white lied. 'We'll have a lovely W-A-L-K, won't we, Bubbles?' I don't know why I bothered spelling it out to stop him becoming hyperactive, he'd heard it enough times to know what the sounds meant. Plus, me or one of my work mates arriving at walkies time almost every day was a bit of a giveaway. He was almost turning himself inside out in his excitement to get outside and find some poor cat who'd been foolhardy enough to risk one of its nine lives by being on the street at the same time as him. 'We'll see you later.' I gave Mrs Parker my most professional smile before grasping the lead firmly, preparing for starter's orders and opening the front door for the off.

I wondered, as I walked him, who would get Bubbles added to their list after I left. It would probably be Natalia who, in spite of being so slender she didn't look strong enough to handle a Chihuahua, was amazingly good with the big and/or physically powerful dogs. I didn't know if she was a secret dog whisperer or if one look just scared them into doing what they were told, but whatever it was, it was certainly working. Talisker wouldn't like her. Talisker would like kind, gentle Daisy. Hopefully Davina would realise that. And I was pretty sure she wouldn't want to disappoint her best customer in any way.

By the end of the day, I'd managed to get over the weirdness I'd felt earlier about tomorrow and was actually looking forward to doing something a bit different with my weekend. This evening was another thing entirely though, and I couldn't believe it had only just occurred to me. Would Marvin be spending the evening in the cottage? Or would he have more exciting things to do in town? Would he expect me, as the uninvited lodger, to put together some kind of dinner? Or would he want me to make myself scarce if he brought this Lizzy back tonight? We hadn't talked about any kind of arrangements for this evening and neither of us had a mobile number for the other.

Daisy and Nick were going out for a drink after work in Nettles, the quietest of the wine bars in Wintertown, where you knew you had a good chance of getting a table. At lunchtime she'd invited me to go with them. I would have gone anyway as I liked them both, but would Marvin think it rude of me? Maybe I should leave a message on the cottage answer phone, just in case he also wasn't sure what to do. I had the phone number in my mobile. Without thinking any more about it, I keyed in the contact and waited for the answer phone to kick in.

'Hi, Marvin,' I started with great originality. 'It's Beth. Just thought I'd let you know I'm going for a drink with some friends in Wintertown after work, so I'm not sure what time I'll be back. See you later ...' If I hadn't only just met him I'd have known how to word a question like 'Do you want me to stay out of the way if you're planning on bringing somebody back?' But I had only just met him, so as I couldn't think of anything else to say, I ended the call.

The very second I put my mobile back in my bag a horrible thought struck me. What if, for some reason or other, Henry Halliday didn't end up staying in Geneva for as long as he'd told Marvin he needed to? What if he got back tonight, before either myself or Marvin? And what if he was the one who listened to my message?

CHAPTER THIRTY-TWO

'Earth to Beth, earth to Beth.' Daisy waved gently at me from across the little table and I realised the waiter was clicking his pen on and off over his pad and looking at me, clearly waiting for us to finish making our order. 'I thought we'd have a bottle of Pinot Grigio and three glasses. Is that all right with you, or did you want something else?'

'No, no, Pinot Grigio's fine,' I said, as brightly as I could. I didn't want her going back down the 'Why does Beth seem so distracted?' route that I'd managed to head her off from this morning.

'You do seem distracted today, Beth. I thought so this morning.' Seemed I was in for a disappointment. 'I suppose you must be missing Alex?'

'Alex? Alex who?' I wanted to say. I actually had been as distracted as Daisy thought today, but it was by the sudden arrival of Marvin Halliday. And in that distraction my runaway husband had, essentially, slipped out of my mind altogether for now. But of course I couldn't actually say that to Daisy and Nick, so I mumbled, 'Oh, you know how it is,' ignoring the voice in my head that told me no, they, in fact, didn't. Here were a happy couple who obviously enjoyed each other's company, having a drink together to unwind at the end of their working weeks. They unwound, as they probably did most things, together. They couldn't be expected to understand the version of Alex's departure I'd given them. And they'd be even less likely to understand what had really happened.

I noticed them giving me sympathetic looks. Blimey! It was bad enough when a female friend thought you needed sympathy, but when her boyfriend thought it too, things must look really bad. 'Don't you two worry about me.' I pumped up the cheeriness level in my voice. 'There was no point at all in me going to Dubai and twiddling my fingers in a hotel room until Alex could find us an apartment. I don't have any work to go to there and I love working at Sitting Pretty, so this was the ideal thing.'

How many times had I told that lie? I was getting a bit fed up with it and actually, having told one person the truth, I was itching to blurt it out to someone else. Or even to everybody and be done with it. What would they say if I came out with 'Hey, you'll never guess what that little shit of a husband of mine did to me?' But if I handed in my notice next week, I still had at least a week to work with Daisy and I didn't want any awkwardness. There was plenty of time to tell her the truth when she was giving me a lift to the station to catch my coach to London.

The waiter brought the wine and poured a little into Nick's glass for him to try. He swigged it back, said it was great, and waited for us all to have been served and the waiter to have walked away before saying, 'I wish they wouldn't do that. Why do they bother? It's a wine bar, what they serve has to be good otherwise they'd lose all their customers.'

Daisy rolled her eyes at me. I knew from our many little chats over lunchtime pizzas or morning cups of coffee that her boyfriend, who was a lovely guy and seemed very outgoing, was actually painfully shy and hated to be singled out for anything. 'Never mind.' She kissed his cheek. 'And just think, if there was ever a disgruntled employee at the winery who put something in one of the bottles and we got it, you could save my life by having that first taste of it.'

'That'll be a great comfort to me while I'm writhing round on the floor in agony.'

Nick grimaced at us both, then smiled as Daisy said, 'Then I could save you by giving you the kiss of life …'

'You'd risk giving me the kiss of life, knowing there might be poison on my lips that could kill you too?'

'Of course I would, Nick. Any woman would for the man she loved.' She looked at me as if expecting me to agree with her. 'You'd do that for Alex, wouldn't you, Beth?'

Not bloody likely, was the first thought that entered my head. Just a few short weeks ago I would have. Now I thought I would just tip the rest of the bottle down his throat and clamp his lips shut with my fingers for good measure. But of course I couldn't say that, so I came up with a rather lame, 'Oh I don't know, I'm useless in a crisis. I probably wouldn't think of it until it was too late. Cheers.'

We clinked glasses and spent an hour or so chatting about work and gossiping about our Russian co-workers like three fishwives. Nick was completely on our wavelength in a way Alex had never been. It suddenly occurred to me just how many couples' nights I'd missed out on because Alex had refused to make any effort to fit in with them.

Daisy and Nick were going somewhere to eat, but I turned down their invitation to join them, thinking they should be left to enjoy the rest of their Friday evening without me playing gooseberry. So after I'd switched to orange juice and they'd polished off a second bottle, I paid my share of the bill and drove Harriet carefully, and even more slowly than I usually did, through the country lanes back to Netley Parva.

It was a relief to see Marvin on his own in the front lounge through the open curtains as I drove past before parking down the little lane at the side of the church. I wondered if he'd done that on purpose to let me know. Walking back across the dark village green and up the front path, I rang the doorbell – which was a first, but as Eleanor at the shop knew Marvin was here, then the whole village probably did too, so I thought it would look more normal if I behaved like any old visitor popping round on a Friday night.

'Hey, Beth! Come on in.' Marvin ushered me inside. 'Have you eaten yet? I wasn't sure what to do about dinner. I got your message – which I've deleted so Henry can't come across it by accident – but you didn't say if you were eating while you were out or not. I was about to order a pizza from that place in Netley Magna.'

'Pizzicatos?' My eyes must have lit up. Their pizzas were good – much better than the place in Wintertown which we always ended up ordering from at work just because it was nearby and quick. That and the fact that Davina had opened an account with them.

'Yes, here you are.' He handed me the menu, which I would be willing to bet was the first delivery menu ever to cross the threshold of this cottage and not end up straight in the recycling bin. 'I was thinking of a medium meat lovers' feast and cheesy garlic bread. So we could make that a large or you could choose another medium of what you want.'

'No, the meat lovers' feast is just fine by me, thanks,' I agreed. 'But don't add any extra garlic bread for me, I won't be able to manage it.' I wouldn't even have been able to finish a medium on my own – I never had. Usually

I just had a small pizza with a side salad – so I would probably just have a couple of slices and Marvin could pig out with the rest of it.

'There's some white wine and beer in the fridge – I didn't know what you liked. Help yourself,' Marvin said, picking up the phone and dialling the number. So I did just that. It was Chardonnay, not my favourite, but it had been nice of him to think of it. 'It'll be about half an hour,' he told me.' There's nothing worth watching on TV. Do you want to have a look through the DVDs and find something to watch? Nothing soppy though, eh.'

Soppy was the last thing I wanted, so we both agreed on a comedy. The choices in Henry Halliday's DVD collection were rather limited as he seemed to prefer detective series and historical documentaries. If I wanted to learn all about the fall of the Roman Empire I was in the right place, but as far as comedies went there was a choice of *Father Ted, Fawlty Towers, The Fall and Rise of Reginald Perrin, Yes Minister,* and *Yes, Prime Minister.* And yes, they were all in alphabetical order.

'*Father Ted*!' we both shouted at the same time.

We were watching the episode where they enter a lookalike competition and all three of them dress up as Elvis when the pizza arrived forty-five minutes later. I had a vision of twitching net curtains from one end of the village to the other, like a row of falling dominoes – a pizza delivery motorbike turning up at Henry Halliday's cottage? Whatever next?

The pizza was so good I ate three slices, while Marvin demolished the rest of it with no problem at all. I noticed he hadn't ordered garlic bread after all, unless they'd forgotten to deliver it.

'Did they forget your garlic bread?'

'Oh, I changed my mind,' he said, 'as you weren't

going to be having any. I didn't want to be unsociable and breathe garlic all over you.'

I couldn't imagine that would have been a problem – we weren't going to be getting that close – and if he had any plans in that direction he was going to find himself going to bed disappointed. And very much alone, unless Talisker decided to ditch the spare room for the master bedroom.

It was probably silly of me to even think it – he hardly seemed the type of man who needed to jump on an unsuspecting woman whether she wanted him to or not – but Marvin's comment about the garlic made me ever so slightly uneasy. There wasn't a lock on the spare room door so when I went upstairs to get ready for bed, I put the dressing table stool up against it so the door would bang into it if it was opened. Then I thought how ridiculous I was being and took it away again. Who did I think I was, Gisele Bündchen? After the way Alex had left me, I suspected I more in common with *Father Ted*'s Mrs Doyle.

CHAPTER THIRTY-THREE

It took me much longer than normal to get to sleep that night. My brain wouldn't let me relax until I'd heard Marvin come up the stairs, go along the landing to his brother's bedroom, and open and shut the door. Then my ears started straining to hear him moving about. Then they strained themselves even further, listening out for the sound of silence after he'd got into bed. Even then my mind wouldn't let sleep come. Sometimes my imagination was a pain in the backside.

In the morning, I was awoken again by a knock on my bedroom door. Still needing sleep, I desperately wanted to ignore it but as I heard the door handle turn, I suddenly found myself wide awake.

'I don't know, Beth,' Marvin repeated yesterday's manoeuvres with the mug of coffee, milk, and sugar bowl, 'you're not very good at this taking it in turns to make the coffee, are you?'

I hadn't realised I was supposed to be. And if I had, I would have got dressed before doing it, I thought, as I noticed that this morning he'd invited himself into my room wearing only a T-shirt and boxer shorts. He had very hairy legs.

'How long do you think it'll take you to get ready? Quick shower, bit of toast – what, about half an hour?' He started to head for the door. 'Then we can feed those cats of yours on the way.'

Damn! I thought, as he left the room, closing the door

behind him. I'd briefly managed to forget that he was supposed to be taking me to the Isle of Wight today. All I wanted to do was curl up under the covers and go back to sleep, but I had half an hour to get up and get ready, and if I didn't want him coming back in, I'd better get moving.

132

CHAPTER THIRTY-FOUR

'Aren't we going from Southampton?' I asked an hour later, after giving firstly Bella and then Anthony and Cleopatra the quickest visits ever. I'd promised them all that I would stay longer and play with them properly next time – Bella gave me a baleful, disapproving look that made me think she'd be straight on the phone to her owner to complain and demand that she ask for a refund on the grounds of dereliction of duty. Tony gave the impression of feeling very hard done by and kept looking at his toys and then at me as if he couldn't quite believe how cruel and neglectful I was being. Cleo didn't seem bothered at all, as if she had better things to do anyway.

We took the fork that went towards Lyndhurst and Lymington, rather than the one for Southampton. The one and only time I'd been to the island was by Red Funnel ferry from Southampton to Cowes, or was it East Cowes? It had been a cold day then too, and I'd been pretty sure we were about the only people on board who hadn't been on their way to visit relatives or friends staying at her Majesty's pleasure in Parkhurst.

'Southampton?' Marvin glanced briefly at me before turning his attention back to the road and, of course, the ponies who might or might not take it in to their heads to wander in to it at any time. 'Lizzy's in Lymington. We're going to Yarmouth.'

'Oh, right,' I mumbled, feeling a bit daft. This Lizzy couldn't be his girlfriend then, otherwise he'd have stayed with her last night rather than coming to his brother's place. Then he wouldn't have had to drive over this morning. And my imagination wouldn't have kept me awake by grabbing hold of a couple of twos and making nine hundred and seventy-five over a silly comment about garlic breath.

Marvin was wearing a dark-blue, baggy sweatshirt and scruffy, well-worn jeans which looked like they'd had years' worth of some kind of dark oil – engine oil, probably – soaked into them, washed out, and soaked in again. They looked like the same clothes he'd been wearing when he turned up in the early hours of yesterday morning. They weren't, however, because those seemed to have gone into the washing machine first thing this morning, along with another set of the same. He must live in scruffy, well-worn, oil-marinated jeans and dark-blue sweatshirts. And there was me thinking my wardrobe lacked variety. I only wished I'd known that he was going to put a wash on so I could have popped a few things in, too. The launderette in Wintertown was a pretty dismal place to spend an hour or so in the company of one or two others who, for whatever reason didn't have access to a washing machine, each of us pretending not to be watching anyone else's underwear go round and round and round. On second thoughts though, maybe it was just as well.

By the time we reached Lymington it was starting to drizzle ever so slightly and I was wondering if this outing had been quite such a good idea after all. Lovely as it was to be doing something different – hell, anything different – with my weekend, I could have been eating lunch in a warm café, wiping a space in the condensation steaming up the windows to watch other people get drizzled on, before going along to a warm, dry cinema and munching popcorn while slipping into somebody else's life and the dramas it held, for a couple of hours.

We headed for the old town quay which seemed to be full of all sorts and sizes of boats. It looked pretty, even if you weren't a boat-y type of person. There were three swans, floating regally about between the various vessels, as if they were the harbour inspectors giving them all the once-over. Two were spotlessly white and one was a bit muddy looking, as if it had been in the wash with a stray brown sock – obviously the trainee or work experience harbour inspector. There were brown ducks splashing along behind them too – so it could have been Bring Your Ducklings To Work Day. What was the word for a group of ducks? It was something amusing I seemed to remember – paddling? A paddling of ducks?

'You go and have a wander if you like,' Marvin told me. 'I've got to see someone. I'll meet you back here in half an hour.'

So I went and had a wander. There was a quaint little cobbled street meandering away from the quay. I walked towards it, checking the time on my watch. As I passed a ticket booth for Puffin Cruises I picked up a leaflet and scanned it. Apart from the ferry service to the island, there were half hour scenic river cruises and a lunchtime boat that allowed you three hours in Yarmouth – I wondered if that was the one we were going on. Actually, that sounded really nice and it only took half an hour to get there. Then I noticed that the timings on it were for the summer. I couldn't see anything about November. Still, Marvin and this Lizzy must know what times the boats were. It sounded as if they did this sort of thing all the time.

Folding up the leaflet and putting it in my pocket, I carried on towards the cobbles. There were little cafés and restaurants, and a collection of little boutique shops, gift shops, a sweet shop. A few of them had one or two tasteful and pretty decorations in their windows that could have been for Christmas but weren't necessarily so, and none of them were playing any kind of tacky Christmas music. As the narrow road bent to the left, it started to go uphill. I didn't go all the way up to the top – those cobbles looked like they could be slippery when wet, which they would be soon, so I just peered in the windows of the lovely little shops, imagining one day having another proper home to put nice things in again.

That made me wonder what Alex was doing. It certainly wouldn't be drizzly where he was. Would he be having lunch now? Would there be a canteen in his office or would he go to a café? I'd sometimes made him a packed lunch when he was here, but it wasn't something he would ever do for himself. If I could make him a packed lunch right now I'd put egg sandwiches in it. He had a thing about egg sandwiches. He used to love them as a child until his mum had made him some for a school trip once. She forgot to put the boiled eggs in the fridge to cool, so they got that grey sulphurous edge round the yolks, but she must have been in a hurry and mashed them together anyway and when he opened them up at lunchtime they stank the place out and nobody would sit anywhere near him for the rest of the trip. Yes, I think I'd make him a special Mama Petropoulos egg sandwich. And I'd vacuum pack it to keep the smell contained and ready for that blast from the bowels of hell smell when he opened it.

Feeling the ghost of a smile on my lips, I made my way back down to the quay. There was a sign for mackerelling trips I hadn't noticed on the way up. Couldn't say I fancied that much. I wondered if the mackerel got thrown back after they'd been caught, or if the people took them home and gutted and cooked them. No, I didn't fancy that at all.

It occurred to me that maybe I should get three coffees from the little coffee shop. If the trip was only half an hour there might not be anything on board, but I didn't know if Marvin's girlfriend would want coffee or tea, or how she took either of them, so in the end I didn't bother. We could always get something to warm ourselves up once we got to the island.

Marvin was waiting for me, alone, when I got back to where I'd left him. I was about to ask him if Lizzy was on her way when he asked, 'Are you ready for boarding?'

'Boarding?' I looked around us, puzzled. 'But the ferry doesn't go from here, does it?'

'Ferry? What ferry?' Marvin looked at me as if I were speaking a foreign language. 'We're not going by ferry. We're taking Lizzy.'

I looked towards where his head was indicating, at a small to medium sized – in comparison to all the others around it – rather old and scruffy-looking motor yacht. At least I presumed that was what it was, not having any interest in boat-y things. The name on the side suddenly caught my eye – *Tin Lizzy*. We weren't seriously going to sail this thing to the Isle of Wight, were we? It looked like a hand-me-down toy boat that some child would float on Wintertown Park lake for five minutes before it started letting in water and sank. I looked at him, trying to form the question without making myself sound too stupid. After all, I'd thought Lizzy was a girl.

'I know, everyone wants to know why she's called *Tin Lizzy* and not *Thin Lizzy*,' he grinned, obviously mistaking the reason for my confusion. 'You see, she's not named after the band, she's named after the cartoon robot that the band are supposed to be named after!' He paused like a comedian waiting for applause but he wasn't going to get any. I couldn't have cared less what the damn thing had been named after. It, or she, or whatever, wasn't a nice, big, safe-looking ferry with lifeboats and burly sailors on board who knew what they were doing. In fact, the more I looked at it, the smaller and older-looking it got. And we were supposed to get in it, cast it off – or whatever they called it – from dry land and go out to sea in it? My fingers curled wistfully round the Puffin Cruises leaflet in my pocket.

The revolving underwear show in the Wintertown laundrette was starting to look a lot more attractive. I wondered if there was a bus from here.

CHAPTER THIRTY-FIVE

'See, that wasn't so bad now, was it?' Marvin helped me onto the jetty or whatever it was called which was absolutely no help at all as the damn thing was moving about just as much as the blasted boat had been. As soon as one wave of nausea subsided, another, even stronger one started to build up. It felt like my feet and knees had been stolen and replaced with big blobs of jelly and if I didn't stop wobbling about on them soon, we were going to be seeing my toast and marmalade and coffee again very soon. Oh God, I needed to stop making food analogies. They really weren't helping. 'Just sit on that bollard for a moment and you'll be as right as rain,' my torturer advised. If I'd been in any fit state, I'd have liked to rip the bollard out and bash him over the head with it and see how long it took him to feel 'right as rain'. That seemed like a fitting level of justice for the eighteen minutes of hell this man had just put me through.

Ten minutes, he'd told me. Ten minutes at fifteen knots – the liar. Smooth as silk the Solent was, he'd told me. We'd glide along like a knife through butter he'd told me, too – liar, liar, pants on fire. It had been more like surfing on an Eccles Cake at speed through lumpy rice pudding. How I hadn't ended up tossed into the sea, I didn't know. If he thought he was getting me back on that contraption for the return part of the trip he was very much mistaken. No, there was only one thing I could do. I'd just have to stay on the island and live here for ever.

There was sure to be a pub, café, or restaurant who could use a cheap and cheerful pair of hands in the run up to Christmas. I could make myself indispensable during opening hours and then stay behind to help clear up and … well … it wouldn't be the stupidest thing I'd ever done. I seemed to be saying that to myself a lot lately.

'Now, I've just got to go and see someone,' Marvin told me in a voice most people saved for small children or those who were a bit slow. 'I won't be long. You stay here a few minutes and get your land legs back and then we'll go and have some lunch, eh? What do you fancy? I know a place that does the best crab sandwiches on the island. It's not far.' And with that he marched off and left me, wondering if this was his way of punishing me for borrowing his brother's house. Crab sandwiches indeed. The thought brought on another wave of nausea – as if I was about to put anything sea related anywhere near my mouth. If it was, then I thought it cruel and unusual and quite honestly, at that moment I'd rather have ended up explaining my behaviour to the boys in blue. At least there'd be no threat of crustaceans down at the station. And a prison cell wouldn't keep moving around.

'Blimey, mate, she looks a bit green around the gills,' said a voice that wasn't Marvin's but sounded vaguely familiar from somewhere. I realised Marvin had come back with a friend, and tried to smile politely. After all, he was probably of the opinion – even though he couldn't have been more wrong – that he'd brought me on a nice day out. 'Oh, it's you!' the voice said again. 'One of the Doberman girls, from the park!'

I groaned inside as I simultaneously recognised both the smell and the ruddy face of the man who'd been sitting by the lake when I took Wendell for a walk in

140

Natalia's place. The man with the stinky cigarettes who thought I didn't know how to handle a dog. This was all I needed. If he started patronising me again I'd have to shove him into the water, even if the movement did finally bring my breakfast back up.

'Do you two know each other?' Marvin looked from one to the other of us, making me feel dizzy again. I let his friend tell him about our one brief meeting, even though his version didn't tally with the one in my head. I was too busy swallowing air and saving my energy in case that shove became necessary.

The restaurant with the amazing crab sandwiches was decked out in blue, green, and silver – whoever had done it had probably had some kind of Christmas at sea idea in mind. It just looked cold to me. And it wasn't tinsel, although something not far off it and a bit more expensive-looking. Their tree looked very jolly though, although I'd never seen a mermaid on top of a Christmas tree before. To take my mind off the unfortunately seafood-orientated menu that had been placed in front of me, I wondered if there was an angels' union and if there was, what they would make of a mermaid taking one of their jobs.

All I really wanted was a cup of tea and some dry crackers or a piece of plain bread. I did manage a few of the chips from Marvin's plate, with just a bit of salt on them – no vinegar – so he ordered me a soft bread roll – no butter – and I had an impromptu chip butty, which did actually help me feel a bit better.

'So, now you've got some colour back in your cheeks, Beth, what shall we do next?' Marvin asked me. I wondered if it would seem rude if I asked if we could find somewhere to book me a ferry ticket so I didn't have to go back on that torture device with him. 'How about Yarmouth Castle? That's not far.'

'Closed at the beginning of the month for winter,' Mr Ruddy Face, who's name I'd forgotten Natalia had said was Stinky Steve until then, reminded him.

'Actually, I'd be happy to just go for a walk and have a look around here,' I told them, mentally drilling myself not to call him *Stinky* Steve. Or Gnome Man, as Daisy had christened him yesterday morning. Don't call him Stinky Steve – don't call him Gnome Man – don't call him Stinky Steve – don't call him Gnome Man, I chanted inside my head. I was on the boundary of being in enough trouble without insulting Marvin's friend. Even if both nicknames were true.

CHAPTER THIRTY-SIX

It turned out we weren't taking *Tin Lizzy* back to Lymington anyway. Marvin and Steve, for reasons best known to themselves, had swapped boats and we were sailing back on Steve's slightly bigger, although not any better-looking yacht – he did tell me what sort it was but, as with any other boat related information, it went in one ear and passed straight out the other without troubling a single brain cell on the way.

'There you go, Beth,' Marvin seemed to think this slightly smoother ride should make up for the hideous outward journey. 'What did I say, eh? Like a knife through butter.'

'Mm ... hmm.' I gave him a tight-lipped smile, keeping my eyes on the horizon just in case the chip butty decided to make a return appearance.

My jelly legs weren't as bad getting off in Lymington. It was a relief, but not a big enough one to ever make me want to do that again.

'Why don't you go and have a cup of tea in that little café up there?' Marvin gestured towards the cobbled lane. 'I've got a few bits and pieces to do and then I'll come and join you.'

That was something I didn't need to be told twice. It was almost miraculous just how quickly my legs got their act together. They carried me off like a thoroughbred racehorse's legs would have, past my old friend of this morning, the Puffin Cruises ticket booth, and on towards the cobbles and a hot cup of tea. In my head I sounded decidedly middle-aged for a twenty-eight-year-old, but I didn't care. This twenty-eight-year-old had had a very up and down day – particularly in the stomach department and was in dire need of the cup that cheers.

I was feeling more like myself again as we drove back through the New Forest towards Netley Mallow to give Bella and then Anthony and Cleopatra their second visits of the day. Had I thought about it in the morning, I should have driven my car as far as here and left it in the Steadmans' driveway, then Marvin could have driven home and left me to make my own way.

'If you don't mind, I'm going to shoot off and catch up with someone then I'll come back for you a bit later,' Marvin broke into my thoughts before I had a chance to voice them as he pulled up outside the Steadmans' bungalow. 'How long do were you planning on staying here? About an hour or two?'

One hour would have been perfect – half an hour for each house, unless Bella was being stroppy, in which case, twenty minutes per cat. Two was a lot longer than I'd planned but I didn't want to be awkward – my seasickness had probably taken enough of the shine off his day already – so I just said, 'An hour would be great. If you think you're going to be longer than that I could always walk back. It's a lovely afternoon – that earlier drizzle didn't come to anything, so I don't think it's going to rain now.'

'Well, I might be closer to two hours than one, so if you're sure?' He looked a little more relieved than was gentlemanly, I thought, but ignored it. After all, he didn't owe me anything – more the other way round.

I was sure that I didn't want to be hanging around for

two hours – cats weren't known for their long attention spans and I'd already seen enough of my clients' sofas to last me a lifetime. 'Yes, of course,' I told him. 'I'll see you later.' Then I watched Marvin drive off, thankful that Daisy had offered to walk Bubbles for me, and that this was the only thing I had left to do today.

'Tony,' I called, 'Cleo, I'm back.' Anthony was sprawled across the middle seat of the sofa, lying on his back with his front paws stretched over his head as if he was seeing how long he could make himself. His limbs twitched ever so slightly at the sound of my voice – unless he was having a chasing dream and trying to hurry up and catch that mouse – before settling back into exactly the same position. His eyes didn't even flicker – he was fast asleep like a teenager on a Monday morning and nothing short of a biscuit bag shook right in his furry little face was going to get him off that couch.

I wandered through the open bedroom door to where I knew Cleopatra would be, staking her usual claim on the Steadmans' double bed. She was lying on her front, with her paws tucked tidily under her chin, eyes closed in a smiley, happy way. She opened one eye and looked at me as if to say, 'Oh good, you're back. Would you mind giving my head a little rub, just behind the ear, if it's not too much trouble?' Then she closed it again. So I rubbed her head, behind one ear and then behind the other so it didn't feel left out, before she blinked another sleepy smile to say thank you.

With neither cat in the mood to be entertained, I went to the kitchen and topped up their shared biscuit bowl, which hardly needed much adding as I'd already done it that morning. Then I emptied, washed, and refilled their water bowls. There was no point in opening their tins of Fancy Feast until at least one of them was awake, so I went back into the lounge and looked out of the window.

A light wind had blown up out of nowhere, as half-hearted as the spatter of drizzle had been earlier, and was ruffling the surface of the duck pond. The ducks were nowhere to be seen. It seemed like it might be best to walk down the lane and drop in on Bella now, then come here after, as I'd have to go past to walk to Netley Parva anyway.

'I'm just going down the road to see Bella,' I called to the sleeping cats, as if they could understand me, knew or were bothered who Bella was, or cared what I did, even if they had been awake and listening. Of course, if they had, they'd probably have been annoyed that I was, yet again, taking my attention elsewhere. 'I won't be long,' I said, as I pulled my jacket back on and let myself out again. It had gotten colder even in those few minutes I'd been in the bungalow and I walked quickly down the lane.

In contrast to the other two, Bella was still in almost exactly the same spot she'd been in when I'd left her that morning. She looked as if she'd been waiting for me to come back, tapping her paw against the parquet flooring like a mother who'd given her daughter permission to stay out until eleven and it was now past one in the morning. I could see the 'Where the hell have you been?' and the 'What time do you call this, young lady?' look in her eyes the moment I opened the front door.

'Hello, Bella,' I cooed, 'How are you, lovely girl?' I was hoping the tone of my voice might soften her up a bit.

'Don't think you can soft soap me with that "Hello, Bella, here, kitty, kitty, aren't you a lovely little pussy cat" nonsense,' her hard emerald eyes replied. 'I've got your number, missy, and I'll be passing it on, don't you think I won't,' they added for good measure.

'How about we get you something nice to eat?' I tried

again, making for the utility room, where an array of every top end brand of cat food filled a whole shelf. 'What do you fancy for your supper today, Bella? Gourmet Perle rabbit and game? A little Fisherman's Delight? How about some Dreamies while you make up your mind?' That should do the trick. I hadn't met a single cat who didn't roll over and purr its head off for a few Dreamies. I didn't know what they put in them, but most cats would tickle *your* tummy for a little handful of them.

But apparently not this one. She still hadn't moved. I couldn't see her eyes any more but the disdain with which she held her head as she continued to stare in the direction of the front door left me in no doubt as to how she felt. This cat had made up her mind about me. This cat had decided that I was no good. And this cat was not for turning.

There is only so much silent treatment anyone can put up with and I didn't even make it to twenty minutes with Bella. She was still glaring at the front door when I walked through it to leave. Her 'Good riddance! Don't let the door hit you on the way out, you complete waste of space!' was almost palpable in the air.

Of, course, among the many cats I'd worked with at Sitting Pretty, the majority had been an absolute pleasure to look after and had made my workday seem not like work but more like a series of visits to very cuddly, small friends. They made my days fly by and my not particularly wonderful wages feel worth it. I had also made the acquaintance of quite a few less pleasant cats, with a variety of unfortunate attitudes between them but Bella, with her determination to be displeased with absolutely everything, was a first.

'I'm back!' I trilled as I opened the Steadmans' door

for the third time that day. The wind had become a bit more brisk and I'd walked quickly from Princess Grumpy's house. The same silence greeted me. Anthony didn't appear to have moved a muscle since I last looked at him. Cleopatra had rolled on to her side, but both paws were still tucked under her chin and her smiley eyes were still resolutely closed. 'OK,' I said, 'I can't hang around here like a spare part all evening waiting for you sleepyheads to decide to wake up. I'm going to put your supper out now and you can eat it when you feel like it.'

Back in the kitchen I opened two tins of Fancy Feast, one savoury salmon and the other tuna and chicken, and mashed one into Tony's dish and one into Cleo's. At least they had a choice of two flavours.

'Bye-bye, then,' I called out, as I left them for the last time that day. 'Don't worry your little furry heads about giving me a complex, will you? I'm absolutely fine about all of you wanting to ignore me today. It was worth getting out of a comfortable car to come and watch you sleep and now I'm perfectly happy to go and walk through the cold, dark forest to get back. It's all fine. It's all good.'

Silence. Apparently irony was lost on cats. Which I thought rather ironic in itself, as they themselves were unwittingly so damned good at it.

I did my jacket up to my chin as I walked down the driveway. It was definitely getting colder and I was starting to regret telling Marvin that I would walk back. Would that thought occur to him and make him decide to come back for me? His car would be a welcome sight right now. The duck pond was starting to look quite bleak, and I could imagine its usual inhabitants huddled together in the church porch, grumbling about today's nip in the air, the worse cold to come, reminiscing about last spring and looking forward to the next one – they were English ducks, after all.

At the end of the village, the trees started to close in over the road, making a sort of tunnel, even with their lessening November foliage. I crossed the road so that I was walking on the right and facing any on-coming traffic, stuffed my hands into my pockets for warmth, and kept on walking. I'd only been going for about five minutes when the heavens opened and the trees proved just how little protection they could afford against the downpour.

CHAPTER THIRTY-SEVEN

'Bloody hell, Beth! Look at you – talk about drowned rats!' Marvin started to laugh and then stopped just as quickly as soon as he realised I wasn't joining in. 'Sorry. I've only just got back myself. I should have thought and come back for you. I just assumed you'd stay put until it stopped. Stay there and don't drip on the Axminster. I'll bring you a towel.'

It was nice to know that his brother's carpets took priority over my discomfort. He, Bella, Anthony and Cleopatra should start up a club, although I knew Tony and Cleo would only be temporary members – they loved me, really. In the way cats love anyone who feeds and lavishes attention on them. Dusty, Sooty, and Smuts, on the other hand – the *Hammer House of Horror* cats – would want to be on the committee. They'd be the ones proposing and seconding all sorts of horrible ideas about what to do to their least favourite pet sitter.

Marvin came back down the stairs with a bath towel. At least he'd found a clean, dry one, although it wouldn't be either for much longer.

'Thanks,' I said, as I threw it over my head and tried to squeeze out the worst of the drips before they ruined Henry Halliday's floor covering and got me into the possibility of even more hot water. Talking of which, there wasn't much I wouldn't give for a bath right now.

'Do you want me to make you some tea, or run you a bath or something?'

Was Marvin telepathic? 'That's all right,' I said quickly, before he started offering to come and scrub my back for me – although if he was telepathic he would already know that was never going to be an option. 'I can manage the bath part. A cup of tea would be very welcome though, thanks.'

Talisker was curled up on my bed, also fast asleep – what was it, National Sleep-in Day for Cats? Was there a sponsorship form I should have signed? I mean, anybody working with animals knew that cats could sleep for twenty hours a day, but still, I'd never had a day when not one of my furry feline charges had started head-butting me for a tickle or a rub behind the ears, or even just to get me to hurry up and feed them as soon as I'd walked through the door. Cleo briefly opening one eye earlier didn't count. The rest of her was still sound asleep.

I put the plug in and started running myself a bath, pouring some of the own brand, rose-scented shower cream I'd bought in Asda under the tap – I didn't have any bath stuff, but I couldn't really see what the difference was anyway. And I certainly wasn't using any more of Henry Halliday's expensive toiletries. The hot water looked so inviting and the fragrance coming off it, while not in the same league as what I'd used at Mum's – but then that was Champneys – it was all I could do not to just climb in with my sodden clothes still on. They certainly couldn't get any more wet. But I didn't want Marvin wandering in with my cup of tea and calling the newspapers or texting Sky News to say that the Loch Ness Monster was indeed still alive, but had relocated down south and had just been seen in a bath tub in a village in Hampshire.

'Here's your tea,' called the man himself, wandering into the bedroom and then, clearly as an afterthought, knocking on the door just behind him. 'I put a drop of whisky in it to help warm you up.'

'Thanks,' I said, trying to stop my eyebrow raising in case it made me look like I thought he was trying to get me drunk. Or that he might be disappointed that I hadn't started getting undressed and he'd missed out on copping an eyeful. He'd been very kind to me and I didn't want him to think I didn't trust him. 'You didn't have to bring that up, I was just going to come down for it,' I added, pretty sure I'd managed to do just that. 'Did you manage to catch up with your friend?' And now I sounded nosey too.

'Yes, that's all sorted, thanks. Right, I'll leave you to your bath. If you dump your wet things on the landing, I'll shove them in the washing machine for you.' He turned to go. 'Don't forget to put them on the towel or wrap them up in it, or else Henry will go ape.' He rolled his eyes at what he clearly saw as his elder brother's outrageous idiosyncrasies and off he went.

From what I knew of him, I couldn't imagine Henry Halliday going ape, or bananas, or any other description of it. In my head he was far too well-mannered and gentlemanly for that. To me he seemed more the sort of person who would politely smile and nod, while noticing things and storing them – in his probably photographic memory – for later. Then I imagined he would request whoever had done something wrong to come to his office, where he would say whatever had to be said in private. I saw him as the sort of boss whose standards were high and whose word was law, and who would give short shrift to anyone who didn't come up to scratch, but would do it in a calm and dignified way and look magnificent while he was doing it – where did that come from? Then the employee would go away feeling worse about disappointing the boss than about being in whatever trouble they'd got themselves into.

I put the cup and saucer down on the corner of the bath, and as I peeled off my wet clothes, I wondered what it would be like to work for somebody like that. Davina was a lovely boss but she was fairly temperamental. People had been fired with no verbal or written warnings, over the slightest thing if that was how the mood had taken her – poor Daisy had nearly been one of them. I'd been very lucky during my time at Sitting Pretty. All the pets I'd been given the care of had taken to me – well, except Bella, the grumpy princess, but nobody knew about that and, unless Bella's owner had a nanny cam in her house, nobody was likely to. I'd been very lucky with their owners too – although I wondered how many of them would look at me quite so favourably if they knew what I'd been up to in some of their absences.

I rolled up my soggy clothing in the towel and, checking the landing was clear, dropped it outside my bedroom door. After a look at the still sleeping Talisker, I closed the bathroom door – at least I knew he was there, so there'd be no Andrex puppy-type surprises interrupting this bath.

My whole body started up a Mexican wave of a sigh as I lowered myself into the bath. By the time my shoulders were submerged in the faintly rose-scented, gorgeously hot water, the sigh had waved itself up and down and up a couple of times before mellowing out into a state of tranquil floatiness. I ducked my wet head under the water for a moment before reaching for my shampoo and giving my hair a quick wash, ducking under again to rinse. Then I squeezed a dollop of conditioner into my hand and massaged it through my hair with my fingers. Alex had always told me off for washing my hair in the bath. I couldn't remember what his problem was with it and right now I couldn't have cared less.

Leaving the conditioner on, I picked up my tea and took a tentative sip in case it tasted disgusting. It was a bit stronger than I would have liked, but he must have added just the right amount of sugar and it tasted all right. I swallowed half the cup. The alcohol, along with the hot water, were soothing and I decided to empty my mind and let it relax and float. What had I been thinking about? Oh yes, Henry Halliday ... and Davina ... I'd been about to compare them as bosses. But that could wait. I was going to empty my mind and let it relax ...

Davina didn't look like the boss of any other pet sitting or dog walking agency I'd worked for before. Most of them dressed as if they knew they'd more than likely have to go out and scoop up a steaming pile of dog poo, separate a pair of copulating animals, or climb a tree to get a daft cat down at some point during their day. Never mind that now. Come on, Beth. Float and relax. Float and relax ...

She looked as if she should really be the editor of some swanky fashion magazine with a one-word title – a French, swanky fashion magazine with a one-word French title – where all her employees looked like clones of Audrey Hepburn, and whatever matching lipstick and nail varnish Davina wore on a Monday, they all rushed out to buy and came in wearing for the rest of the week. She should be like Meryl Streep's character in *The Devil Wears Prada*. She should be ... OK, that's enough thinking about Davina. Mind, empty yourself. Think empty thoughts ... Empty thoughts ...

Henry Halliday's a stylish dresser, too. I bet that fancy wardrobe in his bedroom is full of tailor-made business suits and shirts and a dinner jacket with a real bow tie that you have to tie into a bow yourself. A yawn caught me by surprise ... Where was I? Henry Halliday's wardrobe ... I bet even his casual clothes are stylish, if that photo of him with his niece or whoever she is was anything to go by. And I bet all his shoes are handmade by cobblers. Cobblers? Don't they mend shoes? Who makes shoes? Shoemakers, I suppose. And elves. Elves and shoemakers ... wasn't there a story about an elf and some shoemakers? Or was it some elves and one shoemaker? A second yawn ... it was relaxing, this rose-scented bath stuff. My eyes felt heavy. I could so easily fall asleep ...

A rattling sound woke me and I jolted up in the water as if I'd been electrocuted. What on earth was that? I looked round and saw the door handle going down and up ever so slightly, as if it was being operated by a frail old lady. But we were fresh out of frail old ladies here.

'What are you doing?' I called out. 'I'm in the bath! Go away!' The handle went down a bit more and up again. The idea of locking the door had flitted briefly across my mind just before I climbed into the water, but it had seemed a bit nonsensical then. 'Go away! I'm in the bath,' I tried again as the handle went all the way down and the door swung open.

I ducked my body back down into the water while reaching my arm out for the nearest towel and nearly sending the cup and saucer flying. Then I saw who it was.

CHAPTER THIRTY-EIGHT

'Talisker!' My voice didn't know whether to register annoyance at being disturbed, relief that it was just the cat and not anything more sinister, or wonder at how he'd managed to open the door by himself. It sounded a confused mish-mash of all three to my ears – I had no idea how it sounded to his.

The cat strutted across the tiled floor, tail high in the air, purring loudly as if to say 'Look! Did you see me? Did you see how clever I was? Get out of the bath and close the door and I'll do an encore and amaze you again with my dexterity. Go on!'

'How did you do that?' I asked him as he hopped effortlessly onto the edge of the tub. 'How did you open that door, young man?'

He just purred some more and smiled at me as if he was some incredibly popular, talented, and famous film star and I was a chat show host, and he'd taken time out from his fabulous career to come and let me interview him. I could almost hear him saying 'Ask me anything you like, Beth. Any question at all.' So I did.

'Talisker, do you know how naughty it is to open a bathroom door and wander in while somebody is having a bath?' He looked completely unabashed – I might as well have been asking Lindsay Lohan if she knew that excessive drinking and drug taking were bad for you. 'Particularly if it is a person of the opposite sex,' I told him in a sterner voice, although I wasn't quite sure how I was planning on taking this line of debate where two different species were involved. Although as Talisker was unlikely to actually ask me that, it didn't really matter.

He dipped a paw into the bath water, put it up to his face, and started licking it.

'Excuse me! This is my bath water,' I told him. 'And I can't imagine it tastes all that nice with the chemicals it's probably got in it.' It seemed I was wrong, because he dipped the same paw right back in the water and did exactly the same thing again. 'Are you planning on doing all four paws?' I asked. 'Because I don't mind the front two too much, but if you start dangling your back legs in my bath water then one of us is getting out of here very quickly.'

He gave me a look that said, 'Fair enough, it's a deal – front paws only'. And he switched his weight to the first paw and started dipping the second one.

Without lifting my shoulders out of the water, I picked up the cup and saucer before he knocked them off the edge, drained the cup, and put them on the other corner. 'Don't you think it's time you went back into the bedroom? I'm not getting out of here with you staring at me.'

He seemed to give the matter a moment's thought before deciding I was right. He then jumped gracefully down with the same economy of movement as he'd used jumping up and strutted towards the door, turning to give me a goodbye meow just before he passed through it.

Wondering if I would ever again be able to have an undisturbed bath in a house with an animal in it, I turned on the hot tap, switched it over to the shower setting, and started to rinse the conditioner out of my hair. How had he done that?

I might have been eager to do something different with

my weekend for once, but it seemed to me that I'd had more than enough entertainment for one day. What with seasickness in the Solent, belligerent Bella the fractious feline, a sudden monsoon on my walk home, and a cat named after a whisky trying to drink my bath water, all I wanted now was to get into my pyjamas and have a quiet evening in front of the TV. No more dramas for me today, thank you.

CHAPTER THIRTY-NINE

The next day, being Sunday, the church bells woke me before the alarm and I momentarily wished I'd taken Daisy up on her offer and let her walk Bubbles today as well as yesterday. With only the three cats to feed today, there would have been no need to get up early. Anyway, I hadn't, so I hauled myself out of bed and went downstairs to make coffee.

The rain had stopped some time during the night, but everything outside was still very wet and shiny, as if the whole view had passed through a car wash. Walking Bubbles would be fun.

'Are you decent?' I called as I knocked on the other bedroom door. 'I've brought you a coffee.'

'Come in,' I heard Marvin yawn. 'Completely and boringly decent, as you can see,' he added, as I took his coffee to the bedside table and put the cup and saucer down on a coaster – only Henry Halliday would have a coaster on his bedside table, surely?

'Very glad to hear it,' I told him in my primmest voice.

'Of course, if you were interested, it wouldn't take me long get indecent ...' He treated me to a *Carry On* style wink.

'Tempting as that offer may sound – in your own head at least – some of us have dogs to walk.' I threw his cast off sweatshirt from yesterday at his head. 'I'll be a few hours, do you want me to bring anything back for lunch?'

'No it's all right, I'll probably be out, but I'll cook

something for dinner. You know you're a cruel, heartless woman, Beth … Beth …'

'Dixon,' I informed him. 'Now shut up and drink the coffee this cruel, heartless woman bothered to bring you.' And I shut the door and left him to it.

Bubbles was, as usual, a complete nightmare. The rain had washed away the scents from all his favourite trees and he couldn't make up his mind which one to pee on first. Plus, with it having rained so heavily all evening, there were no tasty, tossed aside treats in any of the rubbish bins for him to rootle out and wolf down. He kept looking around, disappointment written all over his mischievous face. I didn't envy Mrs Parker – he was going to be a pain in the backside all day.

Anthony and Cleopatra were much more lively than yesterday and I stayed and played with them for half an hour. Bella was her usual miserable self – I did my best with her but there was just no cheering that cat up.

Marvin had gone out by the time I got back, so I made myself a cup of tea and got my laptop out. I needed to stop delaying the inevitable and start looking for jobs in London. I wondered where I might end up working next. Wherever it was, it wouldn't be a patch on Sitting Pretty. The dog walking service that I'd been working for in London when I met Alex was a possibility, but going back there would feel like taking a step backwards. Plus, people there had got to know Alex. If any of them were still there, they would ask questions and look at me pityingly, whatever variation on the truth I told them. And if I told them the actual truth, they probably wouldn't believe me.

As I was lunching solo, I started off a jacket potato in

the microwave and then put it in the oven to crisp the outside up. While I was waiting, a couple of trickles of rain appeared on the kitchen window and I watched them race each other down the pane. It was turning into a steady drizzle by the time my potato was ready. And by the time I'd cut it in half, sprinkled some grated cheese on it, and put it back in for a couple of minutes, the drizzle had turned into another solid downpour. Afternoon walkies was going to be fun.

I wasn't quite as drenched when I got back that evening as I had been the day before – more soggy than sopping. At least I'd gone out prepared for the rain today, and I'd had my car with me.

'Mmm, something smells good,' I found myself sniffing the air like a Bisto kid on speed as I walked through the front door. Marvin could be heard clattering about in the kitchen and my stomach decided it was looking forward to whatever it was he was making.

'It'll be about five minutes,' he called out.

I went upstairs and changed out of my clammy work clothes and into my warm pjs, thinking I should probably give my hair a quick blast with the hair dryer but unable to keep myself away from that delicious smell. So I followed it down the stairs, hoping Marvin wouldn't mind eating dinner opposite someone wearing aesthetically challenged, kitten and puppy print pyjamas. I hadn't realised just how hungry I was until the smell wafted its way up the stairs and in the direction of my nose as I was getting dressed. All thoughts of drying my damp hair were abandoned in the face of this delicious aroma. And my stomach had rumbled its agreement that hair drying and any other titivating could wait. Well, I supposed it had been a long time since that jacket potato.

'I knocked up some pasta.' Marvin indicated the large saucepan he was stirring on the stove, as I walked into the kitchen. He was clearly a one pot type of cook. 'It's my signature dish. I know you love cheese. I hope you like garlic and mushrooms.'

'I do.'

'And cream and eggs.'

'Yes, those too.'

'And bacon.'

'Sounds lovely.'

'Pour yourself some wine then and I'll be ready to dish up in a couple of minutes.'

I didn't need telling twice. I poured myself a glass of wine and Marvin a beer and put both drinks down on the table. Then, as I had time, I ran back up the stairs and grabbed the hairdryer and my bottle of anti-frizz serum, imagining Marvin ladling out the fusilli pasta in its creamy Carbonara-type sauce into two lovely big bowls and setting them down on the table in a few minutes. My stomach rumbled appreciatively.

Squeezing a blob of serum into my fingers, I rubbed my hands together to spread it around, and started scrunching it into my hair and working it through. I was just reaching for the hair dryer when I thought I heard the front door open and close. Marvin must have forgotten the parmesan or something. He should have said – I could have gone and got it.

Wondering if he'd left the pasta on the stove and if I should nip down and give it a quick stir, I headed for the landing. That was when I heard Marvin's voice, very loudly and exaggeratedly saying, 'Hey! Henry! I wasn't expecting you back so soon! Good to see you, big brother. Talisker will be so happy! Are you hungry, Henry? Sit down and I'll dish up.'

No! He couldn't be back. He just couldn't. But he was. What was I supposed to do now?

CHAPTER FORTY

'I thought you said he was going to be away for the whole weekend and part of next week,' I whispered to Marvin, thanking God that I'd happened to be upstairs combing Frizz Ease through my hair and not sitting at his kitchen table stuffing my face when that front door opened. My stomach rumbled again, this time in protest – it wasn't thanking anybody for getting between it and that delicious-smelling food downstairs. It was wishing Henry Halliday had caught a later flight or taken a route from the airport with a traffic jam on it.

And what would have happened if I'd already started using the hair dryer? He'd surely have heard that and wanted to know who was upstairs. My heart was banging so hard I could barely hear the panic in my own voice over it. I could feel it, though, and it felt like a pressure cooker that had been left to slowly build up for weeks and weeks and was about to explode. 'What am I going to do?'

'Don't worry, Beth.' He said it so calmly that I almost did a double take. Did he not realise the seriousness of the situation? His brother wasn't all laid back and 'anything goes' like he was. He would be furious when he found out.

'What do you mean, don't worry?' My whisper went up an octave.

'Look, just stay in here and …'

'What? Hide?' I whisper-squeaked. 'Where? Behind

the shower curtain? In the wardrobe? Under the bed? Those were the first places you thought of looking when you found me here.'

'Yes, but he knows *I'm* here ...'

'Won't he ask why you've been sleeping in his bedroom instead of the spare room while he's been away?'

'Look, I'll just tell him I like the shower better in his en-suite – which I do, as a matter of fact. It's a power shower ...'

A squeak of frustration escaped my lips which I then immediately clamped shut before they did anything else to give me away. Power shower? I'd give Marvin power bloody shower! Did the man have no sense of urgency at all? 'Thanks for the amateur dramatics, by the way. Those loud repetitions of his name didn't sound at all suspicious. I bet you two speak to each other like that all the time.'

'Sorry,' he grinned, risking a beating around the head with the bottle of Toilet Duck. 'I had to make sure you could hear it was him so you didn't come back down. Look, you just stay here, don't make any noise, and as soon as he leaves for his office in the morning you can make your escape.'

'Don't make any noise?' My words were now coming out as the sort of sounds only dogs could hear. 'Have you heard my stomach rumbling? If it gets any louder they'll be able to hear me in Dorset. And where do you think you're going to sleep tonight?' I suddenly had a horrible premonition that he was expecting us both to share the spare bed, which was most definitely not going to happen.

'Look, Beth, we'll have to sort that out later,' he mumbled. 'I'd better get back downstairs or he'll wonder what I'm doing when there's a nice glass of beer waiting for me on the table ...'

'And my wine glass!' I almost shrieked. I'd forgotten about that.

'Don't worry. I'll say I invited a friend round for dinner but she had an emergency and had to go before it was ready. It'll be fine. Just don't make any noise.' And with that he left, shutting the door behind him.

Right. Fine. I'd just stay there and not make any noise. Did he have any other stupid commands for me? I stood where he'd left me, staring at the door and wondering why we couldn't have just said we'd bumped into each other and he'd asked me to stay for dinner. At least that way I'd have had some food. I was starting to suspect Marvin was enjoying this subterfuge a little too much. Henry Halliday would be coming up those stairs to unpack his travel bags – either before or after he'd enjoyed my lovely dinner – and then he'd go back down, and then later on, when he was tired, he'd come back up to go to bed. That would make three times at the very least, that he'd be on that landing, walking past this room, this door. A couple of inches of wood was the only thing stopping him from seeing me. What if he decided he wanted one of his laundry fresh, specially-packaged, hypoallergenic pillows now his brother, who wasn't as borderline OCD as he was had been sleeping in his room? What if he decided to swap the bedding over? Where the hell was I supposed to disappear to while that was happening?

And what if he didn't believe Marvin about the wine glass? What if he thought his brother had brought some girl here and he came in to check? I wondered what other incriminating evidence I'd left in the lounge. All this time, I'd been so careful about not leaving anything of mine lying around downstairs. I'd kept all my stuff as small and together and as tidy as possible. Then Marvin had turned up and suddenly I was treating the place like I was a guest. What an idiot I'd been! How could I have let myself become so blasé? So careless?

I tiptoed around the room, gathering my stuff together and carrying it as quietly as possible through to the en-suite, just in case the owner of the house should decide, for whatever reason, to come into his own spare room. Wiping out the bottom of the bath tub to make sure it was dry, I placed my bag in it, shielded by the shower curtain, and then, with a silent sigh, I took the book I'd been reading off the top of it, carefully put the lid of the toilet down, and sat on it to read – what else was I supposed to do up here?

'Just going to check something on my laptop!' I heard Marvin yell as his footsteps sounded out up the stairs. He really should join an am dram group – they'd love him. It was thoughtful of him to find of a way of letting me know that it would be him opening the spare room door and not his brother, but seriously, could he not hear how strange and hammy he sounded? It seemed a tad ungrateful to tell him that his heavy, clompy footsteps could definitely not be confused with Henry Halliday's much quieter, cat-like tread. I heard the bedroom door open and waited for him to realise where I was.

'Hello,' I mouthed at him when he popped his head round the bathroom door.

'You don't have to hide in here,' he chuckled.

'Shush, he'll wonder who you're talking to,' I whispered. 'What does he think you're checking?'

Marvin shrugged. 'I don't know. Something nautical? He's about as interested in boats as you are, so I could tell him I'm bidding on eBay for a second hand spliced main brace or a double-ended buoy and it'd mean absolutely nothing to him. Which,' he clocked the look on my face, 'is about as much as I can see it means to you.'

'Did he believe you about the wine glass?'

'Why wouldn't he? Why would I lie to him about having invited a girl over for dinner? It has happened before, you know. I'm not so ugly that I can't get a member of the opposite sex to sit on the other side of a table and have dinner with me.' Marvin winked at me. 'After all, you were going to.' He was far too nonchalant about this for my liking.

'You'd better get back down there.'

'OK. I'll try and sneak you up something to eat as soon as I can. Enjoy your book.' And he strolled out, shutting the bedroom door on his way before I could forget about not making any noise and throw it at him.

I was bored with my book and contemplating the ridiculousness of this latest situation I'd managed to place myself in when I heard Henry Halliday come up the stairs. My breath was held as he walked past the door again and on to his own room. A few minutes later, Marvin came up too.

Standing up, rather stiffly – bathrooms don't make the most comfortable places to sit for a couple of hours – and carefully, so I didn't rattle the wooden seat, I edged into the bedroom.

'I brought you these.' He handed me a small, open packet of McVitie's Digestives, not a particular favourite – that would be the chocolate version, and a cup of tea and said,' Sorry. It was all I could get my hands on. A cuppa and some biscuits in bed was the first thing I could think of that wouldn't look too odd.'

'Thanks,' I said, forcing myself not to grab the biscuits. I was grateful right now for anything and kicking myself for not having had a bigger potato for lunch ... I shoved the first biscuit in almost whole, to stem the rising of the next stomach rumble.

And now for the awkward part – well, the more awkward than what had already happened this evening part.

'OK,' I whispered, 'Do you want to use the bathroom now? Then I'll put any bedding you don't want to use in the bathtub and ...'

'You're kidding right?' He looked at me as if I'd just told him I still believed in Father Christmas, the Easter bunny, and the tooth fairy. 'That won't be very comfortable.'

'It'll be fine,' I quietly and firmly protested. I didn't want him getting any funny ideas about us sharing the bed.

'Look, Beth, the bed's perfectly big enough for us to share without touching. I promise you, I'd be on my best behaviour, but if you don't trust me we can always put those spare pillows down the middle.' Too late to worry about the getting any funny ideas thing. I wondered if there was any way at all I could sneak out in the night without making any noise. Although I couldn't think where I'd go. Anyway, chances were I'd trip over Talisker at the top of the stairs, soundly hit each one on the way down and wake up the entire village.

'The bath tub will be just fine,' I repeated as firmly as I could without saying it any louder. 'Now go and do your teeth and ... whatever else you need to do. I don't want you needing to use the loo in the middle of the night. That's an image and a sound I really don't need in my head.'

He shook his head as if in bewilderment at my half-baked madness but did as he was told, before coming

172

out and saying, 'Look if you're that against us sharing the bed, you should have it and I'll sleep in the tub. I'm a sailor, after all, I'm used to sleeping in awkward spaces.'

'No, I'm much smaller than you,' I argued. 'And in any case, if there's the tiniest chance of your brother coming in because … because he's forgotten to tell you something, or whatever, it needs to be you in that bed rather than me, doesn't it?'

Marvin's last words to me before I shut the door and climbed into my makeshift bed were, 'Should I be offended that you were perfectly happy to share this bed with a cat who, although perfectly clean for an animal, has never used toilet paper, soap, or toothpaste in his life, but you'd rather give yourself a stiff neck sleeping in the bath than share it with me?'

'One, I am a married woman. Two, you are not cute and furry. And three, I am treating that as a rhetorical question,' I told him, then shut the door. And locked it.

CHAPTER FORTY-ONE

He'd been right enough about the stiff neck. Boy, oh boy, had he been right. While the tub had been rendered quite snug by the spare pillows from the wardrobe and the bed, my neck had, during the night, slipped between two of them. It was indeed feeling very sorry for itself and making sure that the rest of me knew about it. I was gingerly rubbing it, trying to alleviate some of the stiffness, when I heard Marvin scrabble gently at the door – well, at least I hoped it was Marvin. I found myself doing a very poor impression of Quasimodo as I tiptoed over to open it.

'Thank God,' Marvin rushed in past me. 'I'm absolutely busting for a ...'

I closed the door with myself on the bedroom side of it before I could hear the rest of that sentence. Looking at the little alarm clock on the bedside table, I saw that it was five to seven. I'd have to get a move on. All I needed was for Henry Halliday to go to work and leave the coast clear for me to get down the stairs and out of the house.

A worrying thought suddenly struck me. What if, after his troubleshooting trip, he decided to take the day off and give himself a long weekend? If he'd had a stressful time over the last few days, it was possible. Marvin must have clocked the look on my face when he came back out.

'What's up?' He looked from me to the door and back to me again.

'He is definitely going to go to work today, isn't he?'

'My brother, the workaholic? What do you think? Now you go and have a shower. He'll think it's me in there and I can have one after he's gone. Unless …' He raised an eyebrow at me.

'What? I refuse to share a bed with you, but you think I'm going to share a shower with you?' I folded my arms across my chest and put on my best battle-axe face.

'Can't blame a fella for trying,' he chuckled, stepping out of the way for me to go back in.

I was dressed and almost ready to make my escape as soon as it became possible, when we heard the front door bang shut. We looked at each other.

'Coast's clear,' he said at normal volume. 'Have you got everything?'

'Almost.' I picked up my toothbrush and toothpaste and slipped them into my spongebag before zipping it up and pushing it into my bag. Laying my book on top of it, I had a quick look round the bathroom and bedroom. 'Right, well … thanks for … everything … and taking me to the Isle of Wight …'

'My pleasure. It's certainly been different,' he grinned and we went down the stairs. 'Where will you stay tonight?'

'Don't worry about me. The first thing I'm going to do when I get in to the office is to hand in my notice. I'll also tell Davina I have nowhere to stay while I work it. She doesn't want me to leave, so she'll think of somewhere.' She'd probably order one of the others to put me up, but I didn't have much choice now Henry Halliday had come back.

Talisker was waiting at the bottom of the stairs. I picked him up and gave him a cuddle, kissing the top of his head for what was probably going to be the last time.

The thought brought a lump to my throat and a prickle behind my eyes.

'You know, Tal, out of all the pets I've looked after at Sitting Pretty, you've always been my very favourite.' He head butted my chin, loudly purring as if to say, 'Of course I have – who could be better than me? No one, that's who!'

It was hard to put him down but I had to get to the office and say my piece to Davina. I rubbed my cheek against his one last time and put him on the floor. He wandered off towards the utility room, his tail in the air and not a care in the world.

'I'd better be off,' I said, wanting to get out of there before that prickly feeling behind my eyes turned into actual tears. Then I stuck out my hand to shake Marvin's at the same time as he went to hug me.

'What? Not even a hug for the fella who saved your bacon?' He hammed up the disappointed act.

'You know, you really should take up amateur dramatics,' I chided. He wasn't going to give up, was he? And he had been very kind to me.

I put my bag down on the bottom step and opened my arms to give him a quick hug but he enveloped me in his, saying over my head, 'You're one crazy girl, Beth Dixon. That husband of yours has to be the biggest muppet on the planet.'

He was just letting go of me when the front door opened and in, carrying a small loaf of bread and a newspaper, walked Henry Halliday.

CHAPTER FORTY-TWO

He'd gone to the village shop. He hadn't left for work at all, he'd gone to the sodding village shop. What should I do?

After all these weeks of getting away with it, today, this morning, the very last time I was ever going to do this was the time I had to get caught. I looked from one to the other of them. Henry Halliday looked from one to the other of us. And Marvin Halliday just stood there like a big idiot.

'Good morning,' Henry Halliday, ever the well-mannered gentleman said after a pause.

'Good morning,' I feebly replied.

'Oh good, you got some bread,' said the big idiot who by now, thankfully, had dropped his arms to his sides. 'Saved me a walk. I'll put some toast on, shall I?' And with that, he took the bread from Henry's hand and wandered as nonchalantly as you like towards the kitchen, leaving me to face his brother alone.

'I ... I have to be going,' I stated the blatantly obvious then, hit by a shaft of inspiration added, 'Nobody told me you were back so I came to see to Talisker, but I can see you don't need me, so I'll be off.' My pathetic wittering finally over, I ducked past the man I'd been so carefully – or so I'd thought – avoiding and made my escape through the front door. I just about managed to stop myself from running towards the little lane leading to the common, where I'd parked my car in the hope it would just be taken for another dog walker's vehicle.

My hands were trembling as I fumbled with the keys. So was my breath. Once inside, I had to sit a moment to gather myself together before even thinking of starting the ignition – the last thing I needed right now was to drive into the ditch and have to go back and ask for help.

Had he believed my pathetic attempt at an excuse, made even more improbable by what was clearly my overnight bag? What would he do? What would Marvin say? Would Marvin back up what I'd said? Had he even heard me? He'd seemed to be very engrossed all of a sudden in the preparation for making a bit of toast.

I looked through the rear window. There was no angry cat owner marching in my direction. But then, would he? Wouldn't it be more his style to just get straight on the phone to Davina if he hadn't believed me and wanted to know what was going on? Being a Monday, Davina would only be in the office for the morning – she always had somewhere to be on a Monday afternoon, so if he wanted to catch her, these four hours would be the time to do it. Although, as a long standing client, he might have her home number – what was I talking about? He'd have her personal mobile number – she didn't give it out to many clients, but she would have given it to him.

Doing my best to slow my breathing, I started the car, waited for a border collie and his owner to make their way past, and did a clunky five point turn. Then I turned the steering wheel away from the village and towards Wintertown.

Unspoken prayers ran through my head that he wouldn't call Davina. It was one thing, me telling her what had happened with Alex and smoothing over the fact that I had been homeless since he left. I could plead that I

180

had nowhere to stay while I worked my notice and I was pretty sure that resourceful Davina would think of something. A voice in my head was telling me that if I had done that in the beginning instead of worrying what everyone would think, I wouldn't be in this sorry predicament now.

Three ponies wandering in the road, with no evident intention of getting themselves back onto more hoof-friendly ground, made my drive all the slower, giving me even more time to worry. When I got to the car park, however, Davina's BMW wasn't there, which was unusual – just an empty space, as if nobody else dared park in her spot. It was the only space left though, but I didn't risk it, so I drove on to the Asda car park. I'd go in and buy a sandwich or something later.

When I got back to the office, Katya was at her desk, also just for the morning, rummaging disgustedly through the cardboard box of animal themed Christmas decorations she really didn't want to put up, and handing out keys and any extra instructions for the day. She didn't say anything out of the ordinary or look at me strangely, so if anything had been said, it hadn't started doing the rounds of the office.

'No Davina yet?' It was a valid question as she was never late. I just hoped my voice didn't give me away by sounding any more interested than it should.

'No. She had urgent call from client. She had to go sort something …'

'Do you know who the client was?' Try as I might, I could still hear the squeak in my voice.

'No. Why? You lose somebody's poodle?' She smirked over my shoulder as Daisy came bustling in.

'What, Bubbles again?' She looked at me. 'You haven't managed to lose him too, have you?'

'No, I haven't!' I jumped in, my voice slightly more shrill than it should have been. 'Nobody's lost Bubbles. Do you know when Davina will be back?' I turned back to Katya.

'She didn't say. You want to leave message?'

'No, it's all right. I'll try and speak to her at lunchtime,' I told her, grabbing my keys and heading back out of the door. See you later.' My nerves would be shredded by lunchtime. They were halfway there already.

It was half past ten when my phone rang. I had a key in my hand, just about to unlock Anthony and Cleopatra's door. I jumped so much I dropped it. Answering the phone, I nearly dropped that too. It was Henry Halliday.

CHAPTER FORTY-THREE

We managed to get seats at a tiny window table amidst the lunchtime crowd at Dominic's. It felt like a cross between a trip to the headmaster's office and the Mad Hatter's tea party. There was dapper, business-like Henry Halliday, tall and imposing, in the chair opposite me. He was far more handsome than his photograph and smelled deliciously of L'Occitane lemon verbena. I felt suddenly quite gauche for bringing him to a place with dangling sparkly Santa Clauses and snowmen suspended from the ceiling and holly-filled milk jugs with red and green ribbons tied round the handles on every available surface. *Do They Know it's Christmas?* was wafting almost apologetically through the café's sound system, as if it knew that most of the shoppers would very soon be fed up of a constant barrage of Christmas songs, but it just couldn't help itself and it hoped they wouldn't mind too much. Either that, or the volume knob was stuck on low again.

'I've never been in here before,' said the man who could report me to the police for squatting and, presumably, theft of electricity and water, glancing surreptitiously around him. Of course I'd never have imagined otherwise – he would probably feel very out of place with a chunky mug of builders' tea in his hand. Maybe it was a mistake asking him to meet me here when he called me, but it was all I'd been able to think of in my panic – taking him to a crowded café and throwing myself

183

on his mercy. Surely he was far too much of a gentleman to shout at me or have me arrested in such a public place?

'They do a good all day breakfast,' I heard myself say and immediately wondered why on earth I'd thought a man who eats in all the posh places he must eat in would possibly care.

'I suppose you've had to rely a lot on places like this lately?' His expression gave nothing away and I wondered how much his brother had told him. Was he cross? Furious? Disappointed that I'd betrayed his trust so badly? I wouldn't want to play poker with this man.

'Well … yes. I suppose I …'

'Didn't know how to use my cooker?'

'No, it wasn't like that.'

'Then why don't you tell me how it was?' He sounded like a television interviewer or a journalist. Was he going to lull me into a false sense of security with polite, statement of fact type questions and then … Bam! In for the kill?

I was granted a slight reprieve as a waitress arrived at our table with a well-laden tray. Henry Halliday smiled politely at her as she deposited my latte and cheese toastie, his pot of tea for one, jug of milk, crockery, and a couple of warm mince pies with pastry forks on the side on our table. I'd never been offered a pastry fork in here before – didn't even know they had them. Did they keep them specially for posh-looking customers? That'd explain why I'd never seen one.

'Thank you,' he said to her as she turned to walk away. 'The pies look nice.' He proffered the plate towards me. I knew they'd be nice – I'd eaten enough of Dominic's home-made pies while living in Wintertown, coming in with Alex for a coffee on a Saturday morning, or on my work lunch breaks, to know how nice and crumbly the pastry was and how they didn't stint on the filling, but I didn't think I could swallow the tiniest bite of it, or my toastie, come to that, not without choking on it, however much my stomach was rumbling. I took it though, to be polite. Maybe I should eat it anyway, or wrap it up and put it in my bag for later – they weren't likely to be giving out mince pies at the police station. I'd have to eat it before they took me through to the cells or they'd confiscate it, and it might be the last Christmassy thing I'd get to eat this year.

I suddenly noticed he was looking at me patiently, and realised he was waiting for my explanation. Taking a sip of my coffee, I tried to remember all the things I'd planned to say to him, the order I thought I should say them in and where I'd decided I should start.

'I'm supposed to be in Dubai right now,' I looked at him, 'with Alex, my husband.'

'I didn't know you were married. But then, there's no reason why I should, really. What happened? I wouldn't normally pry, of course, but under the circumstances ...' He raised a questioning eyebrow and waited for me to carry on.

'He went without me.' The words sounded so stupid out loud – *he went without me* – as if he left me behind like a bag of shopping forgotten on a bus.

'On holiday?' Henry Halliday looked puzzled. As well he might. I wasn't explaining myself very well.

'No. To work.' *I was a bag of forgotten shopping that wasn't even worth going to the depot to collect. I was a flimsy carrier bag with a hole in the bottom of it, an inch away from shedding its dented tin of economy baked beans, special offer bargain basement washing powder and half price – because it's reached its sell by date – bread.*

'For how long?' He was frowning now, probably wondering what type of badly written soap opera-type character he'd been allowing into his home to look after his precious pet. Probably worrying, too, what treasured ornaments I might have helped myself to, to flog down at the market.

'As far as I know, for good.' Wasn't this where the *EastEnders* theme song was supposed to ring out?

'I take it this wasn't a joint decision?'

'Not unless he made it jointly with somebody else,' I sighed. 'We haven't been married that long. He was offered a job in Dubai and we decided to get married so I could go out there with him. We were living together anyway, so although it was probably a bit too soon, we decided to go for it. And then,' an unladylike little snort escaped me, 'without thinking it might be important enough to mention to me, he decided to go it alone.'

'So, what … he just left without you?'

'Phoned me from the plane as the announcement for passengers to turn off their mobile phones was being made. I could hear it in the background. Probably timed it to the second so he wouldn't have to face any awkwardness, like me trying to call him back and argue with him.' I noticed his mouth open a little in shock. This probably wasn't how people behaved in his world. 'Of course,' I tried not to sound bitter as I added, 'that was just after the removal company had left the flat with all our furniture and stuff in their van to ship to Dubai.'

'You mean he literally left you with nothing?' Henry Halliday shook his head in disbelief.

'Oh, I had my clothes packed up in the car.' I took a swig of my coffee. 'The car I was about to hand back to Davina, what with me having handed in my notice to leave for Dubai. I assume Alex thought a cardboard box in the Sitting Pretty office doorway would do as a bed for the night for me, and that in the morning my bags and I could hitch a ride up to my mum's in London.'

'But you didn't. So where does your mother think you've been all this time? Presumably she doesn't think you're in Dubai?'

'God, no! I've actually been up to stay with her, the first weekend I wasn't on duty. I took the coach up on the Friday evening and came back again on the Monday morning. It was really nice and relaxing. We baked and watched our favourite films. She and Alex have never really got on that well, so it was probably the first time we've spent that long together since Alex and I became a couple. She knows that Alex has gone to Dubai. I couldn't bring myself to lie to her and the coward in me couldn't face telling her the truth. So, while I know how pathetic I'm being, I've just sort of been letting her think the same thing I've been telling everybody else …'

'Everybody else?'

'Well,' I could feel myself blush. 'Davina and the girls at work.'

'And what have you been telling them?'

'That it was decided it would make more sense for me to stay on here and work for the time being while Alex went on ahead and settled into his job and found a suitable apartment.'

'And, what is it, a month later? Nobody's questioning the fact that you're still here? Where do they all think you're living?'

'It's not been as long as that,' I felt my face flame. 'Well … it's three weeks. I think they've all just assumed I'm still at our old flat. And to be honest, Davina doesn't really give much thought to anything outside of the business, so she's probably forgotten I was supposed to

187

be going somewhere anyway.'

'So what put the idea into your head of staying at my place when I was away? And where do you go the weeks when I'm home? Do you alternate between us? Have you put together some kind of rota?' His expression was inscrutable.

My fingers played with the handle of my mug as I ploughed ahead. 'Davina called me from the office just minutes after Alex's call. The girl who was supposed to be replacing me lost control of somebody's dog and couldn't go and feed Talisker. I didn't really know what else to do, so I just got in the car and went round to see to him.'

'That was conscientious of you, considering what had just happened,' he nodded, pouring his tea. It was the first time I'd ever seen anyone pour hot tea from one of those individual stainless steel teapots without the spout leaking all over the table, or them burning themselves on the handle.

'I don't know if it was conscientious or I was just on autopilot, but while I was there, Talisker was so comforting. I had a lovely cuddle with him on the sofa and it was as if he knew something was wrong and was trying to cheer me up.' I saw an almost paternal smile creep up his face – only a true pet lover would give credence to such a statement, but it was absolutely true. 'I went to wash my face as I'd managed to cry mascara everywhere, and I got it all over one of your lovely white towels, so I needed to wash that. I think it was when I sat back down with Talisker again, wondering what else could possibly go wrong that day, and where I was going to spend the night, that the thought came to me that it wouldn't be doing any harm if I just stayed on your sofa that night and left in the morning. It just seemed so simple at the time – like an extra-long pet sit – and then the next day I'd be gone. No harm done.' I took a sip of my coffee and carried on. 'Talisker didn't leave me all night – we cuddled up on the back room sofa and dozed on and off. My brain must have been in overdrive. I was shocked and upset of course, but I just got angrier and angrier. I'd been prepared to turn my life upside down for Alex and he'd just thrown it back in my face in the most cowardly way possible, apart from doing it by text maybe. By the morning I'd convinced myself that if I could just stay on at Sitting Pretty I could save up enough money to either rent a little flat, or follow him out there …'

'Follow him out there?' Henry Halliday looked at me askance. 'Whatever for?'

'Closure?' I shrugged, embarrassed. 'An explanation to my face …' I trailed off as a hot flush washed over my face and I realised how utterly stupid and ridiculous I must sound. 'I thought I could stay on your back room sofa at night, have coffee and biscuits in the office for breakfast, get a hot meal here at lunchtime, then buy sandwiches or salads to eat in the evenings, nothing that needed cooking – I didn't want to use any more electricity or water than was absolutely necessary – just very quick showers in the morning. If the weather got too cold, I knew you always left the central heating on for Talisker.'

'I expect he enjoyed the extra company.'

'Did you know he can open doors?' I realised I'd interrupted him and felt a little flustered.

'Oh, he's a very clever cat. And he can jump really high, so if he wants to get into a room it doesn't take him long to do a few practice jumps and get enough height to grab at the door handle. Then his weight pulls it downwards. Why? He didn't burst in on you in the bathroom, did he? That's one of his favourite tricks.'

189

I nodded, biting my lip to stop the grin spreading. The words, 'I was in the bath, actually,' came out of my mouth before I could stop them. He must think I'd been really making myself at home in his cottage.

'I hope he didn't scare you too much.'

'Well, he did make me jump. But I think I was part scared, part amazed, and part relieved. I mean ... I mean ...' I trailed off, feeling my face get hot again, unable to finish that sentence without disparaging this man's brother.

'That it wasn't Marvin?' Henry Halliday tilted his head to one side. 'My brother did behave himself whilst you were both there, didn't he?'

'Oh God, yes! Yes, of course he did. Yes,' I stumbled over my words. 'That wasn't what I meant at all. No, he ...'

'Maybe you could clear up a little mystery for me,' he jumped in to my rescue. 'I notice Talisker's put on a bit of weight, and yet he hasn't seemed to be getting through his food as quickly as he usually does ...' That questioning eyebrow went up again.

'He was always so pleased to see me when I got there in the evenings, I gave him extra biscuits. I bought more, it was the least I could do, and it was the easiest way of giving you something back without you actually knowing about it.'

'I see,' he nodded. 'And when I was home? What did you do then?'

'I've been staying in other client's homes and doing the same things – buying whatever I can slip in to their existing pet supplies so they won't notice. One night I went out with the girls from work, for one of their birthdays. They've always been in the habit of staying half the weekend at each other's places if they go out on a

Friday night. So there's always been that option if I'm on duty so I can't go up to my mum's. I think they just assume I'm lonely without Alex – they never ask any questions. If I did that, I'd insist on buying them a takeaway or paying for the taxi from wherever we'd been, so I wouldn't feel too much like I was taking advantage.'

'But what if you decided to use your wages on a flight to go and have it out with Alex ...' Henry Halliday looked uncomfortable. 'I don't want to sound pessimistic, but ... wouldn't you just be in the same boat again when you came back? I mean, how long did you think you'd be able to keep up this extraordinary lifestyle?'

'I'd already started asking myself that same question. I was actually going to tell Davina this morning and hand in my notice. Then I was going to go up to my mum's and tell her, and stay with her until after Christmas, then play it by ear.'

'Play it by ear?' His exclamation was loud enough, and the Christmas music, at that particular moment, muted enough, to draw attention from Dominic's other customers.

'I've been really stupid, haven't I?' I mumbled, before hiding my still flaming face behind my mug under the pretext of finishing my coffee.

'Do you know what I think, Beth?' He lined up his pastry fork with his teaspoon and the handle of his teapot. 'I think you should eat that toastie before it gets any colder.'

CHAPTER FORTY-FOUR

My mind was most definitely not on my work that afternoon. After my lunchtime chat with Henry Halliday, it wouldn't have surprised me if both the dogs I was walking had taken one look at me and told themselves that today was a good day for slipping their leads and running from this dopey woman for some fun and games.

The man whose home I'd taken advantage of most had sat and listened to my story in much the same way I could imagine him sitting and listening to an episode of *The Archers*. What, however, he planned to do about me, I had no idea.

After his phone call this morning, poor Anthony and Cleopatra had ended up with such a cursory visit I returned in a convenient gap between afternoon dog walks. I fed them an extra biscuit snack, talking complete gibberish to them. Cleopatra, clearly not wanting to hurt my feelings, washed her face, pretended to listen for a while and then decided my feelings were less important than her beauty sleep and took herself off for a nap. Anthony just stuck his leg in the air and licked his bottom.

My nerves were jangling like wine glasses on a moving tray as I drove back to our office. My phone's shrill ringtone startled me so much I almost veered into the hedgerow. It was Henry Halliday again. There was a lay by on the other side of the road and no other traffic, so I quickly pulled over into it, took a deep breath, and answered it.

CHAPTER FORTY-FIVE

'I've been speaking with Davina about you.' Henry Halliday turned from his state of the art coffee machine and put what looked like a perfect latte on the counter in front of me. 'Decaf latte, no sugar, correct?'

Blimey! A man who paid attention and remembered how somebody he'd only met properly once liked her coffee. Still, I supposed attention to detail was important in his line of work.

When he'd called as I was heading back to the office with the day's keys, he'd asked me to come round to the cottage that evening for a chat. As if there was any chance I was going to say no to him. I was almost at the fork in the road, where I could turn right for Wintertown to carry on to the office and take the keys back, or left, to go straight to Netley Parva. Without a second's hesitation I'd turned left. His tone had given nothing away and I didn't know whether I should expect to find a policeman waiting for me or not. It appeared not, unless he was lurking in the front room.

'Yes,' I gulped. 'Thank you.' I wanted to ask him if I should be worried, but didn't want to sound flippant, so I went to take a sip of my coffee and scalded my lip instead.

'Shall we?' He ushered me through to the front room, too much of a gentleman, of course, to comment on my sloppy drinking habits. 'Please sit down.'

'Should I be worried?' I heard myself ask as I perched

on the oh, so comfortable sofa where I'd cuddled Talisker the day my husband deserted me, mentally cursing myself the moment the words left my disobedient mouth.

'Not at all. Davina speaks, as she did when she first sent you to take care of Talisker for me, very highly of you. She says you're an excellent people person as well as being very good with animals. And that you have more common sense than anyone else she's ever employed.'

'Oh?' That was praise indeed, coming from Davina. I wondered where this was going.

'Tell me, Beth, do you know what a secret shopper is?'

'A secret shopper?' I hadn't expected that. 'Well … it's someone who goes into shops and pretends to be a customer while they secretly spy on the staff and make sure they're being polite enough to the customers and … er … not helping themselves from the till? That sort of thing?' I trailed off.

'Loosely that sort of thing.' He emphasised the loosely and I felt as if I were being laughed at, but not in an unkind way. Henry Halliday coughed gently. 'You know I run a vacation club?'

'Yes,' I nodded. 'Davina always gives us an outline of anything that might be relevant to our clients' packages – especially with regular customers like yourself. I always thought it must be lovely to have your own upmarket timeshare, except with lots of places to choose from instead of just the one.' The inane words finally stopped tumbling out of my mouth. I noticed him wince ever so slightly when I said *timeshare,* but the words queuing up inside my head just wouldn't stop until they were out.

'There's a little bit more to it than that, Beth,' he said politely, as I cringed for equating his posh holiday company to some dodgy timeshare. I really was my own worst enemy – I'd squatted in this man's house and now I was insulting his business. All I needed to do was kick his cat and the brown stuff really would be all over the fan.

To hide my embarrassment I took a gulp of my coffee while, as if my thoughts had summoned him, the cat flap in the back door gave a little rattle and a flump. Then the sound of biscuits being crunched came from the utility room.

'Anyway,' Henry Halliday carried on. 'Regarding your current and rather unusual predicament, I have a proposition for you – a job which I think would be perfect for you and for which I believe, given your skill set, imagination and resourcefulness, you would be perfect.'

I nearly dropped my drink. I'd gone from half expecting to be carted off to the cop shop to being offered a perfect position. Of course, his idea of what would be perfect for me might be very different from mine. But I didn't think it very likely that he had a secret chain of lap dancing clubs where the dancers needed imagination, resourcefulness and a way with animals, and was planning to put me to work in one of them as a penance for taking advantage of his home in his absence. Trying not to gush and sound too girly and unprofessional for whatever he had in mind I gushed, 'I'm all ears.'

'Tell me, Beth.' He crossed his legs and picked what seemed to be an invisible cat hair off his trouser leg – and they were very nice trousers. 'What do you look for when you stay in a hotel? What would be the three most important things to you that could either make or break your holiday experience?'

'Er ...' I suspected *generous measures in the bar* wasn't the reply he was looking for. 'Fluffy, white towels and having them changed every day? Or,' I added quickly, as the thought popped into my head, 'the option not to, if I want to be eco-friendly.'

'I see. What else?'

'Friendly staff?' I ventured. 'Especially at the reception desk – it's horrible having snooty receptionists looking down their noses at you because you're not booked into a suite or your luggage isn't fancy enough.'

'Hm. Anything else?'

'Flexible check out times without being charged a fortune for it. After all, if your flight home isn't until the evening and you want to enjoy your last day by the pool or on the beach, you're going to want a shower before you head to the airport, aren't you? But some hotels charge a whole extra night for it.' I ground to a halt, hoping I hadn't just criticised something that he might indeed do in his own company.

'Interesting choice,' he nodded gently. 'Why the towels?'

'Well ...' Oh God, I thought, why had I said about the towels? Think, Beth, think. 'Well, when you're on holiday you want to feel a bit pampered, and fluffy white towels feel luxurious. And,' I carried on, warming to my theme, 'if the towels are spotlessly clean and fresh it gives the impression that the cleaning staff are doing a good job. But if you're the sort of person who feels guilty about having fresh towels every day, you should have that option too.'

'Very good,' Henry Halliday nodded again and I found myself ridiculously pleased that he liked my answer. 'Now I take it you've had experience of snooty receptionists?'

'On our honeymoon,' I gave an involuntary grimace. 'We got married in Greece because Alex has a bigger family than me, and we went round some of the islands for a couple of weeks. Mostly it was fab. We stayed in a windmill on Mykonos, a cave on Santorini, and some of the places upgraded us because we were on our honeymoon – they were really lovely. But by the time we got to the fancy hotel we were staying in on Crete, for the last couple of nights, we'd run out of clean clothes and we must have looked a bit travel worn. The receptionist looked down her nose at us as if we weren't good enough to stay there. It put a bit of a downer on the last days.'

'I'm sure it did.' Henry Halliday sounded indignant on our behalf. 'And if I caught any member of my staff making a guest feel like that, they'd be out the door like that,' he clicked his fingers.

'That was the place that wanted to charge us a whole extra night for keeping our room on until the early evening.' I remembered with embarrassment the loud argument, accompanied by Mediterranean gesticulating, Alex had had with the receptionist about that, thankfully in Greek, so I'd only understood the odd word. Although some of the hand gestures had been all too clear in their meaning.

'Hm, that's a tricky one. It's often left up to the discretion of whoever's on duty, if, of course, the next guest booked into the room isn't checking in straight away.' Henry smiled as Talisker padded into the room and leaped up onto his lap, turning a couple of circles before kneading at his master's thighs, flopping down into a comfortable position, and turning his head towards me, slowly closing and opening his eyes. There'd be more than one cat hair on those trousers now. 'To my mind, if the room is available for those extra hours, it should be complimentary.'

'That's what we said,' I agreed.

'So, if you were the hotel equivalent of a secret shopper, it sounds like you'd have no problem reporting on the checking in and checking out processes and keeping an eye on the cleanliness of the rooms. What about F & B, that's food and beverages? Restaurant service and room service.'

'Right.'

So instead of being in the trouble I'd expected to be in, I was being interviewed for a job as a secret hotel guest. This was surreal. I was suddenly going from being a guiltily secret, uninvited guest, hoping to not be found out, to a top secret, mystery guest who ... well, for very different reasons was also hoping not to be found out. It sounded like a dream job, and it had fallen into my lap!

I wondered if he had any hotels in Dubai. That high balcony I'd thought about shoving Alex off could be within my grasp.

CHAPTER FORTY-SIX

The miniature flat above Henry's Wintertown office was like something out of a catalogue on chic capsule living. Bijou: I think the estate agents' term for its size would be. It was lucky I wasn't the sort of person who'd ever want to swing a cat, because even if I stood right in the centre, I don't think there'd have been room to do it without hitting the poor creature's head against the walls in this ... well, studio I suppose was the correct name for it, with a tiny en-suite shower and toilet and dinky kitchenette on the side.

I certainly wasn't complaining, however, because not only was it a legitimate roof over my head, but it was also surprisingly nice – far better than anything I'd been imagining. And it was extremely kind of him to let me move in at once, knowing I had nowhere else to put my head down that night – he'd been horrified about my spending the previous night in the en-suite tub in his spare room and I wouldn't want to be in his brother's shoes when he got home.

The tiny space was tastefully decorated in neutral cream and biscuit tones and looked more like a finished miniature property in *Homes Under the Hammer* than an unused box room and couple of cupboards upstairs from commercial premises.

'It's a useful space for anyone who needs to stay overnight,' Henry had said to me as I followed him up the stairs. 'I've even stayed here the odd night myself, if I've been working late and felt too tired to drive home.'

'It's just so much lovelier than I was expecting,' I heard myself gush. 'I was expecting to be squeezing myself into a kind of dog-leg shape to sleep in between boxes of holiday brochures and office supplies.'

Henry laughed. 'Well, there is a stationary cupboard on the mezzanine floor if you'd feel more at home in that,' he chuckled. He had a lovely chuckle – it made you feel safe and like everything was going to be all right.

'No thanks,' I jumped in quickly, throwing my shoulder bag down on the bed as if to stake my claim on it. 'This'll do me just fine.'

Henry left me to unpack my case with the wonky wheel, which I'd noticed him glancing at. Of course he was far too much of a gentleman to comment on it. I could almost see him biting his tongue.

He'd kindly stopped so we could pick up a few essentials from the supermarket on our way there, and so as soon as he left I went into the miniature kitchen and ran some water into the travel kettle to make myself a proper cup of tea.

Whoever had designed and fitted this Lilliputian space had done an amazing job. The fridge was like a hotel mini bar, just big enough for my litre of milk, tub of easy spread Lurpak, half a dozen eggs, and packet of cheese. The letterbox-sized ice section would hold one ready meal, and I happily posted my individual lasagne into it, looking forward to a hot meal that evening – that for once, wasn't pizza – like a child looking forward to Easter. Above the fridge was a very shiny, two ring electric hob that didn't look as if it had been used yet. A pair of sparklingly new saucepans, one small and one medium sized, hung from hooks off a rail above that and below an eye level shelf, on which stood the dinkiest microwave oven I'd ever seen. It looked like something out of a Wendy house. Henry had told me it was a combination oven when he caught me looking longingly at the frozen meals in the supermarket. Above that was a cupboard containing a dinner plate, side plate, bowl, cup and saucer, a wine glass, and a tumbler.

To the left of the fridge, a compact sink sat over a cupboard containing a few cleaning things and a brand new iron, still in the box. Above the sink was an empty cupboard where I put my tea bags, bread, marmalade, and baked beans. That instantly made the place look tidier.

Leaving my tea in the kitchenette in case I knocked it over, I hauled my case up onto the bed and started to unpack. There were two deep drawers that each took up half the length of the sofa bed, which was a god send, as the wardrobe in the corner of the room was, out of necessity, slim. Most of the contents of my case would fit into the drawers, and I divided T-shirts, jumpers, underwear, and pyjamas between them, but I hung up my two jackets, jeans, trousers, and the least scruffy of my clothes on the hangers provided. Thank God the job came with a clothes allowance – I could hardly imagine any of the places Henry would be sending me to, letting me through their doors dressed like a bag lady.

Everything I owned needed ironing – it hadn't mattered while working for Sitting Pretty, but I'd have to take a lot more care with my appearance in this new job. Then I balanced the empty case on top and hoped it wouldn't fall off in the night and give me concussion.

The en-suite consisted of a slender shower cabinet, loo, and a sink, the size of which I've only ever seen in a caravan. There was a ribbon of shelf over the sink where I lined up the contents of my sponge bag, glad I'd never

been a hoarder of cosmetics. One thing about this place –
it was going to force me into being a much tidier person –
there really was no alternative!

CHAPTER FORTY-SEVEN

'So you're *really* going to leave us this time?' Davina pouted across her desk the following morning. She clearly couldn't understand why anyone could possibly want to work for someone other than her. We'd been through all this before, of course, only last time the fact that Alex and I were moving abroad stopped her taking it quite so personally. Telling her that Henry Halliday had offered me a job in his company had gone down about as well as if I'd told her I thought her fancy new shoes made her ankles look fat.

'Yes, Davina, I'm sorry but this time it's really happening.' I'd had to fudge a bit about not going to join Alex in Dubai. I couldn't bring myself, after three weeks, to admit to Davina and the girls that he'd left me, and that I'd stayed on as part of a bizarre plan born out of sheer bloody-mindedness. I'd just told her that Henry and I had got chatting about his work a few times and that I'd thought it sounded like something I'd like to have a go at. She seemed to find this a poor reason for abandoning all my furry customers, as if my leaving meant they were all going to starve and spend days crossing their little paws because nobody was going to be there to take them for their walks.

'Well, you will work out your notice before you toddle off and desert me, won't you?'

'Of course I will,' I assured her. I'd already discussed this with Henry, and he'd agreed completely. He was the sort of person who valued loyalty and I think he'd have been disappointed if I'd even thought about not working my notice.

Davina seemed to be satisfied with this. I had a sneaky feeling, though, that she was expecting me to do another turn-around in a week and stay working for her. But this time she was going to be disappointed. Henry Halliday was no Alex Petropoulos.

CHAPTER FORTY-EIGHT

The next ten days took on a kind of surreal quality. In fact, I sometimes felt like pinching myself to make sure I hadn't fallen asleep and was having another of the weird dreams I'd been having since Alex left.

Whilst working my weeks' notice, I was also spending my evenings with Henry while he coached me in the art of being a mystery guest. This had to be the jammiest apprenticeship ever. I kept waiting for him to decide that I wasn't really the right girl for the job after all, thus sending me back to my life of un-wantedness only with the added humiliation of knowing what a lovely job I could have had if only I'd been a bit wittier, a bit better dressed, or a bit more posh.

We ate out at a different type of classy restaurant every night, so I could familiarise myself with fine dining menus and the etiquette they required, and which wine I should order with which food. The first was a French restaurant, called L'Escargot, where we ate *Escargot á la Bourginion* – snails in garlic butter, which were absolutely delicious, accompanied by glasses of light and lively – Henry's words, not mine – Petit Chablis. Next came the *Cuisses de Grenouille* – frogs' legs, which really did taste like chicken. With these we drank gorgeous appley and melony – my words, not Henry's – Pinot Gris. And to think I'd always been a Sauvignon Blanc kind of girl, and at the cheaper end of the market at that – stick a Buy One Get One Free label on a bottle and it practically shrieked out 'Beth! Beth! Come and get me!' from its supermarket shelf. This new job was broadening my horizons before I'd even started it. It would be broadening my waistline too if I had to eat too many dinners like this. I'd have to watch that – my fancy-pants clothes allowance wouldn't go far if as soon as I bought something I started bulging out of it!

'I hope you won't be offended, Beth,' Henry said to me, after the waiter had finished clearing the entree plates from our delicious chateaubriand – its accompanying glass of Medoc Rouge serving to remind me how much I preferred white wine, however fancy the red was. Here it comes, I thought. I'd known this was all too good to be true. My table manners were worse than the Tasmanian Devil's and I'd managed to splash garlic butter all over the pristine table cloth. Add to that the fact that I was clearly a wine peasant and of course he couldn't bring himself to let me loose in one of his posh hotels. 'I'd like to book you an appointment to get your hair done before you go on your first assignment.'

'My hair?' I supposed it was looking less than its best at the moment, and split ends would definitely not be *de rigueur* where I was going to be staying. He went on, however, to mention a much more upmarket hairdresser than anywhere I've ever been able to afford. It did need a bit of a tidy up – well, probably a lot of a tidy up – but yikes! It was going to be the most expensive hair cut I'd ever had in my life. Would he give me an advance on my future wages to pay for it? There was no way I would have enough money. And while I was busy worrying about how much the hair cut would cost, he started talking about a facial, manicure, and pedicure. Double yikes! It was starting to look like this job was out of my league for reasons other than the ones I'd already come up with. I needed to let him know – maybe I could get away with just the hair cut for now, with an advance, and when he'd paid me for the first assignment I could afford the facial?

'Er, Henry.' I swallowed the tiny morsel of pride I had left since I'd taken to a life – well, a few weeks anyway – of sofa squatting crime. 'I hope you know how very grateful I am that you've offered me this job ...'

'Let me stop you right there, Beth.' He put his hand up to silence me but in a nice, friendly way. 'In my line of work I deal with a lot of people, and I think it's made me a pretty good judge of character. I've already been impressed by the way you looked after Talisker when I was away. You were the only one who always bothered with all those little things like rinsing out and refilling his drinking water every day, not just topping it up – you know how slimy the inside of a cat's water bowl can get, and you'd be amazed how many so-called pet sitters don't bother. That was one of the reasons why I always asked for you. But then you told me what your husband had done and how you'd reacted to it and the difficulties you'd put yourself through so you could stay here and do the job you enjoyed and, well, I thought that showed a kind of gumption you just don't see very often. It took imagination and initiative and a fair amount of guts to do what you did, Beth, and I'd say you've got all of those in spades.'

'I don't know if all the other customers whose sofas I borrowed would agree with you,' I shrugged, feeling my face flush at being complemented for doing something which was basically wrong.

'Anyone with half an ounce of imagination and empathy would appreciate the respect you showed their homes while you were doing it. You certainly went the extra mile with Talisker,' he started to argue, pausing as the waiter came back with the dessert menu. 'I can recommend the *Soufflé au Grand Marnier*,' he said as he looked down at his menu. There were dessert wines too and I worried that if I had any more alcohol he'd have to carry me out of there. I should have said no when he offered me an aperitif.

'Actually, I'd love the *Crème Brûlée*,' I told him, hoping there wasn't a wine to go with that.

'One *Soufflé au Grand Marnier* and one *Crème Brûlée* please,' he ordered. 'And I think we'll have a glass each of the Muscat.' He handed the menus back to the waiter and smiled at me. He wouldn't be smiling if, after all this rich food and wine, I threw up in the taxi back to Wintertown. I mentally crossed my fingers that I could distract him somehow and tip my glass into his. There's never a handy plant pot around when you need one.

'Henry,' I bit the bullet. 'About my hair cut ...'

'Oh yes, I'll need to get a move on and book that for you, but they know me there so it shouldn't be a problem. It'll have to be an evening appointment, to fit in with your other work commitments, won't it?'

'It's just, well, the thing is ...'

'Is there another salon you'd rather go to? They have an excellent head stylist.'

Oh my giddy aunt! He didn't just want to book me into probably the most expensive salon in the whole of Hampshire, he wanted me to see their probably even more expensive head stylist. How much of a dog's dinner did I look right now?

'That sounds lovely but very ... expensive,' I trailed off. My face must be Santa Claus red if the heat I could feel in it was anything to go by.

'I have an account there,' Henry said, looking a little

nonplussed for a tiny moment before it seemed to dawn on him just what I was worrying about. His mouth opened and then shut again. 'You didn't think I was expecting you to pay for it, did you, Beth?'

'Well …'

'This is on company expenses. I'm sorry, I should have explained. As part of your assignments you'll have to use and report back on all the beauty facilities in the spas at most of the hotels you'll be staying in. It'll help you to fit in if your skin, hair, and nails look like they're used to those sorts of treatments. Also it will give you a level against which to judge the spas you'll be visiting. It may sound like an extravagance but believe me, it will be money well spent. Especially if any of the spas at any of my hotels are falling down at all in what they are doing for the guests. You need to go in there, armed with the knowledge of what they should be doing, and how they should be doing it.'

I think he was too polite to tell me that someone who looked like an ex squatter who walked dogs and scooped poo for a living would look out of place in any of his establishments. He was clearly trying to turn this sow's ear into the closest thing to a silk purse he possibly could before letting me loose amongst the shiny-haired, tiny-pored, mani-pedied posh people.

CHAPTER FORTY-NINE

The following night, before taking me to a seafood restaurant, where I was praying he wouldn't force me to try oysters, Henry took me clothes shopping. No chain department stores for him, although I was allowed to have a look through Designers at Debenhams. I felt a bit like Julia Roberts in *Pretty Woman* – except I was a pet sitter, not a prostitute. Come to think of it though, now I was spending time with Henry, I'd realised he wasn't just some stuffy-sounding fuss-pot in a suit. I'd noticed that he did have a bit of a mid to late thirties, shorter haired, Richard Gere look about him.

'How about this one?' Henry held up a beautiful cashmere sweater which looked like it would cost more than my wages for a month. 'This colour would look great with your eyes.'

The dark purplishpink wasn't a colour I'd ever have picked for myself – I'd always been a practical blues and browns and greens kind of dresser. In fact, I could probably get dressed in the dark and find that whatever items I'd grabbed from the cupboard, drawer, back of the chair, or the floor all still went with each other. Not, of course, that clashing clothes would be a problem when pulling a reluctant dog away from its favourite tree, or trying to crush a cat's worming tablet into its food without it noticing and developing a sudden and stubborn eating disorder. As long as you were giving them food and attention, animals wouldn't care if you turned up wearing gold lamé leggings, Noel Edmonds' worst jumper, Pat Butcher's loudest earrings, and a pair of yellow, purple, and orange stripy knickers on your head.

'I'll give it a try,' I said, with more enthusiasm than I felt for something that would more than likely make me look like I'd been rolling around in beetroot juice.

'What size are you, a ten?'

Bless him. 'Ten to twelve, depending on the make,' I told him, flattered that he'd had me down as a ten. I put my hand out to feel a sumptuous sea green version of the jumper he was holding. It was so soft. It felt like stroking Talisker.

'You know, Beth, you don't have to dress for practicality any more, not in this job. You're not going to be worried about getting covered in pet hairs, or mud or whatever. You can feel free to express yourself. Well ...' his top lip flickered ever so slightly, 'just as long as you don't have an inner Goth waiting to get out. You might just stick out a bit then.'

Catching his eye, I couldn't help smiling. I liked his dry sense of humour. Henry Halliday had such a warm, easy-going way about him for a boss. He was going to be great fun to work for, I just knew it. Half of me wanted to keep pinching myself to see if this was real. But the other half wouldn't let me, just in case I woke up and found myself back on a client's sofa with a hairy animal stretched out on top of me with its head on my chest. If this indeed was a dream, I was happy to let it go on for as long as possible.

I didn't like to tell Henry that the earth colours he'd always seen me in probably expressed me down to the ground – no pun intended. He might give up on me as a bad job and find someone else to train up as his new mystery guest, someone who could locate and embrace her inner Joanna Lumleyness while I was still racking my brains trying to remember if I ever had one. And if I did, wondering where it had been hiding itself all this time.

'Here you are.' He handed me the selection of knitwear he'd picked out. 'Try these on and see what you think.'

It was funny, I thought as I carried the jumpers and a couple of long, pretty, floaty cardigans I'd never have looked at in a month of Sundays to the changing room. If Alex had ever picked out clothes for me to try on I would probably have been quite annoyed, but the way Henry did it wasn't high handed or chauvinistic. It was a bit like shopping with a British, slightly older, and a lot calmer Gok Wan, which got me thinking – was Henry gay? That might explain why there was no wife, fiancée, or girlfriend on the scene.

Spending all this time with Henry, I'd come to learn what a lovely man he was – not the OCD, anally retentive fusspot that Davina, probably inadvertently, treated him as – he was just someone with high standards. And why shouldn't he be? Apart from being quite handsome in a well-clipped and groomed kind of way, he always smelled so good – lemon verbena, orange, and geranium, a scent I now recognised, thanks to my one-time foray into his pristine bathroom. I flushed, wondering if he had any idea about me helping myself to a dollop of his L'Occitane shower gel that first morning I'd slept on his sofa. It was the one thing I hadn't been able to replace.

He was smart. After all, he'd spotted a gap in what some might think of as an already overcrowded market and created a tailor-made company which seemed to be doing all the right things at all the right times in all the right places. He was incredibly kind, as evidenced by his offering me this job, and taking so much trouble over helping me to get ready for it. And he had that pithy, witty sense of humour which was worthy of Stephen Fry. And yet with all this, this man was single. How could that be? Yes, the more I thought about it, the less straight Henry Halliday seemed.

It occurred to me that I'd better get a move on or he'd be wondering if I'd got my head stuck in an arm hole, managed to stumble into the mirror, and was now lying on my back on the cubicle floor like a concussed tortoise with a bleeding forehead. It wouldn't be the most stupid thing I'd ever done, and going on my recent behaviour, he would probably think it was just par for the course.

The assistant who'd shown me to the cubicle had hung everything up, in order of shade, on the neat row of hooks on one side. On the other, between two more hooks with Yes and No signs over them, and above another whose sign said Maybe, there were a couple of chiffon scarves hanging up, with a little notice asking customers wearing makeup to use them while trying on their selected garments. You didn't get that in Primark.

I wondered which of these girly shades I should get out of the way first. The palest one was a sort of marshmallow pink and I could just see me wanting to hurl myself head first into a chocolate fountain wearing it. Pulling off my own dark green jumper which, although my best one and definitely not one I would have worn for work, was probably already suffering from a massive inferiority complex at being so close to these much fancier items, I gently removed the marshmallow one from its hanger. It really did feel like it was made from the hair of particularly fluffy kittens.

As we were going on to dinner afterwards I was, in fact, wearing lipstick, so I put the scarf over my head and gingerly tried on jumper number one. It was like being enveloped in a soft, downy cloud. Stroking my arms, there was no denying how gorgeous and luxurious it felt, but I was right about the colour – I hated the pinkness. Taking it off even more carefully than I'd put it on, as I definitely wasn't having it, I put it back on its padded hanger, hung it on the No hook, and took the next one. This was more of a Battenberg cake shade of pink. I hated it on me, but thought I was definitely getting hungry.

It wasn't until I got to the raspberry coloured one that I started to get a glimmer of what Henry had said about my colouring. This polo necked creation did indeed bring out the bluish-green of my eyes and I surprised myself by rather liking it. I stepped out of the cubicle to show Henry.

'Oh yes, that colour really suits you,' he smiled, 'and they've got some lovely scarves over there if you'd like me to find you one to go with it.'

'Oh, er, yes thank you,' I dithered, as he went off to look at what appeared to be silk scarves, before I turned and headed back to the changing room. I didn't dare think how much all this was costing him, or rather his company. I just prayed that I would be able to do justice to his faith in me. And that it would all be tax deductible enough to make up for my failure if I didn't.

CHAPTER FIFTY

When Henry and I arrived at the seafood restaurant, the maître d' kindly took my bags and stored them safely in the cloakroom for us. They contained the raspberry jumper, a deep-purple cardigan, and a beautiful white silky top to go under it, a silk scarf which would go with both, a pair of very upmarket – for me at least – jeans, and a pair of boots I'd never have dreamed of looking at, let alone trying on, from a shop I'd never have dared to go into on my own.

'Now then, how do you fancy starting off with half a dozen Whitstable oysters?' Henry asked me before he'd even opened his menu.

'Mm hmm,' I gulped. And not in a happy-to-swallow-an-oyster kind of way. Was he really going to make me do this?

'They also do a fantastic *Moules Mariniere,* and their chargrilled razor clams are delicious.' He was starting to sound like Billy Bunter on his way to the just-about-to-open-for-business tuck shop. 'Or do you fancy sharing the *Plateau de fruits de mer* – the seafood tower, with a bit of everything?'

I wondered if that would be a better way of getting out of eating the bits that I didn't like without him noticing.

'Anyway, have a look and see what you think.'

'Mm hmm,' I nodded and opened up the beautifully crafted menu I'd been given and searched for this sampler tower of torture. *Oysters Kilpatrick* jumped straight off the page at me. As did *Oysters Rockefeller*. There were also lobster, crab claws, crayfish, scallops, and grilled prawns– yes, yes, yes, yes, and yes again. There were mussels – I could eat those if I really had to and there weren't too many of them. Ditto the clams, razor or otherwise. But those blasted oysters kept rearing their ugly heads off the page and jeering at me. *We're slippery and slimy and we're going to slither down your throat and make you gag and throw up in front of your nice new boss. We might even make you throw up all over his shiny shoes.* It was almost as if they knew how disgustingly ill Alex had been when he tried them at some fancy brunch buffet, just after we'd gotten engaged. Even after they'd finally stopped coming back up and bringing everything else he'd ever eaten or drunk in his life with them, he'd been in bed for days, sweating and moaning and clutching his stomach. The very thought of emptying one of those shells into my mouth and trying to swallow its contents made me go hot and cold all over.

Henry and the waiter were discussing wine. I heard champagne, Chablis, and Chardonnay mentioned, but my ears pricked up properly when I heard the words Sauvignon Blanc. It would be a treat to try one from the higher end of the market. As soon as the waiter left I said, 'It all looks absolutely delicious, Henry. I do have to confess that I'm not a big fan of oysters, though.'

'Had a bad experience with one before?' Henry sounded sympathetic. 'If that happens the first time you try them it can put you off ever trying them again. Don't worry about the oysters, are there plenty of other things on there that you do like? Or would you rather order separate dishes?'

'No, no the tower would be lovely,' I gushed, full of relief.

'And how about something non seafood for a starter? Maybe the griddled fresh asparagus with hollandaise sauce and a poached quail's egg?'

'That sounds great,' I enthused, thankful that after last night's rich dinner I hadn't been hungry enough to do more than pick at some fruit at lunch time.

'I expect all your Sitting Pretty clients will miss you after this week,' Henry said when the asparagus plates had been cleared. 'Davina tells me you're one of the most requested sitters and dog walkers she's ever had.'

'Really?' That was news to me, but it was a nice thing to hear. No wonder she hadn't wanted me to leave. She was still giving the impression that she didn't really believe I would go this time, although what she thought I was doing going out for meals and shopping with Henry, I couldn't imagine.

'You've been very popular with the staff, too.'

'I will miss Daisy,' I confessed. 'She's a lot of fun and good-hearted and I'm hoping she'll be the one to come and look after Talisker for you after I've left.' I'd already mentioned this to Henry so I was pretty sure that Daisy would be my replacement. He'd probably already sorted that out. 'I expect I'll even miss Katya and Natalia a bit …'

'Ah yes, Natalia,' Henry's right eyebrow raised ever so slightly.

'I didn't realise you knew Natalia.'

'Oh I don't,' Henry said quickly. 'I just hear bits and pieces from Marvin.' His eyebrow moved again.

'Oh?' I was intrigued now, but he was saved from having to say anything else as the three-tiered tower, absolutely crammed with mouth-watering seafood – as long as I ignored the oysters which had arrived separately in their own serving dish as they were hot and everything else was on ice – made its arrival. Blimey! Was that just for us two? We'd be here all night. And when they wanted to close up so the staff could go home, they'd have to phone for one of those winch things to hoist us out of our seats – and after all this food, I would probably be firmly wedged into mine.

'Bon appetite!' Henry indicated that I should help myself first. I wasn't sure where I should start so I just pulled off a crab claw and a couple of prawns.

'Well?' I asked, once Henry had helped himself to some of his yucky oysters.

'Well, what?'

'Are you going to elaborate or are you going to leave me guessing?'

'About what? Oh! You mean your friend Natalia,' he suddenly realised what I was talking about. 'Oh, there's no mystery there. It's just this rather dodgy friend of Marvin's …'

'You don't mean Sti … Steve, do you?' I stopped myself just in time.

'How do you know this Steve?' The easy smile had slipped down a notch.

'I don't,' I said, quickly. 'He was sitting in the park one day when I happened to take one of Natalia's dogs for a walk as a favour. It was a very badly behaved dog and he made some comment or other, I can't remember what. I probably wouldn't even have remembered it but then, when Marvin took me out on that horrible yacht, we bumped into him on the Isle of Wight.' I just stopped myself saying that he came and had lunch with us. Henry certainly didn't seem to like the man.

'I know it's not my place to tell you what to do, but I'd advise you to stay away from Steve. He's a smuggler.'

222

'A smuggler?' I laughed, thinking he must be joking. This was all a bit *Jamaica Inn*.

'Yes, really. He gets up to all sorts in that old fishing boat of his. How he hasn't got caught I don't know, but it's only a matter of time, which is why I don't want my brother getting mixed up with him. I wouldn't trust that man as a far as I could throw him. Marvin knows I won't have him in my home. But Natalia seems to be spending a lot of time with him. The two of them seem to be as thick as thieves.'

That was curious. Natalia always had an opinion about anyone she met, and she'd never, to my knowledge, been shy about voicing it. She'd seemed completely uninterested in Stinky Steve when I'd mention him to her in the office. All she'd said was that he was harmless.

I hoped Henry didn't notice that I spent quite a lot of the rest of the meal wondering just what Natalia had managed to get herself caught up in.

CHAPTER FIFTY-ONE

'Katya?' I was glad to find her on her own when I got to the office the next morning. 'Is everything all right with Natalia?'

'Yes, of course. Why it should not be?'

Did Katya sound cagey, or was it my imagination making her words sound that way? I decided to try another tack. 'Do you know this guy called Steve?'

'Stinky Steve?' Katya's nose looked as if I'd just wafted a carton of month old milk under it. 'Why you want to know about him?'

'No reason,' I lied. 'It was just that ...'

'What? You hear something bad about him? So, he get his hands on some black market DVDs. So what? Is not crime.'

The way I could feel this conversation was going, there was no way I was going to be Miss Goody Two Shoes and remind her that actually, yes it was. After all, it was none of my business and anyway, Natalia would laugh her head off at the thought of little old me trying to look out for her.

So I kept what Henry had told me to myself and told myself I would keep an eye on whatever might be going on. But from a distance.

CHAPTER FIFTY-TWO

'Good morning. How may I help you?' The smartly-dressed receptionist at the New Forest's smartest hotel and spa smiled at me from between two beautiful arrangements of Christmas flowers in gold-coloured vases. I wondered if she could sense that the sleek Samsonite spinner being wheeled effortlessly alongside the hotel porter like a well-trained Labrador was not mine, but lent to me because my own shabby excuse for luggage had been deemed unfit to be seen in public. Or that just ten days ago I had been a homeless pet sitter caught squatting in one of her customers' homes and that, luckily for me, the customer in question had turned out to be a knight in shining armour. What would she think if she knew that I had spent the last week pet sitting and dog walking by day, but by night, being coached like Eliza Doolittle by Henry Halliday's Henry Higgins?

'Oh, good morning.' I tried to sound as if this was the type of place I wandered into all the time. 'I have a reservation, Beth Dixon, but I'm probably a bit early for check-in.' Test number one – would they make me wait until check-in time, and if so, would they offer me a complimentary drink while I waited?

'Beth Dixon,' the receptionist repeated. 'Just a moment please.' *God Rest ye Merry Gentlemen* played gently in the background as she checked my reservation on the computer. 'No, that's absolutely fine, Miss Dixon,' she smiled again. 'If you could let me have the credit card you used to book, then the porter will take you up to your room.'

I mentally gave check number one a ten out of ten, as the lift smoothly took the porter and I up to the third floor. He commented on the seasonally cold December weather and enquired if I'd travelled far, then made no further conversation until we got to the door of my room.

'Room three twelve,' he announced, slotting the key card into the lock and opening the door for me, standing back to let me go ahead. While he hefted my case onto the luggage rest, I fumbled, slowly and deliberately, in my handbag for my purse. Test number two – would he slow down and drag out his duties for as long as possible until I found and handed over his tip?

'Sorry, I just ...' I mumbled, pretending to be embarrassed, which was very easy because I was – the two pound coin had been in my hand when I arrived and I would much rather have just handed it over. Especially as he was indeed dragging this out, wandering around the room, showing me where the mini bar was and how the light switches worked, opening the en-suite door to show me where it was.

'Oh, here we are,' I hammed it up, when I could stand it no longer. 'Thank you so much!' I pressed the coin into his hand and watched him give a brief nod of acknowledgement and withdraw from the room like a tide ebbing swiftly away. I wondered how long he would have hung around if I'd had the nerve to pretend any longer – would he have run the taps in the en-suite to show me how the water worked? Would he have put the little kettle on and made me a cup of tea?

I got out the tiny file Henry had given me, found the

check list and filled in my comments straight away while they were still fresh in my mind. Then, as he'd instructed me, I programmed my chosen code into the safe in the wardrobe, tested it, put the file in it, and locked it.

This was far too easy a way to earn a living, I decided a couple of hours later, as I sprawled out in my fluffy, white bathrobe on the comfortable king-sized bed with the pillow top mattress – ten out of ten – watching *How to Train Your Dragon* on the huge TV screen, the remains of my room service tray – only eight out of ten as my first choice of starter wasn't available and the soup I ended up ordering wasn't as hot as it should have been – on the bedside table. I'd had a luxurious soak in the bath, marinating myself for at least an hour in the fancy bath foam then slathering myself with the matching body lotion. The complimentary spa toiletries had scored ten out of ten as they both smelled and felt delicious. Of course, it was up to the chambermaid to keep that ten out of ten by replacing the products that had been used. The shampoo and conditioner were still untouched as I'd washed my hair at the little studio flat before setting off, not wanting to arrive with it looking greasy, but I'd give those a try the next morning.

As soon as the film finished, I got dressed in my new jeans. Henry was right, they were a very good cut and a whole world away from my old ones. I could see now why he gave me what I'd considered to be a huge clothes allowance – every item of clothing I'd owned before would have screamed out that I didn't belong in a place like this. Dressing the part was really helping to give me the confidence to play it. With my brand new hiking boots, warm jacket, scarf, and gloves to complete the outfit, I headed downstairs and looked around for somebody to offer assistance. Even though I already knew where it was, I had to ask for directions to the park nearby.

When you reach the end of the drive turn right, Ms Dixon,' the man, who I guessed was the concierge, told me. 'Then drive for about five minutes until you see the sign for The Barn Owl pub. Take the next left, then the first right, and then after a couple of minutes, the entrance to the park will be on your right. Enjoy your walk.'

I thanked the man and set off in the lovely clean car Henry had hired for me – you don't notice just how whiffy and hairy a car that gets used for transporting animals is until you drive one that isn't – following his instructions exactly. About ten minutes later I pulled into a parking space next to Henry's car – also hired, and changed regularly, he'd explained to me, so he could arrive at any of his UK hotels without his car being recognised and putting the staff on guard. Sneaky, I'd almost said, but had managed to stop myself just in time.

We wound down our windows almost simultaneously. It felt like being in a spy film and I bit back the urge to giggle.

'How's it going so far?' Henry asked me.

'Really well. It's absolutely gorgeous,' I enthused. 'They let me go up to the room straight away and …'

'That's fine, Beth,' he stopped me. 'You don't need to tell me now. Are you marking it all up in the report file, like I showed you?'

'Yes, and I've put it in the safe, like you said.' I forced myself to stop gabbling in case I annoyed him and made him think better of offering me the job.

'Any questions? Anything you're not sure about?'

'No, not that I can think of.'

'Excellent. Well, I shall look forward to reading it.

Enjoy the spa tomorrow.' He smiled at me, closed his window, and pulled out of the parking space.

I watched him drive away, wondering if he checked up on all his staff's first assignments or if it was just me.

CHAPTER FIFTY-THREE

Dinner last night was sumptuous and I rather missed having Henry sitting across the table from me; it was one thing wandering into Dominic's on my lonesome, grabbing a table, and shovelling their pasta of the day down my throat – it was something else doing this fine dining lark at a table for one.

My starter of hand-dived scallops, served on black pudding with little cubes of chorizo and squiggles of green pea puree, more than made up for the weeks of living off pre-packed salads and sandwiches. The Dover sole, filleted at the table, just melted deliciously in my mouth. And as for the trio of desserts, my taste buds thought they'd died and gone to heaven.

It looked as if breakfast was going to be just as delicious. I was torn between the full English – although where I'd put it after last night's overload of scrumptiousness, I wasn't sure – and the kedgeree. But then there was poached haddock topped with a poached egg – which sounded yummy – or grilled kippers. It was so hard to choose and yet I had to look as if I ate like this all the time and it wasn't anything out of the ordinary.

There was a buffet of fresh fruits – including some I'd never even seen before, yoghurts, cereals, and all kinds of breads and pastries for guests to help themselves to while their hot breakfasts were being cooked. It all looked so fresh and colourful and inviting – I did my best to keep my bottom jaw from straying too far away from the top one.

After being seated, I ordered a freshly squeezed grapefruit juice, as it wasn't something I would normally have in at home, a decaffeinated latte – I couldn't bring myself to say 'decaf' – and I decided at the last minute to go for the kippers, as that was something I would never cook for myself. Then I took some berries and Greek yoghurt from the buffet, as I was going to be spending time in the spa and didn't want to be lying down on a full stomach for my massage or burping all over the masseuses and therapists.

The spa oozed elegance and serenity. The air was fragrant with rubbed, scrubbed, cleansed, toned, and moisturised, elegance. The soft tinkly music gently wafting in the air was serene and calming. It felt as if nothing bad could ever happen in a place like this.

I was so glad Henry had made me go to those beauty appointments while he was training me for these assignments. All the girls who worked here, from the receptionist to the girl who showed me around and explained what was what, to the massage therapists, they all had skin which seemed to glow – they were a wonderful advertisement for the place. If I hadn't had the previous treatments, my skin would more than likely have looked and felt like coconut matting to them. They'd have been drawing straws not to be the one to have to put her lovely hands on crumbly me.

My spa experience began with an exotic lime and ginger salt scrub. The girl applying the scrub had soft, gentle hands, and the scrub itself smelt fresh and zingy.

'Are there any areas you would like me to pay special attention to?' she asked me, in such a soothing voice I wasn't completely sure she'd even spoken.

'I'm sorry?'

'Do you have any problem areas, such as elbows or heels, that you would like me to spend more time on?'

I thought of the state of my feet a few weeks ago and sent Henry another telepathic thank you. 'No, I don't think so, thank you,'

She didn't speak again until the scrub was over. I supposed it wasn't like being a hairdresser where you chatted to your clients while you worked on them. This was far more intimate and it would probably be a bit strange asking an almost naked client where she's planning to go on holiday while you spend half an hour rubbing citrusy, salty paste all over her body.

After the top layer of my epidermis had been scrubbed to within an inch of its life, I was directed to a shower cubicle to wash away all traces of the scrub – and probably a few million dead skin cells, although it could have been a lot more – before my next treatment. This was going to be a Swedish massage, and a vision of a muscular Scandinavian man with strong hands had been floating around my head ever since I booked it.

My masseuse came in, reading the health check form I'd been asked to fill in when I booked the appointment. She was neither Scandinavian or a man, but she did have very strong looking hands.

'You would prefer oil or lotion?' she asked, in an accent so similar to Katya's and Natalia's that I had to look at her face again just to make sure that neither of my old workmates were moonlighting here.

'Lotion please,' I told her, remembering how slippery I'd felt after the first time with the oil – although I still wasn't sure that the masseuse where Henry had sent me for my first massage hadn't been a bit too heavy-handed with the stuff. I mean, loads of people have Swedish massages all the time. They can't all come out feeling like a penguin in an oil slick, or else they wouldn't keep doing it.

So there I was, face down on the massage bed, glad I hadn't had a big breakfast, and looking forward to a relaxing hour. After all, I'd practically fallen asleep last time. The next thing I knew, one of those strong looking hands was ploughing a line down my upper back as if it thought it was Moses and my shoulder blades were the Red Sea. The force brought my head up, like a cat's does if you stroke down its back really hard. Except that a cat does it – usually – in pleasure. In my case, I think all my vertebrae were having a sudden panic attack.

'You must relax. You are very tense,' the masseuse told me, bringing her hand back around in a circular movement. No kidding! Having someone try to break your neck with one hand will do that.

'That's actually a bit hard,' I winced, as the other hand started to do exactly the same thing, veering off to circle the other way.

'You have very stiff neck,' she insisted.

Better a stiff neck than a broken one, I thought, trying to get up, and failing miserably. She really was very strong. 'That is definitely too hard.'

'Lie down.' She pushed me – actually pushed me – back onto the bed. 'I have your form here. You have stiff neck. I know exactly what you need – deep tissue massage.'

'There's nothing on my form about a stiff neck.' I tried to move sideways but was stopped by the first hand pinning my neck firmly back down while my head did the cat thing again. This could be dangerous. You can do somebody physical harm by manhandling their neck badly, I'm sure of it.

'Would you please stop!' I said as forcefully as I could while lying on my diaphragm and having a heavy weight bear down on it from behind. 'Just stop!'

My voice must have been loud enough to be heard outside over the tinkly music, as another girl came rushing to the door to see what was going on.

'Is anything the matter?' came one of the daftest questions she could have asked.

There was a simultaneous 'yes' from me and 'no' from the heavy-handed masseuse. The new girl, who had clearly trained in the school of believing that the customer was always right, came all the way into the room.

'I think you should stop that for now, Nadia,' she said. 'What seems to be the problem, Ms Dixon?'

'No, this not Ms Dixon,' old Heavy Hands interrupted. 'This is …'

'I'm Beth Dixon,' I swung myself round and upright. 'And you must have the wrong form.'

'This is form I was given,' Heavy Hands insisted. 'Is not my fault.'

The new girl sighed. 'I think we'd better call the manageress,'

'Please do enjoy your facial, Ms Dixon,' the manageress smiled confidently as she left me in the capable hands of their very best beauty therapist. I knew she was their very best beauty therapist because the manageress had told me. About half a dozen times. 'And please accept all your treatments today on the house. We will, of course, book you another massage, free of charge, at any time during your stay. I hope this will go some way to making up for your discomfort.'

'Thank you very much,' I said as she padded away. I

wouldn't want to be in that masseuse's shoes right now, the amount of free treatments they were giving me to make up for her mistake. I had tried to tell them that just a free massage would be more than enough – accidents do happen – and that I was perfectly happy to pay for my other treatments. But they wouldn't hear of it. There had also been a whispered conversation about a gift basket, which made me start to wonder if they had some idea what I was really doing here.

My facial went as smoothly as my skin felt after it. She really was their very best beauty therapist.

'Thank you so much, Ms Dixon,' she smiled as I stood up.

'No, thank you. I've really enjoyed myself.' And apart from the one little hiccup, I had.

CHAPTER FIFTY-FOUR

'This was a very full and inclusive report you wrote, Beth.' It was Monday morning and Henry was peering over the top of a pair of spectacles I'd never seen him wear before. He looked rather like a wise owl, but in a cute way. And was it my imagination, or was his top lip twitching ever so slightly?

'Thank you,' I ventured, trying to watch out for further traces of lip movement without actually looking as if I was looking.

'Perhaps next time you don't need to include quite so much extraneous detail.' There it went again, twitching ever so slightly. 'I know I told you to attach an extra page for comments if you felt it necessary. However,' he shuffled the pages in front of him, and a warm flush started to creep up my neck, 'the bare fact, on page one, that your waiter at breakfast on Sunday morning had a small stain on his tie would have sufficed. The fact that it was coffee coloured and shaped a bit like the Live Aid guitar, and that you'd recommended Stain Devils to him, wasn't strictly relevant.'

'Sorry,' I mumbled, the flush creeping higher. I felt like the school swot having been called into the kindly headmaster's office to be gently told off for being too swotty.

He shuffled the pages again, clearly searching out the worst examples of my excessive wittering. 'Your praise, on page four, for the management's idea to serve complimentary sherry and mince pies in the bar while somebody sang Christmas songs at the piano, was perfectly justified. But,' both his lips were trembling now and I could see him clamping them together momentarily, 'your description of the singer sounding just like Shakira, and the following two paragraphs explaining how Shakira is a singer who some people think sounds like a sheep ...' A snort of laughter escaped his throat. It seemed to take him by as much surprise as it took me and we both ended up hooting with laughter as if it was some massive joke.

'I'm sorry,' I breathed, a moment later. 'I suppose I was a bit over enthusiastic.'

'Would it surprise you to hear that I do actually know who Shakira is?'

'I didn't think that would be your sort of music,' I mumbled, hoping he didn't ask me just what I thought his sort of music would be.

'What do you think would be my sort of music?'

'Well ...' I floundered, trying to remember if I'd noticed his CD collection at all and wishing I'd been a bit nosier while I'd been working and staying in his home. My memory came up with a big fat blank. Would he be into opera? Classical, maybe?

'I suppose I look like a fan of Gilbert and Sullivan?' He must have clocked my blank look, because he added, 'They wrote light opera, or operetta. *The Pirates of Penzance*? *The Mikado*?' He suddenly grinned at me – it made him look a lot younger and a lot less stuffy. 'Sorry, I'm teasing you. That's the sort of music my wife liked. It wasn't my cup of tea at all, but she left some CDs behind when she left. I thought you might have seen them.'

'No.' He had a wife – or rather an ex-wife. So he'd been married. I wondered what had gone wrong. I supposed that meant he wasn't gay – unless that was why they split up?

'Actually I like all sorts of music, from Eric Clapton and The Beatles, to Coldplay, Gnarls Barkley, Adele, Emeli Sandé ...'

'Oh, I loved her at the Olympic ceremonies,' I jumped in, 'And I love Coldplay ...' I petered out, realising I'd just interrupted my boss.

'I'm glad you approve, Beth. Now, shall we get back to your report?'

CHAPTER FIFTY-FIVE

The next Halliday Vacation Club property I was sent to, a couple of days later, was in Leeds – well, just outside it, really – a lovely country house hotel set in seven acres of woodland, with, of course, the usual spa amenities and indoor and outdoor pools. They did golf too, although I was highly relieved that Henry wasn't expecting me to try and look as if I knew anything at all about that – other than that you have to wear funny trousers, and that golfing establishments have some very outdated ideas about women.

Henry drove me to Southampton station to catch the half past eight train – he'd been highly amused by my wanting to book an advance ticket and save him money. I'd been gobsmacked when instead of doing that, he'd upgraded the Kings' Cross to Leeds part to first class. That was when he'd explained to me that it would look better if I left a first class ticket from London lying around in my room than an advance economy from a station in the same county where the Halliday head office was. Sneaky. Again.

Under his instructions, I'd phoned and booked a hotel car at the other end for when I arrived. The Samsonite spinner was packed with a different set of clothes which, once again, looked far too posh for the likes of me. I wondered if the expectation for the hotel staff to think me a con-woman who'd shoplifted or pick-pocketed all these fancy things would ever go away. Must be my guilty conscience getting to me after my recent spate of squatting – however nicely – in other people's homes.

The train was on time and, as Southampton was its starting point, empty when I got on, so I grabbed a table seat and slotted the Samsonite under the end of it as it wouldn't fit into the luggage rack above the seat. I felt an itch to make a note of that in my report, as a Victor Meldrew voice in my head asked what was the point of a luggage rack that wouldn't hold anything bigger than your average briefcase? I'd have to watch that voice. I'd already handed in one over-zealous report. I didn't want Henry to think that they'd all be like that.

Brightstone Hall was absolutely gorgeous. The driver, who'd been waiting for me holding a sign with my name on it as I walked out of the station, drove me up the sweeping driveway and I gazed at the beautiful building, which had been requisitioned as a convalescent hospital for officers during the first world war.

Hark the Herald Angels Sing was playing very softly in the background while the receptionist checked me in. There were understated Christmas flowers on the desk and a couple of small tables and a beautiful, real Christmas tree in the corner where the stairs curved upwards, decorated in classic red and gold. Dinner was already being served in the main dining room, she informed me, although I could, of course, eat in the piano bar or order room service. Henry had suggested I try out the main dining room first and, having read their menu online, I was more than happy to do so. So I only went up to my room long enough to leave my coat and use the bathroom before coming back down again.

The crusted mackerel fillet I had for my appetiser was

very good, but the monkfish-wrapped in Parma ham with cockles and red wine jus I ordered for my main course was sensational. I thought the desserts at my first assignment would be hard to beat so I went for the Yorkshire cheese plate, which was excellent. I could see I was going to have a hard time finding any fault with the food.

By the time I went back up to my room after coffee and liqueurs in the piano bar, where an excellent pianist alternated Christmassy music with gentle jazz classics, my bed had been turned down, my slippers and dressing gown had been laid out, and there was a chocolate mint on my pillow which there hadn't been in the first hotel. I'd have to make a note of that.

I ran a bath while I unpacked, and a cloud of jasmine scented the air in the bathroom and wafted through to the bedroom. The fluffy white towels awaited me on a rail by the bath tub, and there were flowers in a vase on a little shelf. I could really get used to doing this for a living.

Henry wasn't going to be lurking on the side-lines for this midweek trip – this was my first solo assignment – although of course he was just at the end of a phone call or an email. I wondered what he and Talisker were doing.

After sleeping soundly on my pillow top mattress, the next day followed pretty much the same format as the Hampshire hotel, only minus the misunderstanding with the massage therapist.

In fact, I was on my way back to my room after my afternoon in the spa when my fancy new work mobile rang. The caller display said it was Henry, so I hurried to open my door and go inside before I answered.

'How's it going, Beth?' Henry asked, before I had a chance to say hello.

'Very well,' I replied, slightly out of breath from rushing – I would have thought with all the dog walking I'd be fitter than that.

'Any problems with the spa?' I could hear the smile in his voice – he'd had a good laugh when I described to him how I'd been manhandled by Heavy Hands. I'd tried to make it sound funnier than it was as I felt sorry for the masseuse, however I suspect she might have been in for a verbal warning about not confirming the guest's name against their health check form – she could have caused somebody an injury.

'None at all. It was absolutely first class – just like everything else here. I'm so relaxed I probably won't need the return half of my ticket. I could just float home tomorrow. It's going to be difficult finding anything wrong to put on the check list.'

'That's a good thing, Beth,' he said, as if he thought I was worried about not finding anything wrong. 'Listen, I need to ask you a favour.'

'Fire away,' I instructed him, cheekily.

'I have to go to a ball tomorrow night. It's the Hampshire Hogs for Hope charity fundraiser. I know it's very short notice as your train doesn't get to Southampton until twenty-two minutes past four, but I was wondering if you would accompany me … That is, unless you already have plans for the evening? Like I said, it is short notice.'

'I'd love to, Henry, but are you sure you want to take me? I don't have anything to wear to that sort of do.' A ball? Me? Had every other woman he knew turned out to be busy and he was left with just me? I wasn't the sort of woman who got taken to balls. I was the sort of woman who walked the dogs of the women who got taken to balls. Or rather, the voice in my head said, I used to be.

'Don't worry about that. I know your size and I can get two or three sent over ready for you to try on and see which one you like best.'

'That would be great,' I said, a frisson of excitement battling it out with a tremor of anxiety. I was going to a ball!

'Lovely. See if they can fit you in for a wash and blow dry in the salon before you leave in the morning.'

'I'll do that right now.' I had a sudden panic that they wouldn't be able to fit me in and that I'd turn up looking a mess.

'Thanks, Beth, see you tomorrow.' And with that he hung up.

The salon would be busy most of the morning and in the afternoon, but the first appointment of the day was available and so, after an early breakfast, I was packed and leaning back having my already perfectly clean hair washed with what smelled like the same shampoo as that amongst the toiletries in the room. Another perk of this job, I'd realised, was that I'd never need to worry about taming my frizzy hair back into its bob, there always seemed to be a hairdresser around to do it for me.

Of course, what with this being north, it being almost the end of November, and me coming out of a hairdressers and on my way to something fancy, the rain was pouring down as if there were stagehands on very tall ladders outside chucking never-ending buckets of water about when I came out from my appointment. Not good. Not good at all.

The receptionist caught my anxious look and within seconds of my checking out, the concierge was holding an umbrella close to my head while I got in to the car that was going to take me back to the station. And with the driver performing a similar service at the station entrance, I sighed in relief as I headed, blow-dried hair still in place, for my train.

'Ladies and gentlemen, we regret to announce the eleven forty-five train to London Kings Cross from platform eight has been cancelled due to an incident on the line. The next train to London Kings Cross will be the twelve fifteen from platform six.'

Oh great, I thought, wheeling my case back along the platform. We'd specifically chosen the quarter to twelve train because it involved less changes. Now I'd end up making the extra change, which all added to the journey time. It wouldn't have mattered normally, but if I got back too late I'd let Henry down.

I pulled my phone out and sent him a text to warn him I'd be on a later train and that I'd let him know as soon as I could what time I'd be due in. A moment later I got one back telling me he'd pick me up from Winchester and save a bit of time.

The twelve fifteen crawled into Leeds station as if it had all the time in the world. It was probably just reluctant to get there because it turned out there were three sets of passengers wanting to travel on it rather than the two I'd thought, as the train before mine had been cancelled too. The incident on the line must have been a serious one. Reservations suddenly became meaningless, especially if yours was the same seat as two other people, either one of which could shout louder than you. I found myself extremely thankful that Henry had booked me a first class ticket for this leg of the journey – at least the scrum in this carriage wasn't as bad as what I could see going on further down the train. We eventually pulled out of the

248

station at twenty-five to one and I sent Henry another text to let him know.

The train was already quite full when we stopped at Wakefield and more people got on than got off. From my window seat I could see the drinks trolley being pulled off one carriage and onto the next, so the carriages further down must have been too full for it to pass through. It did the same thing at the next stop, Doncaster, then Grantham, then Stevenage.

When we reached Kings Cross at six minutes past three, there was another undignified scrum as everyone tried to get off first. There was no way I was going to make my three fifteen connection at Paddington for the Reading train, so I stayed in my seat and sent Henry another text message until it subsided.

CHAPTER FIFTY-SIX

Henry was waiting for me as I walked out of Winchester station at half past five. It was such a relief to see him standing there. And also that it wasn't raining.

'I'm so sorry …' I started to say.

'Don't be silly,' he jumped in, opening the passenger door for me – a habit his brother hadn't picked up from him. 'You couldn't help the trains. It's my fault. I should have thought. I could have booked you an appointment at the hairdressers here and changed your ticket to an earlier train.'

'That wouldn't have made any difference,' I told him, doing up my seat belt. 'The one before mine was cancelled as well, so I'd still have got here at the same time.'

'Anyway,' he started up the car, 'you're here now and we're not running that late. I'm just sorry to have given you such a stressful journey.'

As we drove back to his cottage, chatting about the ball and my trip to Leeds, I thought how nice and calm he was about all this. I couldn't help thinking how in the same situation, Alex would have niggled on all evening about how I'd kept him waiting. Alex. How long had it been since I'd given him a thought? I couldn't even remember the last time I'd looked at his Facebook page. And now here I was, off to get ready for a ball I was about to attend with another man. OK, so the other man was my probably gay boss, but he was handsome, witty, and sensitive. Alex only scored one and a half out of three on those qualities.

'The gowns are hanging up in the spare room,' Henry said, taking my case out of the boot. 'Don't worry, Marvin's on his boat at the moment. There's a small selection of accessories too, so hopefully there'll be something you like.'

I hurried up the stairs, bemused that he'd gone to all this trouble. Although of course, if there was to be a chance of me not showing him up at this do, he probably thought he needed to.

'Oh my god!' I couldn't help exclaiming, having another *Pretty Woman* moment when I saw the ball gowns he'd picked out. There was a pinky-purple one in a lovely fabric – I thought it might be taffeta but I wasn't really sure – which was straight and fitted at the waist, with a V-neck at the front and, I discovered when I lifted it down, at the back too. A less fitted design in a beautiful sea green hung next to it and then there was a raspberry coloured one with a fuller skirt and a rounder neck.

Underneath each dress were a pair of shoes and an evening bag to match, and on the bed were three pashminas and some costume jewellery boxes. Henry really had thought of everything. The shoes were even the right size – he must have remembered from buying those boots. No straight man could put together outfits like these for someone he'd only known a few weeks.

'How are you getting on?' Henry called from the landing. 'Would you like me to bring your case in? There are probably things you'll need in it.'

'Henry, these are gorgeous!' I turned to see him in the doorway. 'I can't believe you thought of shoes and bags and things. And everything matches!'

'I thought that was the idea,' he laughed, putting a plastic laundry cover on the foot of the bed and lifting my case onto it. 'I'll leave you to sort yourself out. Call me if you need any help or anything. We need to leave by seven.'

CHAPTER FIFTY-SEVEN

The Hampshire Hogs for Hope was a charity run by Hampshire business owners to raise money for the local children's hospices. The money they raised helped the families of terminally ill children to take them on a holiday or to enable them to perform an activity that would otherwise be impossible. The annual pre-Christmas ball was the main fundraising event in their calendar and raised thousands of pounds to give the children in these hospices the very best Christmas they could. That was what I'd read on the internet after Henry's invitation.

It looked like it was going to be a very glamorous affair indeed. I was grateful to Henry – left to my own devices I would never have looked as if I fitted in with these well-dressed and stylish people. Although part of my brain couldn't help wondering how much of the money spent on these clothes could have gone into the charity's coffers instead. Fortunately, for once, my mouth didn't blurt out what I was thinking.

As Henry was being talked at by a throng of attractive women who nodded politely in my direction when he introduced me and then completely ignored my existence, I caught sight of Davina across the room. She looked stunning in a hot-pink satin sheath of a gown. I indicated her to Henry and started to edge my way through the crowd. By the time I got to her she was on her way to the Ladies, so I followed her in.

I caught up with her by the mirrors. Looking at her in

that dress, with her hourglass figure and shiny, blonde, perfectly behaved hair glistening in the lights around the mirror, I felt for a moment like the poor relation in the borrowed, albeit beautiful, frock. She didn't even recognise me out of my dog hair-covered trousers and T-shirt. I was about to slink away as she started dabbing into her cleavage and behind her delicate ears with a deliciously sensuous perfume sample, but she caught sight of me in the mirror. 'Beth? My goodness, is that you? You look amazing!' She did indeed look amazed. 'That dress is to die for,' she gushed, probably not in the best taste, considering the purpose of the function we were attending. 'Working for Henry certainly seems to agree with you. Is he here tonight?'

'Yes, I came with him.'

'Oh?' Now she looked even more amazed. 'Well, I hope you have a lovely time.' She peered into her teeny tiny, hot-pink satin evening bag, daintily pulling out a miniature lip gloss which I recognised as her favourite, Candy Shimmer, and adding a coat to her already shimmering lips before pouting at the mirror. I was sure she hadn't meant to sound patronising – she was just being Davina.

'I'll see you later then,' I said and left her to it.

'Hey, Henry!' A tall, plump, sandy-haired woman who looked about fifty and whose ample cleavage looked about fifty-five, was calling him over to table twenty as I stepped back through the double doors. I could only just hear her over Cliff Richard's *Mistletoe and Wine* and the greetings of mingling revellers. 'We're on this one. Come and sit next to me!'

'I've just got to say hello to someone,' Henry called back, smiling sadly as if sitting next to her right now was the thing he wanted to do most in the world. He made his way towards me, calling. 'See you in a minute,' over his shoulder.

Clasping my wrist as if it were a tiny life jacket, he gently led me in the opposite direction. 'I *can't* sit next to that woman, Beth' he whispered frantically at me. So that's what I was here for, crowd control. 'If she's saved me a seat, please promise me you'll sit in it. You're *so* good with people; you can talk to anyone.' Yep, I was his personal bouncer. Maybe I should just tell him that if he wasn't so charming to all these women they wouldn't keep draping themselves over him and hanging on to his every word

We were near one of the four bars – there was one in each corner – so Henry looked inquiringly at me and then smiled at the barman. 'Two glasses of champagne please.'

'Two champagnes, sir. Enjoy your evening,' the rather camp bartender beamed at Henry as he handed him our drinks. The man was getting it from both sides tonight – mind you, he did look devilishly handsome in his dinner jacket – and I'd been right about the bow tie. We melted back through the throng. Henry, in no hurry to return to our designated table smiled, kissed the cheeks of friends nearby, and waved his hellos to those further away.

Feeling redundant, I glanced back at our table. It was starting to fill up. People were making their way to their tables now and seating themselves instead of milling around, air-kissing each other. I followed Henry back to ours, praying that the woman – or more likely the women – Henry had brought me here to protect him from wouldn't all gang up on me for spoiling their fun.

The table looked stunning but crowded before the food even arrived. Its ornate Christmas centrepiece of lush greenery, flickering gold candles, and red velvety ribbon was flanked by glistening ice buckets, tempting bread baskets, and little dishes of butter pats. Tucked amongst these were copies of the menu, lists of raffle prizes and of course, Hampshire Hogs for Hope donation envelopes.

Wine waiters started circulating with bottles of red and white, pouring for people and leaving full bottles on the tables. Henry, who'd finished his champagne, had white, so I followed suit, thinking that I couldn't go far wrong if I copied him.

Suddenly, more waiters flocked towards us with the starters and a huge plate appeared in front of me. In the centre, a tiger prawn looked up from its cushion of smoked salmon. Drizzles of pink and green made pretty patterns in the vast expanse of whiteness around it. While I waited for everyone else to start, I wondered why they needed such big plates if they were only going to use the middles. Henry nudged my elbow, whispering conspiratorially, 'They could have used smaller plates and saved on the washing up.' I giggled, tickled that he'd been thinking the same thing as me.

While everybody else at the table picked up their prawns with their fingers, Henry performed a faultless head-tail-and-shell-ectomy with his fish knife and fork. I tried to do the same and nearly ended up with it in my lap. Fortunately for me, the organisers of the ball chose this moment to introduce themselves and while the rest of our table were looking towards the little stage, Henry gallantly swapped plates with me and performed his prawn procedure for a second time.

I'd always thought there was something rather intimate about a man peeling a woman's prawns for her. Though as poor Henry was surrounded by women who'd clearly be happy to peel anything for him and he'd brought me here to keep them at arms' length, it wouldn't be very helpful for me to start thinking things like that.

The welcome speeches took ages. People finished eating – Henry's prawn was delicious – and the waiters removed the plates, disappearing through the huge side doors, then swiftly returning with the next course. After we'd finished clapping, we turned back and found tiny green salads awaiting us.

'Micro salad! Hmm.' Henry nudged me again. 'They should have put this with the prawns and ...'

'Saved on more washing up?' I chuckled. 'Your concern for the kitchen porters is very touching!'

'And the environment!' Henry teased. 'I am very eco-friendly!' He picked up his glass and clinked it against mine, 'Santé!'

'Santé!' I grinned happily back before we both tucked in to our dinky salads. This was turning into a really lovely evening. Although Henry was so much smarter than me, we seemed to be on the same wavelength. Here was a man I could relax and have a laugh with.

After the salad plates had been cleared away, the elegantly minimalistic turkey course was served. The turkey was a bit on the dry side, so everyone opted for extra gravy to soften it up. The three halves of Brussels sprout were definitely al dente, so they needed a bit of gravy too. And I was about four mouthfuls in when my knife slipped, shooting my stuffing ball into the table centre greenery.

'Good shot!' Henry chuckled, topping up my wine glass and that of the woman on his other side – who was here with her husband and therefore not simpering over him like most of the rest of the table – before doing his own. 'I'll give you mine to get rid of when no one's looking.'

Before serving dessert, they called the raffle. Henry had bought a stack of books and I'd bought as many as I could afford. Before I could stop him, he picked up my few and added them to his pile.

'There,' he announced, fanning them out between us. 'Now we've both added to our chances of winning something.'

'Seems a bit of an uneven deal.'

'Not at all,' he took a sip from his water glass. 'I never win anything, so I'm hoping you'll bring me luck!'

There were about twenty prizes and about forty tables full of people who'd bought many books so I doubted that. Until the fourth ticket was called.

'Blue, number four zero one!' came the announcer's voice.

'That's us!' Henry pulled out a blue book with number four hundred on the top ticket. He folded it back and there was number four hundred and one. 'Come on!' He tugged me by the hand towards the stage. We returned to our seats with an envelope. I didn't even know what our prize was, but at least it wasn't anything in a jewellery box – that would have been embarrassing. Henry opened the envelope and showed me a voucher for a romantic dinner for two at Hetherin Hall country house hotel with pre-dinner cocktails in the terrace bar. A romantic dinner for two – how ironic.

CHAPTER FIFTY-EIGHT

Henry held the taxi door open while I climbed in, hoping I didn't look as tipsy as I felt. I couldn't imagine how he sounded so sober when he'd had just as much to drink as I had.

After the raffle we'd had tiny dolls' tea party-sized mince pies served with quenelles of brandy butter. Then they'd brought out the coffee, but by then the band had started up and I'd somehow found myself on the dance floor.

We'd jived, extremely badly in my case, wiggled our hips and had great fun going in, out, in, out and shaking it all about, before ending up in a conga. I'd carried on until a stitch sent me sinking to the nearest chair, clutching my side. Henry, almost as out of breath, had dropped more elegantly into the next one – he looked like he should be in a black and white Madonna video.

'Your case is at the cottage. Do you want to come back there? The spare room is Marvin-free at the moment, so you're very welcome to use it.'

Suddenly I really didn't want to go back to my little studio. I wanted to curl up on Henry's spare bed with Talisker, just like old times. 'Yes please.' I hoped I wasn't slurring.

Henry held the taxi door open for me. He was very good at this door holding lark. Gay men were so nice, I thought. They had lovely manners and they knew what colours went together. I gave an unladylike yawn.

'Come on, Beth. Time you went to bed I think.' Henry led me up the stairs and into the spare room where Talisker was indeed on the bed. It was almost as if he was waiting for me.

A glass of water appeared on the bedside table. It was on a coaster, which made me want to giggle.

'Goodnight, Beth,' I heard Henry's voice say.

'Nighty-night, Henry,' I mumbled before unzipping my dress, pulling it off, and getting straight into bed. I closed my eyes. The room didn't spin so I wasn't drunk, just a tiny bit squiffy.

He was a lovely man, Henry. Six foot three or four, slender, and he had the most perfect forearms I'd ever seen on a man. And lovely shoes. He looked to me like he should be tap dancing his way through a 1940s musical. I wondered what it would be like to be his leading lady.

Oops, I'd have to be careful, otherwise I might end up being a teeny tiny bit in love with Henry. And that wouldn't be very good, would it? Especially if we'd got to go on a romantic dinner together. He might be charming and have a very cute bottom when he danced, but there was no point in getting any ideas about him. Henry Halliday wouldn't be interested in anything on my menu.

CHAPTER FIFTY-NINE

Gritty eyes from going to bed with my makeup on, a mouth like the inside of a kettle in need of descaling, a headache, and the feeling that there was something I couldn't quite remember greeted me when I woke up in the morning. Half an hour in the bathroom put most of that right and I felt and, hopefully looked, a bit more human when I went down the stairs. There was a little girl in the kitchen with Henry.

'Amelia, this is Beth.' Kneeling beside her, Henry introduced me to the little girl I'd seen in the photograph. She looked adorable in her red, green, and white snowman jumper, tinselly bobbles in her milk chocolate coloured, ringlets, making it look like she had bunches of slightly melted Curly Wurlys growing out of her head.

'Hello, Amelia. I like your jumper,' I looked down at my own. It was more stylish and classier than my usual winter woollies thanks to my clothing allowance, but plain. It was definitely missing a Christmassy touch.

'It's a snowman.' She looked up at me uncertainly, clutching Henry's hand but clearly wanting to show off her Christmas jumper.

'It's a lovely snowman,' I agreed. 'Has he got a name?'

Amelia put her head on one side for a moment and frowned in concentration, 'Olaf, only he isn't from *Frozen*. This Olaf's just a normal snowman. He can't talk.'

'Well, he's very handsome,' I smiled at her. She really was the cutest little girl.

'You had a Father Christmas one last year, didn't you, Amelia?' Henry ruffled one of her Curly Wurly locks.

'That was when I was a little girl,' she rolled her eyes at him. 'I'm four now,' she told me, letting go of his hand.

'Four!' I exclaimed, feeling this was probably the right way to react to the news and being rewarded by a giggle and a cheeky grin.

'How old are you?' She made it sound like a really important question. Still, I suppose when you're four, any question you ask is really important.

'Amelia!' Henry pretended to scold her while trying not to laugh. 'You mustn't ask ladies how old they are!'

'Why not?' came the perfectly reasonable reply. I too, was curious as to why it was considered perfectly all right to ask a man his age but not a woman – or a lady, as Henry so delicately called me, putting me in mind of David Walliams in *Little Britain*, flouncing about in a dress and wig, saying 'I am a lady!'

'Well,' he began, looking to me as if he wished he hadn't started that conversation. 'It's not very polite.'

'What's polite?'

'Polite is when you say "Please" and "Thank you" and "Excuse me", 'he explained.

'I always say "Please" and "Thank you",' she announced proudly.

'I'm sure you do,' I told her. I could see when she grew up there was every chance Henry's niece was going to be a proper little madam.

'Amelia and I were just about to have brunch, weren't we?'

Amelia looked at me as if trying to decide if I knew what brunch was. 'That's like breakfast and lunch all mixed up together. You can have boiled eggs and soldiers *and* fish fingers!' Clearly I looked like I needed the explanation.

'Wow! That sounds lovely,' I laughed as much at Henry's face as at the food combination.

'You will join us, won't you, Beth?' Henry asked, busying himself with the coffee maker.

'Thanks, I'd love to. I love boiled eggs and fish fingers!' I winked at Amelia.

Half an hour later the three of us were indeed tucking into perfectly soft boiled eggs, toasty soldiers, fish fingers, and tomato ketchup. There were also croissants, pain au chocolat, yoghurts, and a bowl of fruit.

'What's your favourite ice-cream?' Amelia looked at me, dipping a fish finger in her egg, sending yolk dribbling down the sides. 'Mine's mint choc chick.'

'Mint choc chip,' Henry corrected her, smiling.

'Why? It hasn't got chips in it.'

'They're chips of chocolate,' he tried again.

'Chips aren't chocolate, silly. They're potato. Everybody knows that.'

'Well, my favourite is banana,' I announced.

'I like bananas in chocolate sauce. Are you Daddy's girlfriend?' She nibbled the yolky fish finger end.

'Amelia!' Henry looked horrified.

'I don't know who your daddy is ...'

'That's Daddy,' she pointed at Henry with the rest of the fish finger, dripping yolk on the table – which would drive him nuts – and looking at me as if she thought I must be more stupid than she'd suspected.

So this was Henry's daughter, not his niece. He can't have always been gay. Maybe he swung both ways? That would make sense. Thanks for the look of pure horror though, Henry. Was that why I needed so many facials?

'Beth works for me, darling,' Henry explained, wiping up the yolk with a damp cloth.

'Like Mummy used to?' She nibbled off a bit more fish.

'Yes,' he sighed. 'Like Mummy used to.'

Hmm. Interesting. I wondered what she did.

'Mummy used to be a spy,' she told me in what was clearly her best hush-hush voice. 'She used to go and spy on Daddy's hotels ...'

'Thank you, Amelia.' Poor Henry looked flustered. 'If you've had enough to eat you can get down now.'

266

CHAPTER SIXTY

After a few more home assignments in Cheshire, Derbyshire, the Cotswolds, and the Lake District, Henry gave me a real challenge for my first international foray – a four-day cruise from Piraeus, visiting Mykonos, Rhodes, Crete, and Santorini. He assured me that the cruise ships all had stabilisers and that seasickness would not be a problem. He also bought me a pair of Sea-bands anti motion sickness bracelets and a packet of Dramamine, which he promised me I wouldn't need.

It would feel strange to go back, alone, to three of the islands where Alex and I had spent our honeymoon. Henry had hummed and hawed about sending me somewhere like Paris or Rome instead, but I surprised myself by finding I actually wanted to go to Greece. I'd only ever been there with Alex, going where he recommended, doing what he wanted, and doing it all the Greek way. Now I could go back as one of those annoying cruise ship tourists and do it my way.

As Henry was jetting off on a business trip too, we flew as far as Athens together. It was the first time I'd enjoyed the luxury of a taxi to the airport – I'd always done my travelling to airports by coach.

'I'm so sorry business class was full,' Henry apologised for the umpteenth time as we waited for the drinks trolley. 'It's because it's so close to Christmas. I should have booked the tickets earlier.'

'It really doesn't matter,' I repeated, also for the umpteenth time. Premium economy was a step up from the way I usually travelled anyway. In fact, where flights to Athens were concerned, EasyJet was the way I'd always travelled. Business class on a regular airline was something other people did.

'And you're sure you'll be all right going back to …'

'I'm sure.'

'And you really don't mind working over Christmas, when you come back?'

'You'll be saving me from Christmas dinner with my mother's hundred-year-old neighbours.' I grimaced.

Henry had no idea how much I was looking forward to our Christmas assignment – a festive package at a swish family hotel in North Wales. It was his turn to have Amelia for Christmas so the three of us were travelling to Llandudno the day before Christmas Eve to one of the latest hotels to join the Halliday Vacation Club. We'd booked a three-room suite and, as far as the hotel staff were concerned, Henry was a Mr Johnson and I was Amelia's nanny. I'd never spent Christmas with a small child before – experiencing the Santa Claus anticipation through Amelia's eyes would be fun.

'Bon Voyage!' Henry kissed me on both cheeks as I went to walk up the gangplank to board the cruise ship. His business would keep him in Athens overnight before going on to Turkey, so he'd come with me to the Port of Piraeus by taxi and escorted me to the right berth – and that was without me telling him about my daft dream where I'd been running around the port trying to find my boat.

'Thank you, Henry. Hope your trip's successful.'

'Don't forget, any problems I'm only an email away.'

I knew I should go on up and make him leave – he didn't want to be standing here waiting for the boat to take off, or whatever it was that boats did – but my feet didn't seem to want to move.

'You've got your Dramamine, haven't you?'

'Yes, in my bag.'

'And your wristbands?'

'Those too. Do you think I should put them on now?'

'Time to board, miss,' came a voice from behind me.

I looked round and saw I was the last person to go up. 'Bye, Henry,' I said quickly and hurried up.

My cabin was pretty much what I'd expected – bed, bedside table, wardrobe, chair, porthole, tiny en-suite. The little television screen was a surprise, but I supposed if I was going to end up in here feeling sick, I'd need something to keep my mind off it. My bags had been brought to my cabin, but I'd unpack later. First, I wanted to put my wristbands on, go on deck, and watch mainland Greece get smaller and smaller.

There was a lifejacket drill and meet and greet with the main members of staff and crew before lunch. It was done in Greek, English, Spanish, and French and, to be honest, I'd zoned out by about halfway through. A photographer was wandering around, taking pictures of passengers in their lifejackets – never a good look – but he was quite entertaining and kept the bored children quiet.

Lunch was a buffet with a lot of salads. There were cold meats and seafood and breads and plenty of fruit, so I didn't think we'd have to worry about scurvy.

My phone bleeped a text message while I was wandering around a cold and windy Mykonos that evening. *How are you feeling? Are you on Mykonos yet? – H* was the message from Henry.

'*Fine thanks, lunch ok, Mykonos good, walking round town now, B,* I replied. I didn't tell him I'd found the shop where Alex and I had bought the most delicious hot *loukoumades* doughnuts, and that I was greedily stuffing my face with one.

I got on the last of the tenders back to the ship. It was dinner time and I was second sitting so I went to my cabin and freshened up first.

'Ladies and gentlemen, welcome to our first night's show,' the entertainments manager boomed out in four languages. Now there was a woman who didn't need a microphone. 'And here with our opening number, all the way from Russia ... our dancers!'

I sat back and watched six pretty, thin, bored-looking girls in skimpy costumes perform a simple-looking routine with six chairs, to that song *Willkommen, Bienvenue, Welcome* from *Cabaret*.

Looking around the tinselled ballroom with its obligatory Christmas tree in one corner, I could see the average age of the passengers was about double mine. What was I doing here? And more importantly, what was this floating holiday camp doing as part of Henry's company? After the hotels I'd visited, I just couldn't see it. Hopefully tomorrow would be a bit less *Hi-de-Hi!*

How was your first night? Hope entertainment and dinner good – H. Henry's text came in while I was deciding whether to bother with breakfast or not.

Average, average, and average. Haven't been sick yet tho☺ B. I thought I'd better put the smiley face so I didn't sound too grumpy. At least today we had the whole day on Rhodes, an island I hadn't been to before. And we

270

would dock in the port, so no ship to shore tenders.

Skipping breakfast, I was first in the queue to disembark and I practically skipped down the gangplank. Now to find something nice for breakfast.

Sounds like it will be an interesting report – H. I read as I sat down to look at the breakfast menu in a lovely café in the old town. Now this was more like it.

I texted Henry back, *No. It will be AVERAGE!!!*

CHAPTER SIXTY-ONE

I arrived back in UK a couple of days before Henry, so I had plenty of time to work on my report before showing it to him, doing a little Christmas shopping, and meeting Daisy for lunch.

'So, Miss Jetsetter,' she gave me a hug and we both sat down at the table I'd grabbed in Dominic's. How's it going?'

'Well, the places I've visited for him *here* have all been fabulous, but four days on a Greek cruise ship was just ...'

'I thought you get seasick?'

'I was all right on this boat – evidently stabilisers do work. No, it was everything else – the whole Butlins in captivity thing I couldn't stand. And the endless buffets with the same food every day. Going ashore each day were the only bits that kept me sane. And fed.' I nodded at the menus. 'Shall we order?'

'Vegetarian lasagne and a hot chocolate, please,' Daisy told the waitress.

'Steak and kidney pie and chips and a decaf latte, please,' I added.

After the waitress had gone, Daisy said, 'It looks like you left Sitting Pretty at about the right time.'

'What do you mean? Davina's not selling up, is she?' Henry hadn't mentioned anything, and surely he'd know. He knew all the business goings on in Wintertown.

'I don't know. Nothing's been said, but there's

something in the air at work at the moment. And we're not taking on any new clients or sitters.'

'What, no new Christmas clients?' There were always new clients at Christmas with people wanting to go away and spend the holiday with relatives.

Daisy shook her head. 'It's like she's trying to run the business down, but I don't understand why.'

'I'll see if Henry knows anything,' I told her. 'If anyone can find out what's going on, it's him.'

CHAPTER SIXTY-TWO

Henry didn't know anything but said he'd look into it when we got back after Christmas. He'd had a good chuckle at my report and confessed that he'd been thinking of disassociating himself with the cruise line and that my report had been helpful in making up his mind.

Now we were on a cold morning train to Birmingham, with three very welcome hot chocolates and bacon rolls in front of us. Amelia was telling me all about her Sunday school nativity performance.

'And my wings were bigger than the other angels and when I turned round they knocked baby Jesus out of the crib.'

'Oh my goodness,' I laughed, while Henry put his hands over his eyes – he'd been there to see it and was evidently trying to forget. 'What happened next?'

'Mary picked him up to put him back in, but his leg fell off and one of the shepherds picked it up and wouldn't give it back …'

Amelia entertained us – and the other passengers – most of the way to Birmingham, en-route to Llandudno Junction. It was a bitterly cold day and it turned out to be a blessing that our train got in just late enough to cut our half hour wait into ten minutes.

'Are we nearly there yet?' Amelia asked soon after we'd boarded this one.

'Uh-oh,' Henry whispered to me, after telling her that

no, we weren't nearly there yet. 'Now she's started asking, she won't stop until we get there. Are you any good at I Spy?'

The hotel looked so welcoming as our taxi trundled towards it, the three of us huddled in the back despite the heater being on full blast. An elegant Victorian building – it overlooked the promenade and out to sea and there was a stylish red ribbon-festooned Christmas tree welcoming us into the lobby.

We'd arrived in good time for afternoon tea and, after choosing our rooms and unpacking our bags, we were soon sitting around a table with a mouth-watering selection of finger sandwiches, cakes, mini mince pies, and slices of Yule log.

'Have a sandwich first,' Henry told Amelia as she reached straight for a piece of chocolate log.

I reached for a sandwich too. 'Mmm,' I mumbled, 'turkey and cranberry. Lovely. What have you got, Amelia?'

'Ham. I like ham. Do you like ham, Beth?'

'Yes, I do.'

'Do you like my daddy?'

Poor Henry didn't know where to put himself.

The hotel had a child-minding service, so Henry and I were able to enjoy a quiet dinner overlooking the wintery sea. The conversation however, was a bit stilted and I hoped he didn't feel awkward around me because of what Amelia had asked.

'How's your salmon?' he asked, picking up his wine glass.

'Delicious. How's your sea bream?'

'Excellent.'

276

I hoped we'd be able to get back the easy camaraderie we'd fallen into before. Should I tell him that it was all right? That I knew he was gay, or at least bi, and that I didn't want anything from him other than the friendship we'd started to have? I wanted to, but I didn't know how to start up a conversation like that, let alone finish it, so I kept quiet. Things were still a bit stilted when we said goodnight and went to our rooms.

The next day was Christmas Eve and whether it was Amelia's excitement or not, everything seemed to be back to normal. In the afternoon there'd be a treasure hunt in the lounge, bar and reception for the half a dozen children staying, with mulled wine and mince pies for the adults, so after a splendid breakfast, the three of us wandered into the town to make a few last minute purchases. I'd packed wrapping paper, so I went back to my room before lunch to wrap the handmade chocolate bells I'd bought. Then, after a light lunch of Welsh broth, the treasure hunt began.

There was much laughter and a few squawks of indignation from children and parents alike as a lot of good-natured cheating – obviously to make sure each child found a prize – went on.

'Gorgeous mulled wine.' Henry offered me a top up.

'Mmm, thanks. Another pie?' I held out the plate for him.

'Go on then, just one more.'

'Look, Daddy!' Amelia shrieked with excitement at the surprisingly tasteful snow globe she'd found as her prize. 'It's snowing inside, look!' She shook it up again and giggled in delight as the little white bits floated around and down.

She was still clutching it when he tucked her up in bed and I went in to say goodnight.

Dinner that night was much more fun – nothing to do with the mulled wine, I was sure.

'How do you fancy sharing a lobster Thermidor?' Henry asked me. It was on the Christmas Eve special menu as a dish for two.

'I'd love to,' I smiled, happy that things were back to normal. I raised my glass and he clinked his against it.

'Looking forward to seeing what Santa's brought you in the morning?'

'I don't think he'll have brought me anything. He wouldn't know where to find me this year.'

'Oh, I think Santa Claus is a very resourceful man,' he smiled enigmatically.

'It's Christmas! Father Christmas has been!' Amelia's cries probably woke up anyone else who might have been asleep in the hotel – they certainly woke us up as we both went running to her room, trying to shush her as we went. 'Look, Daddy, look, Beth!'

'That's lovely, darling. Aren't you a lucky girl,' Henry said. He'd done what my mum used to do when I was little and left a pillowcase at the bottom of her bed with presents in it. She was already tearing the paper off a *Frozen* Olaf hot water bottle.

'Look, Daddy, it's real Olaf. He won't melt when Mummy puts hot water in him, will he?'

'No darling. He's a special Olaf. He won't melt.'

I slipped away to let them enjoy this time, especially as he only got to do this with her every other Christmas, only to find a pillowcase at the bottom of my bed too. A big grin spread across my face. Henry had done that for me – that was so sweet. I was glad I'd bought a selection of travel size L'Occitane men's toiletries to go with the cashmere scarf and gloves I'd bought him. I quickly unwrapped the bundle of bathroom products and rewrapped them individually, then I took the pillowcase off the spare pillow and put the little parcels and the bigger one in and crept towards Henry's bedroom.

'Beth, come and join us,' he called out.

'Just a minute,' I called back, slipping the pillowcase by the end of his bed and going back to collect mine. 'Look!' I exclaimed, as I went back into Amelia's room. 'Father Christmas brought me something as well. Do you think he's left something for Daddy, too?'

Amelia raced out of the room as Henry grinned ruefully at me and said, 'I doubt it, he doesn't usually.'

'Look, Daddy, look!' His daughter came haring back in. 'Father Christmas left something for you too!'

The look of surprise on Henry's face was priceless.

The hotel's chefs surpassed themselves with their Christmas dinner. The turkey was the moistest I'd ever eaten and the crackling on the pork was as salty and as crispy as it could possibly be. There must have been a dozen different vegetables, all cooked to perfection – not a grey sprout in sight.

'I don't think I'll be able to eat again this year,' Henry rubbed his washboard stomach. 'What a good idea to serve the pudding a couple of hours after the dinner. That way we can enjoy both.'

'Not being able to eat again this year didn't last very long,' I teased, looking down at the gorgeous, smoky-grey, pewter broach of a cat that had been one of the gifts in my pillowcase. It looked so like Talisker – I loved it.

Henry saw me looking and smiled. 'I'm glad you like it. I thought of you the moment I saw it in the shop. Tal's very fond of you.'

'Nothing to do with me giving him food, by any chance?' I stroked the broach – it was lovely.

'No. He's had other sitters and he's never bonded with any of them the way he has with you. And that was even before you … you …'

'Turned your spare room into a squat?'

He laughed and I couldn't help joining in.

'What are you laughing at?' Amelia looked up from the game she was playing with some of the other children. It had kept them quiet for all of five minutes.

'Nothing, darling; you enjoy your game.' Then he turned to me and raised his glass. 'Merry Christmas, Beth.'

'Merry Christmas, Henry.'

Boxing Day was never a good day to travel so we'd booked to stay another night. We took the opportunity of walking up the zig-zag road of the Great Orme and enjoying the windswept views. It was breathtakingly refreshing up there. The cable car ride was closed, but we had a fantastic walk. We were ready for our dinner when we got back to the hotel.

'I like Christmas here, Daddy. Can we come back next year?' Amelia stopped spooning beans into her mouth to ask.

'Maybe the year after.'

'Will Beth come back with us?'

I held my breath, hoping he wasn't going to get embarrassed again.

'I don't know, darling. Two years is a long time away. We'll have to wait and see.'

CHAPTER SIXTY-THREE

'I don't like the idea of you going there right now, Beth. I should find somebody else to go.'

After we got back from Llandudno, Henry had received a comment from a guest staying in one of his Dubai hotels. He got staff to collect guest feedback from all his hotels and he took it very seriously. He didn't tell me what the comment had said, but I did know that if Alex hadn't been in Dubai, Henry would have already booked me a ticket to go there.

'Look, Henry, Dubai isn't a small place. What are the chances of me bumping into him there unless I actively went and looked for him?' I reasoned. 'And do you know what? Since I started doing this job, I've hardly given him a thought. I'm not the silly girl who thought camping out on people's sofas was a good idea any more. I can bump into him there or not. I really don't care.' Although the thought of giving him a gentle shove off one of those high balconies was a rather satisfying one.

'Are you really one hundred per cent sure? I'd go myself, but too many people working there know me.'

'I'm sure.'

'I'll have to book you an open ticket. You'd probably end up being out there on your own for New Year's Eve.'

'New Year's Eve doesn't mean much to me. It's just another day.'

'Well, if you're positive.'

'I'm positive. Now book that ticket.'

CHAPTER SIXTY-THREE

CHAPTER SIXTY-FOUR

'Ladies and Gentlemen, welcome to Dubai International. The local time is five minutes past eight in the morning, and the temperature, twenty-one degrees. The cabin crew and I would like to thank you for choosing Emirates Airlines and look forward to flying with you again. Please take care whilst opening the overhead lockers and make sure you take all your belongings with you. Disembarkation will be from the forward cabin.'

My fingers couldn't help surreptitiously stroking the shiny walnut surround of my comfortable recliner one last time. My fellow passengers all looked nonchalant, as if they flew business class every day of their working lives. Having spent the last few years flying EasyJet to and from Athens, I didn't think I'd ever get used to this whole other world of business class travel. It felt like some kind of private club I'd suddenly become a probationary member of, and I had to hide my excitement when I was offered a glass of fizz before take-off in case they all thought I was far too gauche to be there.

I'd never been able to sleep on a flight before, cramped elbow to elbow, as I always had been, between Alex and some random stranger – somehow, it had always been my turn to have the middle seat. The person in front of me would always have their seat leaned back so far their head was in my lap and I'd be tempted to ask them if they'd like a head massage. Behind me, of course, would be the inevitable restless child or someone with long legs who just couldn't help kicking the back of my seat every time they moved.

This was my first night flight with my new job and despite that rush of excitement that kept flooding my stomach, I'd had the most refreshing night's sleep. As I'd drifted off to the land of nod I'd wondered what on earth it must be like in first class, if it was this comfy in business. Drowsy after a couple of champagne cocktails and a delicious Kir Royal, I'd snuggled down, imagining golden chambers with fluffy clouds for beds and pillows filled with angels' wings. There the passengers would be fanned by unicorns while vestal virgins hand peeled grapes for them and gently popped them into their mouths, accompanied by harpists playing soothing lullabies and fairies sprinkling magic dust and smiling gently. Although, come to think of it, I might have actually been asleep by then and dreaming all of this.

My first thought on being woken up for breakfast was that I wanted to snuggle back to my cosy dreams, until the realisation that we would soon be landing in Dubai shook me fully awake. Dubai and my most exciting assignment!

'Thank you! Goodbye!' the cabin crew smiled as we edged our way off the plane. I pulled my lovely cabin bag on its wheels like a puppy on a lead, reminding myself of my first assignment in the New Forest. In some ways that felt like so long ago and in others as if it had only been last week.

Dubai International was full of activity. Henry had told me it was competing with Heathrow to be the world's busiest airport and I could believe him. As the travellator smoothly slid us towards passport control, I could see over the glass walls and down to the various departure lounges and Duty Free on the floor below us. It was bustling with shoppers, even at this time of the morning, all milling about. Everywhere was so bright and shiny and colourful, and so very clean.

At the end of the human conveyor belt were a small group of smiling people in pink and grey uniforms holding up big pieces of card with names on them. Henry had told me to make myself known to them.

'Marhaba.' A young woman I guessed to be from the Philippines welcomed me as I slowed down, wondering which one to approach.

'Yes,' I smiled back. 'I'm Beth …'

'Ms Dixon Beth? Come with me.' She reached for the handle of my cabin bag and I didn't know what to do – she was very petite and although the bag wasn't heavy and was on wheels, it felt very lazy to let her pull it for me.

'Oh, that's all right, I can …' I started to say, but she had already taken control of it and was ushering me ahead.

'Welcome to Dubai,' she said, leading me towards an escalator. 'First time you come here?'

'Yes, it's my first time.'

'Marhaba means welcome. You here for business or holiday?'

'Business,' I said after a brief pause. It felt slightly strange saying it, as if I were pretending to be somebody else.

'Where do you stay?'

'Oh … just in a hotel,' I gabbled, probably taking the whole mystery guest thing a bit too far. 'A driver's meeting me and taking me there.'

I hadn't realised quite how long the queues at passport control would be, and I was relieved when she led me to a much shorter queue, obviously of people who had used the same service. I'd have to remember to thank Henry when I checked in with him later.

CHAPTER SIXTY-FIVE

The car that took me to the hotel was very swish. Sitting back on the soft leather seats felt like sinking into butter. That feeling of being an imposter and wondering when somebody was going to find me out kept tapping me lightly on the shoulder, just in case I should forget. It gave up tapping and started punching when the car pulled up outside the destination of my new mystery guest assignment.

I'd never seen anything like it. It looked like a Hollywood film set of a sheikh's palace and grounds. As we drove up the long drive, I'd been more than half expecting to see magic carpets floating past us. The unicorns with the fans wouldn't have looked out of place here, either. There was no way I wasn't going to stick out like the big, fat proverbial sore thumb.

The member of staff I was supposed to be keeping an eye on was the manager of one of the restaurants. The customer comment had suggested that he might be taking bribes for booking tables in the busy and popular restaurant. It was the sort of place you had to book up months in advance but it seemed it might be possible to get a table for a little backhander.

Henry didn't believe this was happening, but he saw it as part of his duty to his customers to check it out. And so I was going to try to get a table for two for New Year's Eve. I was going to look very desperate and as if that table was the most important thing in the world to me and see what happened.

CHAPTER SIXTY-SIX

'I'm so sorry ma'am, there just isn't a table available for tomorrow night. It's New Year's Eve. All the tables have been booked up for almost a year. It's the busiest night in the calendar.'

Well, he was making all the right noises. I'd have to try harder. 'I'm going to be in such trouble,' I gasped at him, trying to sound as if I might cry. 'My husband told me to book it at the beginning of the year and I forgot. He's going to be so angry with me. It's our wedding anniversary. Isn't there anything you can do?'

'I'm sorry, ma'am. It's just not possible.'

'It's just a tiny table for two. Couldn't you squeeze one in somewhere? It wouldn't matter if it was cramped. Is there any way I could persuade you?' I ran my finger along my purse, where a thousand dirham note was poking out enough for him and only him to see it. I felt very aware that what I was doing could actually get me into trouble. But if he was taking bribes then I was doing a good thing, right?

The friendly look in his eyes vanished immediately. 'Ma'am, this is a respectable establishment. Please do not insult me or my staff. This is the second time this month that someone from your country has attempted to do such a thing and it only serves to give your country a bad name. Please leave me to attend to my duties and do not come back to this restaurant.'

I was shaking all the way back to my room. What if he called the police and had me arrested for bribery? The laws were a lot stricter out here. I phoned Henry.

'Beth?' He picked up almost at once.

'Henry, I did it and he was very angry. He said that someone else had tried to do the same thing recently. What should I do? Can you book my return? I think I should leave.'

'Beth, take a deep breath and calm down. It's all right. Remember I told you that a lot of the staff there know me? I'll call one of them as soon as I get off the phone and they can pass on to this man that you were working under my instruction to check a customer's comment. You won't be in any trouble. Are you in your room?'

'Yes.'

'Then make yourself a cup of tea and I'll call you back in a few minutes.'

Those few minutes felt a lot longer. I put the little kettle on and shoved one of the fancy silk teabags into a cup. Why hadn't he rung back? What if he couldn't get hold of the person he wanted and the restaurant manager decided to make an example of me?

When the kettle boiled I poured the water without taking my hand away and nearly scalded myself. The police could be on their way right now.

The phone rang and I nearly dropped the kettle. 'Henry?' I yelped into the receiver.

'It's fine, Beth. It's all taken care of. He's being told right now. Next time you go downstairs he'll be all smiles again. Now why don't you forget that tea, open the mini bar, and pour yourself a proper drink?'

So I did. I poured myself a very large, very good quality Sauvignon Blanc and sipped it slowly while I waited for my heart rate to return to normal.

And that was when I did it. That was when I did the

290

foolish thing I'd promised myself I wouldn't do while I was there. I switched my laptop on, logged into Facebook, and went on to Alex's page.

CHAPTER SIXTY-SEVEN

My stomach was fizzing like a glass of Alka Seltzer – one where someone had put too many in and it was in danger of frothing over the top. I'd tried taking deep, calming breaths, I'd tried breathing slowly – in, two three four five six seven eight, out, two three four five six seven eight. I'd even tried not breathing at all, but none of those things had helped. The effervescence wouldn't even subside, let alone go away and leave me in peace to get on with getting ready. I was in danger of arriving at my destination foaming and frothing at the mouth like a dog with rabies.

There was also a thumping in my chest that skittered about between a vague salsa rhythm and an even vaguer hip hop beat. And as if that wasn't enough to contend with, my tongue and the roof of my mouth felt as dry and ragged as pages torn out of an old, yellowing newspaper.

This was ridiculous. I should never have gone on Alex's Facebook page yesterday. If I hadn't, I wouldn't have seen that it still said *Relationship Status – Married to Beth Dixon*, and still had the photo of us, petting those damn donkeys on Santorini on our honeymoon. And I wouldn't have seen that he was going to be at a party at the Dubai Marina Yacht Club tonight. And I wouldn't have started wondering if I could get him close enough to some railings to push him over. Or if the music would be loud enough to cover the splash.

I looked at my hair in the mirror – the hair I had just

tried to put up in the quick and sophisticated style Henry's hairdresser had once shown me in case I needed to do it myself in an emergency. At the time, I'd laughed – who has an emergency hairstyle? Now a wave of frustrated despair rushed over me. Of all the times to be staying in a five-star hotel whose beauty salon couldn't fit me in because it was New Year's Eve and they were fully booked up with guests who'd had the forethought to book well in advance. If Facebook had told me, well in advance, that tonight I would know where Alex was going to be, then that's when I would have booked an appointment. The elegant little topknot that the hairdresser in Winchester had shown me how to do, with a few twirly-looking tendrils falling daintily to frame my face, was just not working. How she'd managed to get what there was of my hair into any kind of knot on the crown of my head was beyond me. All I was getting was a ratty little pineapple of sticky-out bits which were in no way elegant. And as for my face being framed by twirly-looking tendrils, falling daintily or otherwise, I looked like a scarecrow who'd been dragged through a couple of hedges backwards. I pulled it all out, shook my hair free, and started again.

The air conditioning in the bedroom had, up until about five minutes ago, felt just right. My top lip, however, was now pursing itself in concentration under a fine film of perspiration. The same unwelcome chilly moistness was starting to trickle down my back, and I was glad I'd decided not to put my lovely dress on until after I had finished doing my hair and make-up.

How did some women do this sort of thing all the time? Was it normal to spend this long faffing about in front of a mirror just to be able to be seen in public? I'd always been a wash and go kind of girl – most of the time

I didn't even bother with a hairdryer. A squirt of shampoo, a dollop of conditioner, a run through with a comb, and I was usually good to go. Since working for Henry, however, I'd been introduced to all kinds of sprays and serums and spritzes I'd never even known existed. Products I'd previously marched past in Boots, their labels making no sense, their contents having no possible bearing on my life, had suddenly become recognisable. There was a hell of a lot of stuff out there for people to spend their money on, and then spend even more time and effort messing about with. My new and very full spongebag was twice the size of my old, half-empty one. I just hoped it was all going to be worth it.

Doing my best to ignore the fizzing and thumping, I threw my head forward, scraped my hair towards the top of the back of my head with my brush, and held it in place with my left hand while my right wrestled with the little clear rubber band thing that the hairdresser had given me a couple of. I twisted it round, pulling the bit of hair through five times, each time thinking that this was when it would snap. It held the hair in place and it seemed to be the closest to the right part of my head that I'd achieved so far.

Encouraged by this bit of success, I picked up the little doughnut thing I'd also been given and carefully pulled the hair though that. Now I was supposed to wrap the bits of hair round it, completely covering it, and tuck them under, securing them in place with a few hairgrips. I'd have sworn the hair wasn't long enough to do that if I hadn't seen the hairdresser do it with my own eyes – and it hadn't been cut at all since then so, if anything, it might even be a fraction of a millimetre longer.

Willing it to actually have grown a fraction of a millimetre while being pretty damn sure it hadn't, I started pulling a bit of it over the doughnut and tucking it underneath. It just about went under, but the hairgrip I shoved in after it really had nothing to attach itself to and just sort of sat in my hair like the spare part it technically was. I gently removed it and dropped it back on the dressing table as surplus to requirements, then set about tugging under and tucking in other bits of hair.

The scrunchie-type hair band I had to wrap round it was the same shade of dark purple-pink as my dress. Sending up another of those silent prayers that I wouldn't destroy what I'd managed to do so far, I carefully stretched it over the hair-covered doughnut, twisted it at the back, and stretched it back again. Twice seemed to just do it, thankfully, so I smoothed out the crinkles a bit and stood back to take a proper look.

The resulting style was a fairly distant poor relation to how the hairdresser had done it but, hey, she'd had years of training and experience behind her. This didn't look too bad, and anyway, it was probably about as good as it was going to get, so I gave it a quick spurt of Frizz Ease hairspray, then another for good luck and left it at that. Job done.

I looked at my watch. It was time to get my glad rags on and be on my way. I had no idea how long I'd have to wait for a taxi to Alex's party.

Unwinding my bath towel from round me, I gave my back a final pat down before spritzing myself with the Ted Baker Pink body spray that had been one of the presents in my Christmas pillowcase. Giving it a moment to dry, I gathered my shoes and clutch bag – there's so much to remember to do, with this dressing up lark – checking that my phone, with the destination of the party in it was in the bag. This was where most women would probably have pulled on some lovely new underwear, something like one of the sets I'd bought for our honeymoon. Only there would be zero point in me bothering with any of that. I could be wearing Bridget Jones's biggest, ugliest granny-pants, because even if I did find him, Alex wouldn't be getting close enough for it to matter what I had on under this dress.

Sliding the garment off its hanger, I stepped into the deliciously silky fabric. I'd never in my life even looked at a dress like this and imagined myself in it. This was the sort of dress worn by go-getting women with high-flying careers and fancy cars. This was a Davina dress – she'd have the lipstick and nail varnish to match. It was hard to imagine it ever being a Beth dress. But the woman in Galeries Lafayette had been so insistent that I try it on and she'd already shown me so many other things that I'd said no thank you to. And I'd fallen in love with it the moment I looked in the mirror.

It looked like a completely different version of me standing there, a glamorous, confident version and, although I'd never thought of myself in that way, I rather liked it. And I had to admit that with all these beauty treatments I'd been having, my skin really did have a lovely, smooth glow to it that I hadn't even realised had been missing.

And now, standing here in it, with the right matching shoes and bag, even my silly hairdo didn't manage to detract from how good it made me feel.

Picking up my bag, I took one last look in the mirror. I was dressed to kill and ready to go.

CHAPTER SIXTY-EIGHT

A steady stream of butter-coloured taxis was pulling up to the forecourt, but as fast as each one disgorged its dinner jacketed and ball-gowned passengers, a new set of equally fancy pants people would surge forward to be next to go.

'Is this the end of the taxi queue?' I asked the woman in front of me, who was swaying slightly in scarily high heels and wearing a short, tight, white dress. She looked like the Leaning Tower of Pisa in a frock.

'Yeah,' she said through a mouthful of chewing gum.

I stood in line behind her and counted how many people were in front of me. Three guys – they'd probably share one cab. Then there were two middle-aged couples – that could be one cab or two. All in all, I reckoned there would have to be about eleven taxis, before I got to leave here. I really should have thought and come down a lot earlier. What if Alex didn't stay long at the party and I missed him?

A quarter of an hour later, I found myself at the front of the queue. My taxi dropped off three handsome-looking older women who seemed to have cornered the world market in sequins and beads, before meandering over to pick me up as if we both had all the time in the world.

'The Marina, please,' I told the driver as I got in the back. 'The yacht club.'

He pulled out of the forecourt and I put my seatbelt on and settled back, trying to relax and doomed to failure.

The thought that I was now only about twenty minutes away from where Alex was had turned the fizzing in my stomach up a notch. I was worried that the next time I had to speak, foam would come oozing out of my mouth. My even drier than before mouth.

I pulled the little pack of mints out of my bag and popped one between my lips, forgetting the lipstick until I saw a smear of it on my finger and thumb. Damn! I didn't want to get it on my dress. I wiped it off on a tissue, scrunched it up, and put it back in my bag. Instead of refreshing my mouth, the mint just stuck itself to my tongue. I wondered if it would burn a hole in it, and moved my tongue against my teeth to try and dislodge it.

We'd reached Sheikh Zayed Road, the main artery of Dubai, and the various shapes of the skyscrapers and hotels rose up into the skyline on either side. Almost no two buildings looked alike from this angle – well, except the ones that were obviously meant to be in pairs. I looked up to the left, and watched the metro slide along its track and disappear into a station like a worm into a hole. In the distance, to the right, with a light show playing against it, was the enormous sail shape of the Burj al Arab, the self-titled only seven-star hotel in the world. I wondered if Alex had been there. Alex. Goose pimples started up on my arms as I saw a sign for the marina.

The driver turned right, off Sheikh Zayed Road and took a parallel road. We passed a metro station, then Dubai Marina Mall, which looked tiny compared to Dubai Mall and Mall of the Emirates. While we were waiting at a red light, a tram crawled towards us, on its track between SZR and the road we were on. It looked empty.

We were turning right again, down a little road, then left, and I could see it ahead of us. The yacht club.

Somewhere in that building was a party and one of the guests was Alex. There was a queue of taxis ahead of us dropping people off, and I was itching to get out. Everyone else seemed to be waiting until their taxis were right in front though, so I thought I'd better do the same.

I looked up the steps at the front of the building. And that was when I saw him.

CHAPTER SIXTY-NINE

Everything went into freefall as I stared out of the taxi window at my husband. He was stood by one of the glass doors, talking to a couple of other men and laughing. His hair was shorter, he was wearing chinos and a T-shirt I hadn't seen before, and he looked happy and carefree. And oh, so very handsome. I'd somehow managed to forget that about him.

A sudden jolt of doubt sparked through me. What was I doing here? What on earth had I thought this would accomplish? Even with all my efforts to show him how fabulously I was doing without him, what was I really expecting to happen? This was stupid, even by my standards.

My cab edged forward as I was trying to think what to tell the driver. I should just turn round and go straight back to my hotel, this was a terrible mistake. But he was pulling up in front of the club now and a group of waiting lads, already anxious to be on their way to wherever they were going next, were opening the doors, one of them sliding into the front passenger seat before I could even open my mouth.

I had no choice but to get out. Opening my bag quickly, I fumbled for my purse, pulled out a hundred dirham note, and handed it to the driver. He gave me five dirhams change which I handed back to him and started to climb out. My seatbelt was still done up though, and it yanked me back, causing me to yelp and one of the lads to laugh and offer me a helping hand, just as Alex happened to look in our direction.

Unbuckling the belt, I tried again to get out of the car gracefully. As I stuck my head out, however, unused to even such a tiny bit of extra height on top of it, my topknot collided with the top of the door frame, dislodging it and sending it skew-whiff.

My heart pounding in my ears, I prayed Alex hadn't recognised me, that he'd gone inside, that I could just wait here for another taxi to take me back to my hotel. My reflection in the taxi window before it drove away showed I looked an absolute mess. After all my efforts. I thought of those hairgrips I hadn't used. They might have kept it in place. Or one of them might have dug into my head and reminded me that I'd got the stupid thing on top of it and then I wouldn't have bashed it getting out. How long would I have to wait for another taxi to get away? I stood behind a man with a broad back and looked out into the road.

'Beth?' His voice from behind me sent the goose pimples racing to the surface again. Oh God! Why did you have to let him see me? 'Beth? Is that you?'

CHAPTER SEVENTY

I took a deep breath to give the ground time to swallow me but it didn't, so I had to turn round and face him. 'Hi, Alex.' How I managed to get the words out I didn't know.

The broad-backed man, clearly not realising the importance of his role, had wandered off and there, in his place stood my husband. He looked as stunned as I felt.

'Beth. It's really you.' He bent forward as if to kiss me, so I offered him my cheek, but his head tilted the same way as mine and we ended up banging noses. His second attempt landed on my cheek while my lips ended up hitting his ear. So much for the cool, calm, independent new Beth I'd been determined to show him before turning on my heel – *me* walking away from *him* without a backward glance. 'You look amazing!'

So did he, but I wasn't going to tell him that. 'You don't look so bad yourself,' I heard myself paraphrase. 'Your hair's shorter.'

'I couldn't handle it trailing round my neck in the humidity here,' he replied. '*Me trelathike* – it was driving me nuts. It's not like Greece. The heat here is wet. You should feel how sticky it can get, even at this time of the year ...' He trailed off as he seemed to realise the inappropriateness of his words.

'Yes,' I said with a calmness that belied the churning in my stomach. 'I should, shouldn't I?'

'Alex!' Before he could dig himself out of that, one of the men he'd been talking to called him. 'Who's this?' The friend came sauntering down towards us, smiling. He was wearing a pink shirt and little frameless glasses and looked kind. Before Alex could say a word, his friend put out his hand for me to shake. 'Hi, I'm Steve.' He looked at me far more approvingly than I was used to. 'And you are?'

'This is Beth,' Alex jumped in. 'My wife,' he added, as if that fact had only just occurred to him.

'Oh my God! Hi, Beth,' Steve, now kissed me on both cheeks – a lot less clumsily than my husband had, I noticed. But then Steve had never married me and then dumped me by phone from a departing aeroplane. He had no reason at all to be nervous about what I was suddenly doing here. 'We've all been wondering when you were going to show up. Come on up and meet everyone.' And he put his hand on the small of my back to lead me up the steps.

I caught a glimpse of Alex's face as I turned to go in the direction I was being led. What did his expression say? Surprised? Scared? Confused? Was it very mean-spirited of me that his discomfort gave me a warm Ready Brek glow?

This had already gone so far off my imagined scenario I mentally tore up the script and let Steve steer me through the lobby and on towards what looked like a bar straight ahead. I could feel Alex keeping up close behind. Was he worried I was going to embarrass him? We passed the doorman, who wished us a good evening, and on in to what was indeed a huge bar, its long wall of windows overlooking the marina. We veered right, past a DJ desk with a tiny, Asian female DJ in headphones, nodding along to the music. There was a bar counter ahead, but we turned left and went through a door and outside, onto the terrace.

I wasn't overdressed and I wasn't underdressed. There were so many different styles – and a lot more flesh on display than I would have expected in a Muslim country. This was obviously the place to party.

We were swallowed up into a large, colourful, noisy gathering at the far end of the terrace. Everyone was talking, drinking, and laughing. Some of them were moving in time with the music in a 'sort of liking the rhythm but it being too early to actually start dancing' way, and there were ice buckets with bottles of white wine and fizz dotted around the tall tables.

'Hey! Everybody!' Steve shouted over the music. Those closest to him turned and waved their glasses at him. 'This is Alex's wife,' he shouted a bit louder. 'This is Beth, Alex's wife.'

The notion that in any normal circumstances it should have been Alex introducing me to his work colleagues flashed through my mind, but normal this was not. I'd landed both Alex and myself in some surreal kind of improvisation with a large cast of extras and this Steve was doing a great job. Maybe he was just that kind of guy. He could be Alex's boss, and therefore felt it was his duty to introduce me. And introduce me he did. In the space of what was probably a couple of minutes I must have met and been given the names of about twenty or thirty people, of whom there was definitely a Sarah and a Zara, because they each made a point of telling me that they weren't the other one. I was pretty sure that there'd been a Mark and a Mike, too, but apart from them, all the names had fallen into that big lucky dip barrel where names always ended up when you were introduced to too many new people at once. Then whenever you had to speak to one of them again you'd dip your hand in, pull one out, and hope it turned out to be the right one.

My only intention in coming here tonight had been to have a dignified skirmish with my husband before flouncing away with both the utmost dignity and the last word. Pushing him into the water had been floating around as an optional extra. This, however, I hadn't envisioned, and I decided I knew just how Alice must have felt after falling down the rabbit hole. And judging by the look on Alex's face he was feeling pretty much the same. I could almost feel sorry for him. Almost.

A few minutes later, I was talking to Sarah and Zara – who had both complimented my dress – sipping the glass of Prosecco which Steve had put in my hand, when Alex came up behind me and slipped an arm round my shoulder. My traitorous stomach did a flip. I could feel the hairs on the back of my neck standing to attention and my concentration on Zara's description of the fabulous dress she was having made for some ball she was going to completely disintegrated.

'*Ella na horepsoume* – come and dance with me,' he said in my ear. I didn't know the song, but it sounded suitable for slow dancing, and my outrageously disloyal heart did a little flutter at the thought that he wanted to hold me. My head, on the other hand, warned me that he just wanted to get me away from his friends in case I said or did something to embarrass him.

'Ahh, that's so sweet,' Sarah and Zara chorused as Alex took me in his arms, a few steps away from them, and we swayed together to the music.

'*Mou elipse toso poli*, Beth – I've missed you so much,' he said, his lips even closer to my ear this time.

'That'll explain all the phone calls, texts, and emails you kept bombarding me with,' I whispered ever so sweetly. 'I thought I was going to have to take out a restraining order.'

'Oh, Beth. I was so stupid. As soon as I arrived here I knew I'd made a mistake. But I knew how angry you would be so I thought I'd wait and give you time to calm down ...'

'What, with that explosive temper of mine!' I stopped pretending to move to the music and looked him in the face. 'And how many months were you thinking of giving me to "calm down"?'

'I kept thinking, tomorrow I'll call Beth, tomorrow I'll send an email. Then tomorrow came and I didn't know if you would want to speak to me.' He looked soulfully at me with those big, dark chocolate eyes, reminding me of Rex, which was dangerous territory. 'The more time went by, the more I thought I must have left it too late ...'

'But you didn't think it was worth giving it a go?' I clamped down on my softening heart. 'One phone call?'

'I should have called you, I know I should, but I thought you'd still be angry and you'd tell me to get lost. I'm so glad you came, Beth.' His eyes met mine again and my heart cranked up the flutter to a skippety-skip beat of its own, while my head told it to stop being so stupid. Did it need reminding of what he'd done to me? The position he'd carelessly left me in? So am I, my stupid heart wanted to say, but my head wouldn't let it. All the times I'd played this scene in my head – what I'd say, what he'd say, whether he'd slink away from me, or yell and shout, whether I'd give him hell, or crumple in tears, I'd never imagined this. Here we were, what felt like only minutes from the moment I clapped eyes on him, more or less dancing in each other's arms, surrounded by his new friends, as if the last few months were nothing.

'I can't believe you came all this way to find me,' he

murmured. 'Come home with me, Beth, you don't need to go back to London.'

'I haven't been in London.' He wanted me to stay? What? He thought it was all going to be that easy? He made the mess, I cleaned it up and now everything was all right again?

'*Pou piges*? Where did you go?'

'I stayed in Wintertown.'

'But we let go of our apartment there.' He looked puzzled. 'You gave up your job there. I thought you would go back to London and stay with your mother while you looked for a new job.'

'I got my job back at Sitting Pretty.' Ha! He hadn't been expecting that!

'Where did you stay? How did you afford the rent?'

'Oh, I took up squatting in empty houses, it's remarkably easy if you know when people are going to be away!' He hadn't been expecting that, either.

'Oh, I've missed that English sense of humour of yours.' He pulled me to him and wrapped his arms around me.

Just wait until I told him about my new job. Would he think that was another example of my English sense of humour? Alex had made no secret of the fact that he saw my time at Sitting Pretty as just a little job to keep me out of mischief and in pin money while he went out and earned the real stuff. I couldn't wait to tell him all about my new career with Halliday's Vacation Club.

CHAPTER SEVENTY-ONE

It was too noisy to talk properly at the yacht club and so, after we'd welcomed in the New Year with the flashiest firework display I'd ever seen we ended up sharing a taxi back to his apartment with Mike. Or it could have been Mark. Whichever one it was, he had an eastern European girl draped all over him wearing the shortest skirt and skimpiest top I'd ever seen and a very hard expression on her face. Alex had said she was his girlfriend but she didn't look very friendly. She looked like she could be Katya's or Natalia's cousin.

The taxi ride took forever – Sheikh Zayed Road seemed to have doubled in length while I'd been at the yacht club – but eventually we got to Bur Dubai, where Mike, or Mark got out first at a rather downmarket-looking hotel and quickly disappeared inside with the girl, who I was starting to suspect might not actually be his girlfriend.

We drove round a couple more streets before pulling up outside a huge building called Golden Sands. Alex paid the driver and I clambered out, not having to worry about the stupid topknot, which I'd yanked out in the powder room at the club. It looked like a nice building and I peered up at it, wondering which balcony was his. A smile flickered across my lips as all my bluster about shoving him off one of those sprang into my mind. As if! They still had the death penalty here for that sort of thing.

A security guard greeted Alex with a smile and briefly

glanced at me as we walked through the lobby area towards a pair of lifts. We got out on the first floor and Alex led me along the corridor.

As he stopped at what must have been his front door I caught myself smiling again. This time it was at the memory of him carrying me over the threshold, at my insistence, after our honeymoon and banging my head on the door frame.

Alex put his key in the lock and ushered me into the apartment. The door opened on to the lounge – from what I could see by the light that had been left on through a door to the left. He walked me through the door and past a dark kitchen. The light was coming from the bedroom, where the unmade bed and mess of clothes strewn about took me back to the first time I ever went back to Alex's place in Camden. His room back then had had the look of a student pad tenanted by someone doing a PhD in medium budget designer squalor. The only difference here was that the designer shirts looked high end.

'*Na katsoume sto balkoni* – let's sit on the balcony.' Alex indicated the sliding glass door on the other side of the bed. 'I'll bring some wine,' he added, leaving me to go and get it.

I'd rather have had a coffee, I'd already sunk far more wine and fizz than I was used to tonight. It occurred to me though that the options would be limited – sandy Greek coffee you could stand a spoon in, or syrupy frappe with sickly condensed milk. In my absence there wouldn't be any decaf, or even any fresh milk in Alex's kitchen. So more wine it was.

I fiddled with the window catch and went out onto the balcony. It was long and narrow – just room for a small bistro table with a chair on either side which you would have to squeeze past to walk further along. I supposed it

312

ran the whole length of the apartment. Instead of the road, it overlooked a quad with a swimming pool in the middle and what looked like a nice garden around it. I looked forward to seeing it in a couple of hours when the sun came up. If I was still here then.

'*Katse* – sit,' Alex invited me, as he put a bottle of Cabernet Sauvignon and two glasses on the table. Of course, he preferred red wine so he wouldn't have any white in, but that was fine. He poured the wine. '*Stin yia mas*! – Cheers! Here's to us.' He clinked his glass against mine and downed about half of it in one mouthful. I took a sip of mine. It tasted dry on my tongue – I wouldn't be able to drink much on top of all the Prosecco I'd had at the yacht club, or I'd be fit for nothing in the morning. Putting his glass down on the table he rested his hand close to mine and ran his fingertip along my wrist. Goose pimples shot up my arm – it must have gotten cooler than I realised.

'How long have you had this place?' I asked him, thinking my brain should be sending my arm a message to move and wondering why it wasn't.

'Since the beginning of December. I was stuck in a hotel apartment before that. It was pretty grim – you'd have hated it.' He turned those big, puppy dog eyes on me and stroked my wrist again. 'You really would have.'

Possibly, but I wouldn't have hated this place, I thought, but didn't say. There went the goose pimples again – I should have brought my pashmina out. 'Big pool.' I breathed, nodding down towards it. 'Do you get time to use it much?'

'Yeah,' his fingers started tracing their way up the inside of my arm. 'Most Friday and Saturday mornings I'll go do a few laps before it gets too warm. Some evenings when I get home too, if I haven't gone for a drink with the boys after work.'

'Sounds like you've got in to a nice routine.' I took what was meant to be another sip but turned in to a gulp of my wine just for something to do with my hands. He moved closer. He looked like he was about to kiss me. That so wasn't what I'd come here for. And yet …

His free hand found my thigh and started stroking it. Half my brain was thinking *Mm … yes please*. The other half was trying to protest but couldn't quite remember why and my body was siding with the first half. Then his lips met mine, my brain shut down completely and my body took over.

CHAPTER SEVENTY-TWO

We stood up together and moved as one – a rather awkward, clumsy one – into the bedroom. He started tugging at my dress before I'd even kicked off my shoes. I directed him to the zip and started unbuttoning his shirt while he took care of the dress.

'*Ella agape mou* - my love,' he murmured into my hair before pulling the dress down and tumbling with me onto the bed. He had my bra undone and tossed aside in seconds and his hands were fumbling with my knickers. My big old Bridget Jones granny knickers that I'd worn because this hadn't been part of the plan. He didn't seem to have noticed. But I had. I'd worn them for a reason. I wasn't ready for this. I mumbled something about needing the bathroom as I pulled myself away from him and headed for the en-suite. I didn't have long to wait until he started snoring.

CHAPTER SEVENTY-THREE

When I woke up later in the morning it took my brain a second to remember where I was, then I turned over. Alex wasn't there. I looked at the alarm clock. Twenty-five past eight. That was late for me, but then it was New Year's Day and we had just had a very late night. I'd have to get myself back to my hotel soon.

'Alex,' I called out, wondering if he was making coffee. I couldn't smell any and there was no reply, so I got up, pulled on his shirt from last night, and wandered along the little hallway to where I thought the kitchen was. He wasn't in there, but there was a note on the cramped counter, scribbled on a blank bit of a pizza delivery menu with a key next to it. *Gone to work. I've left you my key so you can check out of your hotel and bring your stuff here. Will be back about 6, so be back before me – A x*

Check out of my hotel and bring my stuff here? A few apologetic words and a quick fumble and then business as usual? I knew I was low maintenance but did he really think I was going to just pick up where we left off and pretend the last few months hadn't happened just because we almost slept together this morning?

I'd started a new chapter in my life and had a great new job. I wasn't just going to throw everything Henry had done for me back in his face because Alex had realised he'd been an idiot. We had to sit down and have a real talk about all this as soon as he got back from work.

Hang on a minute though, it was New Years' Day. Why would he have to go in to work on New Years' Day? I pulled the business card Steve had given me out of my evening bag. He'd scribbled several phone numbers on it that he thought might be useful, including one for reception. I dialled the number and waited.

'Al Jadeed Brinkley, how can I help you?'

Think, Beth, think. 'Er, hello, is Alex Petropoulos there please?'

'Just a moment, I'll put you through.'

'Alex Petropoulos speaking …'

'Oh, hi, Alex … It's Beth … er … I hadn't realised you were going to be working today.'

'Yeah, New Year's Day! Look we'll talk tonight. Gotta go, it's crazy here today. *Yia sou* – bye.'

OK, so he was working today. Actually, now I thought about it, Steve had said something about them all having to do overtime this weekend because of some emergency I hadn't really paid attention to because I'd been too busy listening to Alex.

There were half a dozen texts, including one from Henry which had arrived about four in the morning, wishing me a Happy New Year and saying he'd got me on a flight tonight. That was quick. I wondered if it could be changed to tomorrow night so Alex and I could have that talk. I was sure Henry wouldn't mind, and I could go and check out of the hotel and stay here tonight, so that needn't be a problem. I texted him back:

Happy New Year Henry! Can we delay 1 day? Have met Alex & need to talk more. Can check out of hotel & stay in apartment, no prob. Hope this ok ☺ Bx

The kitchen in this apartment was tiny. His used frappe shaker sat in the corner of the counter, surrounded by a litter of empty biscuit packets, crumpled condensed milk pods, dirty mugs, and teaspoons. Spilled dribbles of ketchup and that sweet sticky milk and grains of sugar added splotches of red and white to the rust-coloured granite work surface. I saw now that this miniscule space was a tip. The sink was full of dirty dishes and glasses – no pots or pans, so I guessed he'd been living on takeaways. The only thing that was clean was his *briki* – his little Greek coffee pot.

A quick search of the cupboards revealed no other coffee and no clean mugs either. Crockery and cutlery-wise, this kitchen had obviously been kitted out with a set of four each of everything, and all four mugs, dinner plates and bowls were dirty on the counter or in the sink. That particular cupboard held a couple of clean side plates and that was it.

Another cupboard held a half-empty box of bags of salt and vinegar crisps, more packets of biscuits, a jar of Kalamata olives, an open bag of sugar with a coffee-tipped spoon stuck in it, some little salt and pepper packets, and a handful of ketchup sachets, which must have come with some of the takeaways. Another flashback to the first time Alex took me back to his place in Camden.

There was some orange juice in the fridge, and I rinsed out the glass he'd obviously used this morning before pouring some for myself. I'd drink that and have a shower. By then I hoped I'd have finished arguing with myself over whether I should tackle the washing up mountain or leave it to the lazy sod who'd created it.

The quick shower I had was an assault on my senses. Alex's lime and lemon shower gel, his shampoo, his deodorant – the scents I'd spent three years living with and almost as many months living without, shot through my sense memories and made me feel like I'd come home. Except that I hadn't and I wasn't ready to start feeling like that.

It felt remarkably like doing the walk of shame leaving Alex's apartment, wearing one of his shirts, tied at the waist, over last night's dress. There was a different security guard on duty and I didn't want to imagine what he must be thinking as he looked at me, but he didn't say anything. There didn't seem to be any taxis coming along that road, so I walked to where I thought I'd remembered a main road and found one quite quickly. The look the driver gave my clothes made me not want to imagine what he was thinking either.

I'd arrived back at the hotel and had an omelette and a proper coffee, and had just got out of the bath, when a text tinged into my phone from Henry:

Are you sure, Beth? I can delay ticket as long as you need but do be careful. Don't check out in case you need the room. Any problem call/sms/email me H

CHAPTER SEVENTY-FOUR

'Mmm, something smells good.' Alex was practically drooling when he got home that evening. 'Is that my mum's recipe?' The level of enthusiasm in his kiss sent goose pimples chasing each other all over my skin.

'What do you think?' As if I would dare make moussaka any other way. As soon as we got engaged, his mother had handed me a notebook in which she had written down all Alex's favourite Greek dishes with exact instructions as to how they had to be made.

'I'll just grab a quick shower.' He kissed me again. 'I won't be long.'

I carried on laying the little outside table which I'd brought up to the lounge end of the balcony. I hadn't stopped since getting back from the hotel this afternoon. The state of the lounge had somehow managed not to make itself fully known to me until I walked back through the front door, when it hit me full in the face. There were a couple of pizza boxes, complete with a collection of unwanted crusts under the coffee table. On top of it, old newspapers and magazines with coffee mug rings all over them, empty beer, and soft drink cans and water bottles left like knocked-over skittles, and some kind of pizza topping trodden in to the rug at the far end of the sofa. I knew it was stupid but I hadn't been able to go back out and buy the moussaka ingredients until I'd cleared up that lot.

The security guard, once we'd established my identity,

had directed me to a lovely little supermarket called Spinneys, about a five-minute walk away. It was one of the ones which had a pork license and so was a bit on the pricey side, but everything looked lovely and fresh and I was pretty sure I'd get everything I needed there.

It was only when I'd arrived back at the apartment with my minced lamb, aubergines, courgettes, potatoes, herbs and spices, a bottle of Greek olive oil, milk, and my one cheat – a packet of bechamel sauce mix – that I realised there was no baking dish to make it in. I'd expected to find the one his mum had given us specifically for baking this and pasticcio, another favourite of his, but it wasn't in any of the kitchen cupboards. So I'd sliced the aubergines and sprinkled salt over them – as instructed by the Greek mother-in-law, so as to draw out the bitter juices – while I went back out to get one.

Once the dish was assembled and ready for the oven, I'd sat and finished off my hotel report for Henry. A germ of an idea had planted itself in my head, but it was far too early to know if anything would come of it. It was a very long shot that Alex and I might be able to find some way of staying together, but if we did, I didn't want to give up my job. It had occurred to me that I could do this job using Dubai as a base, if Henry sent me to check up on his Middle East, Far East and Australian hotels. But like I said, it was a very long shot that I could trust Alex again and I would miss working so closely with Henry. I flicked through the report again. I was pleased with it and left it out on the coffee table to show Alex, as I wasn't sure if he would understand about the job, or quite believe that it was something I could be good at. I was giving it another quick read-through when Alex came back out, smelling fresh and citrusy and looking even more edible than my moussaka.

He wrapped his arms around me and gave me a long kiss, before patting me on the bottom and saying, '*Na fame eh* – let's eat!' Then he sauntered out to the balcony and sat himself down. My mind did a quick flashback to when I'd made a lasagne for Henry – how he'd insisted on helping carry things through to the dining table and he didn't sit down until everything was on the table and I was there too. But then, Alex had never done any of that, so he wasn't going to start now. Just different upbringings, I supposed.

I took the moussaka out of the oven and left it to rest a moment while I carried out the wine and Greek salad and put them on the table. By the time I'd returned with the moussaka, Alex had opened and poured the wine.

'*Stin yia mas*.' He clinked my glass. 'Here's to us, Beth.'

CHAPTER SEVENTY-FIVE

'So, that's why I was in Dubai on New Year's Eve,' I finished my tale and waited for Alex's reaction.

'*Then katalaveno*. I don't understand. You came here as some kind of undercover hotel spy to try and bribe a manager in one of the best hotels in Dubai?'

'Yes, but only to test whether he'd take it or not. And of course, he didn't. But he told me that the guest who'd complained about him had been the one who'd offered the b –'

'*Stamata* – stop, Beth. This is crazy. Who is this man who sent you to do this? Some man with a cat who found you breaking into his home and living there while he was away?'

'No it's –'

'*Accou* – Listen to yourself. This is like some bad television soap opera. It was bad enough having to tell people you picked up dog shit for a living. Now I have to tell them that you spy on people? What have you let happen to you, Beth?'

'What, apart from my husband flying halfway round the world and leaving me behind?' The words were out of my mouth before I could stop them.

'*Ego ftaio eh?* So it's my fault? I told you to go and live like a criminal? I can't talk to you when you're like this. I'm going for a drink.' And he marched out, taking the one key with him.

I was furious, with Alex, and with myself. This was

what he'd always been like. Why had I thought he'd be any different now? Everything had to be done his way.

Of course he wouldn't be proud of me for finding an exciting new job. He'd be angry that I hadn't done what he thought I should do.

Well, if Alex thought he'd trapped me here by taking the only key with him he could think again. I grabbed my bag, stuffed my laptop, night things and toiletries into it and was out of the door just a few minutes after him, slamming it shut behind me.

I should have listened to Henry. He said I was too vulnerable to Alex to come to Dubai and risk seeing him, and he was right. Henry, who'd only known me properly for what, six weeks? He understood me far better than Alex who'd known me three years. He even knew I'd need that hotel room again tonight. Why couldn't I have married a man like Henry?

CHAPTER SEVENTY-SIX

The first thing I did when I got back to the hotel was head to the bar and order a glass of their very superior Sauvignon Blanc. While I waited for it I sent Henry a text – *Sorry. Been stupid ☹ Please book return ticket A S A P. B x*

I thought there'd have been a reply by the time I finished my drink, but there wasn't, so I tried ringing his number. It seemed to be switched off. Either that or my roaming thing wasn't working. I didn't want to stay for another drink in the bar on my own so I ordered a latte and a slice of camels' milk chocolate tart from the coffee shop to be delivered to my room and went up to run another bath. Henry still hadn't got back to me by the time I was ready for bed and I lay there flicking through the channels, unable to concentrate on anything.

Had Alex got home yet and found I wasn't there? Would he come looking for me and make a scene? I'd already rung reception and told them I wasn't to be disturbed if anybody came asking for me, but to be honest I doubted if he'd bother. He'd probably just expect me to come running back to him again once I'd calmed down. Well he'd have a damned long wait.

I must have dozed off eventually and it was quarter to eight in the morning when I was woken up by the sound of someone banging the door closed in the next room. Checking my phone I saw there was still no response from Henry so I got dressed and went down to breakfast.

Last night's moussaka seemed like a very long time ago, and I'd only had a small portion, so I found I was suddenly ravenous. I hit the breakfast buffet with a vengeance. A cocktail of exotic fruit juices, a mountain of fresh pineapple and assorted melon slices, smoked salmon and scrambled eggs and two pains au chocolat, all washed down with a pot of the most deliciously fragrant coffee.

Back in my room I packed my things in case, when I did finally hear from Henry, I'd need to rush to the airport. I was surprised I hadn't heard from him at all – he was normally never far from his phone. Still, it was only seven o'clock in UK. He might be having a lie-in, or be in the shower himself – a memory of lemon verbena wafted through my mind. Stop that, Beth, he's only a friend, he doesn't want anything else from you.

Reception informed me that nobody had turned up asking for me, which was just as I'd expected, so I decided to take the bull by the horns and tell Alex what I was going to do. Although it would serve him right if I just left without telling him, I wanted closure, and this time I was going to get it.

I got a taxi to where Steve had told me their offices were. It was a smart building and, after looking at the sign saying which offices were on which floor, I took the lift up to the eighteenth.

'Good morning,' the receptionist greeted me with a smile.

'Alex Petropoulos, please.' I smiled back before noticing that the girl looked nervous. 'Is there a problem?'

'It's just that he's got someone in with him at the moment.'

The way she said it, it didn't sound like it was

anything to do with work. 'I'm his wife. Please show me to his office. Don't make me walk around looking for him and disturbing people. I can see you're all busy.'

CHAPTER SEVENTY-SEVEN

There were raised voices coming from Alex's office and I didn't know whether to go in and try to diffuse the situation a little, or leave Alex and whoever he was arguing with to it. The receptionist, having done what I'd asked, had left me to it. I didn't blame her.

Indecision kept me hovering next to the water cooler outside his door – should I stay or should I go away and come back later? I was about to walk away when I heard my name. I went closer to the door. That sounded like Henry's voice. But it couldn't be. I pressed my ear right against it.

'She's my wife.'

'Not that anyone would know, for all the respect you show her. You desert her with no warning, then when she gets on with her life, you don't like it.'

'Working for you isn't getting on with her life.'

'She's happy working with me. She has an interesting job, good friends, somewhere to live …'

'What, on your couch?'

'No, the job comes with a studio.'

'Which I bet you have a key to.'

'Alex!' I shouted, bursting through the door.

'Beth!' they both said at once.

'Henry, what are you doing here?'

'I was worried after I got your text yesterday so I got on the first flight.'

'How did you know where to come?'

331

'The internet is a mine of information, Beth. And when my plane landed I called the office number, not expecting anybody to actually be working today ...'

'Whatever!' Alex shouted. 'Enough! Look, *Henry,* Beth's back with me now, so you've wasted your journey.'

'No, I'm not,' I stopped him before he could say any more.

'Yes, you are.' Alex took a step towards me.

'You know what, Alex? After you left for Dubai without me and phoned from the plane like a coward, I was convinced at first that you'd change your mind and I thought that was what I wanted. Then all I wanted to do was come over here and shove you off a tall building. I behaved like an idiot because I was angry and my head was all over the place. But then Henry gave me a job – a really good, interesting, exciting job – and I started to get my self-respect back. But I hadn't got it back completely yet. Henry understood that. He knew I wasn't ready to come here and see you, but I thought I was. It was my mistake. But d'you know what good has come out of it? I've seen that the marriage I thought might be worth fighting for isn't. You're not worth it. And that's what I came here to say to you now. I've packed and as soon as I've got my ticket sorted I'm going home.'

'With him?' Alex glared at Henry.

'If you mean will we be on the same plane, then hopefully yes.'

'You know that's not what I meant,' he snarled.

'Not that it's any of your business, but no, not *with* him. Henry isn't interested in me in that way. Now, I think it's time Henry and I were making our arrangements. Goodbye, Alex. I don't expect to hear from you again other than via a solicitor.'

I took off my wedding ring and tossed it to him before walking out of the room with as much dignity as I could muster, relieved to hear Henry behind me.

'I'm so proud of you,' he touched my arm as we reached the lift. 'I was worried he'd find a way to get round you, take advantage of your generous nature, get you to stay with him, and then hurt you again.' The lift doors opened and we got in. 'But what did you mean when you said I wasn't interested in you in that way?'

This was going to be awkward. 'Well, it's just that … well, you're not, are you?'

'What makes you think that?'

I couldn't think of any other way of saying it. 'Because I'm a woman?'

'You think I don't like women? What? Hang on a minute, you think I'm gay?' He looked so shocked it was almost comical.

'Well, you asked me to keep the women at the ball away from you.'

'Because those particular women could bore for England. What other reasons?'

'You chose those ball gowns for me with matching accessories? What straight man does that?'

'One who still has an account at all the fancy shops where his ex-wife used to spend most of his money, and can rely on the staff to think for themselves when given a few simple instructions!'

'Oh.'

'Anything else?'

'You're the cleanest, tidiest man I've ever met and you always smell lovely.' Even I knew I was scraping the barrel now.

'Er, thank you?' Henry looked at me quizzically.

'I'm sorry. I thought that was why you got divorced.'

'I got divorced because my wife ran off with a timeshare salesman.'

'Ouch.' I grimaced at him. 'You must have hated me when I compared your company to a posh timeshare ...' The lift doors opened on to the ground floor and we stepped out, moving aside to let other people get in and the doors close again before saying any more.

'It wasn't your most endearing moment,' he raised an eyebrow at me. 'Let's get out of here and sort out our tickets.'

'And pick up my luggage.'

'Yes, and pick up your luggage. All of it. We don't need any reason for you to have to come back here.'

CHAPTER SEVENTY-EIGHT

'Would you like the window seat or the aisle?' Henry asked as we boarded the business class cabin. He had a lovely warm smile on his face.

'I'd like the window seat if that's all right.' I couldn't help smiling either.

Henry put our cabin bags in the overhead lockers and sat down next to me, his arm on the wide armrest just inches away from mine. 'You keep smiling,' he observed.

'Do I?' I edged my arm slightly closer. 'So do you.'

'Can I ask you something?'

'You can ask me anything you want, Henry.'

He leant a bit closer and asked quietly 'Why do you think I dropped everything and flew over as soon as I got your text?'

'Er ... because you're a very kind boss who'd do that for any of his employees?'

'I'm not *that* kind and no, I wouldn't.'

'Then can I ask you something?'

'You can ask me anything you want, Beth.'

'Well,' I leant a bit closer too, 'does our conversation by the lift mean that you *don't not* like me in that way?'

'Possibly. Why? Is that something you might be interested in? *Not* being *not* liked by me in that way?' His arm came a bit closer to mine.

'It might be.'

'Well, you've got about eight hours to make that decision. Do you think that'll be long enough?

CHAPTER SEVENTY-NINE

I took one last look in the little mirror. Henry would be picking me up in a few minutes for our romantic dinner for two at Hetherin Hall. I was wearing a new dress in the raspberry colour he liked me in so much and underneath that, a new set of hot-pink underwear I thought he'd like me in even more. I was also wearing the Ted Baker body spray he'd put in my Christmas pillowcase.

It was all I'd been able to do to stop floating since we got back from Dubai. Even the news that Davina, Natalia, and Stinky Steve had been arrested and charged with distributing smuggled goods hadn't been able to keep the smile off my face. Sitting Pretty was safe, along with Daisy's and everyone else's jobs because Henry had bought the company and Daisy and I were running it as a job-share so I could work around my mystery guest assignments. But tonight was my biggest reason for smiling. Tonight was mine and Henry's first real date.

He knocked on my door and I went to open it. There he was, looking handsome and elegant as ever. He had a hand-tied posy of flowers which he held out to me.

'Thank you,' I said, smelling them. 'They're gorgeous.'

'Not as gorgeous as you.' He bent to kiss me, his lips just centimetres away from mine. He smelled so good.

'What time's our table booked for?' I brushed his lips lightly with mine, wrapping my arms round his neck.

'Eight.' He pulled me even closer, his fingers in my hair.

'Do you think they'd hold the table if we were late?'

'I'm sure they would.'

I pulled him gently towards the bed. 'Then let's see if we can make it in time for last orders.'

ABOUT THE AUTHOR

April Hardy grew up on the outskirts of the New Forest. After leaving drama school, her varied career has included touring pantomimes, children's theatre and a summer season in Llandudno as a Butlins red coat. All interspersed with much waitressing and working in hotel kitchens!

After moving to Greece, she spent many years as a dancer, then choreographer, and did a seven-month stint on a Greek cruise ship before working for a cake designer and then training as a pastry chef in a Swiss hotel school in Athens. Whilst living there, she also helped out at a local animal sanctuary.

Relocating to the UAE with her husband and their deaf, arthritic cat, she has lived in both Abu Dhabi and Dubai, where she is delighted to have found herself so unemployable that she has had plenty of time to devote to writing!

Sitting Pretty is the first of her New Forest-set novels.

Rosie Orr

Something Blue

Anna has a grown-up son, an ex-husband somewhere in Australia, and a feckless married lover. Sporting new scarlet underwear, and not much else, she is horrified to open her door one afternoon not to lover Jack but to son Sam and his girlfriend. They have come to announce their engagement – and to tell her that their wedding is only weeks away!

Anna is soon in the throes of preparations for a traditional Irish wedding: keeping at bay the Versace-wearing mother of the bride, dealing with the return of her ex-husband, and wondering whether Jack will ever have the gumption to leave his wife. And then the big day arrives, bringing hotel cats, destroyed crème brûlée and a surprisingly attractive photographer…

Something Blue

Colette McCormick

Things I Should Have Said and Done

Ellen never knew what hit her.

But when a drunk driver runs a red light her life is over in an instant. Her small daughter survives – and Ellen, hovering in the borderland between life and the afterlife, can only watch as her loved ones try to pick up the pieces without her.

Ellen isn't ready to let go. She doesn't want to say goodbye. She is confused, angry and hurting for her family and herself. And that's where George comes in. He is her guide through her confusion as she witnesses the devastation among the living.

With George at her side Ellen learns that even though she is dead she is not helpless. There are things that she can do from beyond the grave to influence what happens in the world she left behind.

Jenny Kane

Another Glass of Champagne

Fortysomething Amy is shocked and delighted to discover she's expecting a baby – not to mention terrified! Amy wants best friend Jack to be godfather, but he hasn't been heard from in months.

When Jack finally reappears, he's full of good intentions – but his new business plan could spell disaster for the beloved Pickwicks Coffee Shop, and ruin a number of old friendships… Meanwhile his love life is as complicated as ever – and yet when he swears off men for good, Jack meets someone who makes him rethink his priorities…but is it too late for a fresh start?

Jenny Kane

Another Glass of Champagne

For more information about **April Hardy**

and other **Accent Press** titles

please visit

www.accentpress.co.uk